DE WITT'S
WAR

DE WITT'S WAR

Hans Koning

Allison & Busby
Published by W.H. Allen & Co. Plc

An Allison & Busby book
Published in 1989 by
W.H. Allen & Co. Plc
44 Hill Street
London W1X 8LB

First published in the USA by
Pantheon Books, a division of Random House, Inc.

Printed and bound in Great Britain by
Anchor Press Ltd, Tiptree, Essex

ISBN 0 85031 954 4 (Hardback edition)
ISBN 0 85031 944 7 (Paperback edition)

DE WITT'S
WAR

There was a war on. Jerome de Witt was waiting for the bus in a driving Dutch winter rain.

The bus stop was right in front of the Amsteldyk town hall and, as De Witt was the mayor of Amsteldyk, his huddling there in his old raincoat and shapeless hat proclaimed to the town that he was out of favor with the powers that be, who had withdrawn the gasoline allowance for the municipal car.

De Witt could have waited in the doorway of the building, but then he would have had to dash down its slippery blue stone steps when the bus finally appeared around the corner. He was in such a vile mood, anyhow, he felt he'd rather stand there in the open and get drenched. He did not even try to put the fat ornamental lamp post, fronting the town hall, between himself and the wind which tore in from the sea over just twenty miles of very flat countryside. He had always hated that lamp post and was certain that the competition in which its designer had won first prize had been rigged.

It was an unusual time in the chronicle of his country, Holland, and his town, Amsteldyk (population 4,534). On the surface, things still looked rather normal. Actually, life was out of joint. The month was January 1941, winter topping a year in which Germany had overpowered the armies of Norway, of Holland, Belgium, and France, and had reached the coast of Western Europe "from the North Cape to the Pyrenees," as the Dutch newspapers always phrased it. Those papers were of course like everything else controlled by the German occupation force. Across from that coast patrolled by German soldiers in their gray-green uniforms, the jackets with the little slits sticking out over their behinds, lay England. England, bombed day and night, was not defeated, although those same newspapers frequently wrote of what the New Europe would be like "when, soon, the German Army is marching through London."

The bus appeared, taking its time to round the corner. De Witt got aboard in the smell of wet clothes. An aquarium with steamed-over windows, he thought, a people aquarium. All seats were taken. He knew several of the passengers at least by sight; some ignored him, others gave him a little nod or even a smile. It depended on whether they disapproved or approved of his cold attitude toward the German authorities. A young man started to get up and offer him his place, but De Witt shook his head. "I'm not that old," he said with a grin that came out a bit tired.

De Witt *was* tired. He was also soon to turn forty, which depressed him. He had always looked younger than his age, thin even before the war, with lank and badly combed hair of a dubious brown color. People used to express their surprise that so young a man was a mayor even of a very small town, but of late that surprise had stopped. He lived alone in an almost bare little apartment at the edge of Amsteldyk; his wife had left him the year before, after somehow proving to him that most of the furniture was hers by right. The apartment saw out on a girls' school in which since the May 1940 invasion German soldiers had been housed. Around and beyond it was a landscape of Dutch pastures and meadows with a row of stunted willow trees along the horizon. A low mist often hung over those fields in the early morning and gave a final unreality to the squads of German infantry that drilled, from sunrise on, in the girls' school basketball court, singing their marching songs. He would stand at the window of his bedroom watching them—he was a bad sleeper—and think: It can't be, I shouldn't believe my senses. Am I in Holland?

"Stadium!" the bus driver called. They had come to the Amsterdam Olympic Stadium, terminal for the suburban bus services. Here De Witt had to change to a streetcar. The wind had abated but the rain kept falling, almost vertically now. It was twenty minutes before two and he was sure to be late for his two o'clock appointment at Amsterdam police headquarters in the center of town. Just let them try and make a remark about it, he thought. The "them" referred to the Amsterdam

4

police president, a newly appointed man in a newly created office based on the German model, directly under a new national director general of police. De Witt had not yet met this police president, who had been dug up by the Germans from the retired army officers list. He was De Witt's superior in police matters. His overall boss under the new regime was a secretary general of justice in The Hague. (Dutch mayors had always been appointed, not elected.)

When De Witt got to the police president's office, it was a quarter past two. Whether as a reprimand or not, he was kept waiting until three. Then a secretary showed him in. He found a red-faced, white-haired gentleman behind a vast, black mahogany desk, a man who looked almost too true to type. There were dark velvet curtains and paneled walls. An incongruous pastel of water lilies occupied the place where the portrait of the Dutch queen would once have hung. De Witt gave a little nod and sat down, his hat in his lap, his raincoat dripping on the parquet floor.

"Mr. de Witt!" the police president said loudly, as if conducting a one-man roll call, and immediately went on, "You are the head of your community's police. In that function, you are responsible to me and are to carry out my instructions."

De Witt toyed with the idea of jumping to attention but decided that was childish. He did not answer.

"I had instructed you," the police president told him, "to provide every assistance to Mr. Cremer, the most prominent member of your community. Mr. Cremer telephoned me yesterday. He informed me you had declined to do so."

It was a well-heated office. No shortage of coal here, De Witt thought. His raincoat began to steam. "Perhaps you and I could have had our conversation by phone, too," he said, shaking some drops from the wet sleeves of his coat.

There was a silence.

The police president put on a pair of glasses and studied a paper on his desk. "I asked you here," he at last said, "because the importance of the matter warranted it."

A "hmm" from De Witt.

"Important not because Cremer is a friend of mine—he is that—but because he and I are aware of the fact that your attitude may be conditioned by Cremer's role in the public life of our, eh, unhappy country. To be precise, by his successful work in getting our economy rolling again. Cremer is doing an admirable job, a very admirable job. Do you know how many tires the German authorities have released for our road transports?"

De Witt pondered several incisive answers but said only, "Mr. Cremer called me about police protection. I have a police force of four and a half men."

"Mr. de Witt, let us not discuss the details of your job. My father used to say, 'Where there's a will, there's a way.' "

"My mother used to say, sir, that the best protection for a person was a clear conscience."

The police president sighed very audibly. "We are now at the core of this matter," he announced. "As mayor of a Dutch community and head of the police of that community, you must understand that a man who collaborates correctly with the occupying German authority has a very clear conscience. The Netherlands army surrendered on May 15, 1940, and all authority now derives from the German state power."

"We're still in a state of war with them."

The police president's voice suddenly jumped an octave. "Pray do not lecture me on military law, Mr. de Witt. Or do you perhaps advocate a war now of *francs tireurs*, something along the lines of what the natives in Java once tried against us? Do you want to see Holland drown in anarchy?"

As he appeared to be waiting for an answer, De Witt said, "No."

"Then there is no alternative but to work with the Germans. You as a civil servant are duty-bound to do so. Cremer is entitled to all the protection he needs for himself and for his family. Precisely because he has chosen a . . . eh . . . an exposed position."

After another silence, De Witt announced, "Maybe I'm not the right man to handle such policies."

To his surprise, the police president pushed a sandalwood cigar box over to him and held out his lighter. "I know you have been a good mayor for some years now, Mr. de Witt."

De Witt blinked at him through a cloud of cigar smoke.

"If you are thinking of resigning, if you resign, our friend the secretary general in the Justice Department will appoint in your place a member of the Dutch National Socialist Movement. A fellow with bicycle clips on his trousers and who can't spell. Do you think that would be to the benefit of your community? What we need right now are men, good men, willing to accept the responsibility for a correct but formal—" He stopped and seemed taken aback by his own loquacity.

The two looked at each other for a while.

"I'll go see Mr. Cremer," De Witt said and stood up.

"Fine," the police president said. He let his chin drop to his chest. "Let's be realists, De Witt. There's only one army left in Europe now. We live in a new age."

2

When De Witt came out of police headquarters, he found that the rain had stopped. But low, black clouds raced across the sky and it was already getting dark. Because of the blackout regulations, not a single man-made light was visible. A townscape, he thought, as has not been seen since the Middle Ages. Not then either. Five hundred years ago there'd have been torches and candles. Grayish figures hurried across the sidewalks; a world of halftones. The last, false light left in the sky was reflected in the canal in front of him.

Did I cave in? he asked himself. No. In a way the man is right. We have to tag along. Like Pétain in France, what did he say, you can't play games with the survival of your country. Of course folks like him are betting on the Germans' winning the war. And how can they not win? I don't want to believe it; it's against nature for them to win; sometimes I think the

Germans feel that themselves. But for all of us here the greatest wisdom seems to be: lie low. If I'm honest, what bothers me most about Cremer is his damn smugness. And what on earth does he expect from our poor police? Sergeant Koos has fallen arches. That little fellow, Piet, is so young his voice still cracks.

He had come to the archway that led to the university, and he turned in there. Here, under a stone roof, some little light bulbs had been allowed which threw a glimmer on the hand-carts piled with books and magazines. The archway used to be the heart of Amsterdam's secondhand book trade but, with the Jewish book dealers banned from the place, only a dozen carts were left. What they displayed was now mostly junk: paperback romances in Dutch and German and shabby schoolbooks. De Witt walked on to the far end where a gate led to the university garden. A friend of his had his stand at that spot, or not really a friend perhaps—a friendship based on the fact that he had once helped the man. "My only case," he always called him: when De Witt was still studying law and thought he was going to be an attorney, this fellow had come to him for help. His name was Adriaan Veen. That was during the Depression. Adriaan had had himself set up as a "promoter" and was about to be arrested on a charge of for-gery; De Witt had gotten him out of it. They saw each other often. During their discussions, De Witt had become quite sure that Adriaan, like him, had been a university student who had dropped out. Adriaan insisted he was just a self-educated salesman, and their talks always ended vaguely in jokes.

"It's the mayor!" Adriaan cried when he saw De Witt ap-pear. He lowered his voice to a stage whisper. "Have you read of the latest German plan for the invasion of England? All our children have to hand in their ice skates at the *Kommandantur* and then, with the first frost—"

"Very funny," De Witt interrupted, and he had to check himself from taking a hasty look behind him in the gloom.

Adriaan patted his arm. "Never mind, Jerome," he said. "It'll all come out in the wash. Here, look at this." He delved into a box under the cart and produced a leather-bound book, which he held up to the weak light bulb.

"What is it?" De Witt asked without enthusiasm.

"An *Imitatio Christi*. Printed in Leyden in 1588."

"I see."

"I see?" Adriaan repeated. "You know what this little book is now worth?"

"No. How much?"

But Adriaan had lost his eagerness. "Oh, never mind," he said. "Just wait till I hold it under the nose of a German officer. They're buying themselves sick, those fellows."

De Witt tried to have a closer look at the book, but Adriaan didn't let go of it. "You mean it's a fake?" De Witt asked.

"No! No." He seemed sorry now for what he had said. "Here, have a look at this then. Keep it. Compliments of the house." Adriaan put the book away, and in its stead he produced a magazine. It was an old *Esquire*, for July 1938, and he pushed it into De Witt's hand. "Let's have a drink," he suggested. "I'm closing up."

"I can't. I have work to do."

The bus journey home was painfully slow and De Witt, who had a seat in the back, used his flashlight to study the cartoons and especially the advertisements in the magazine—all those products for sale, people asking, *pleading* with you to buy whole hams, cigarettes, cars! An amazing, vanished world. He stared at a liquor ad in which a blond girl in a green evening dress was clinking glasses with a young man against a brilliant skyscraper skyline, at another of a girl on a white beach; he stared, oblivious to the jolting, to wet coats brushing his face . . . until his flashlight began to dim and he hastily turned it off.

When he finally found himself in Amsteldyk again, it was six o'clock. The sky had partly cleared and a half moon was shining through ragged clouds, which made getting along almost easy. He decided he might as well go straight home. In his apartment he left his wet shoes and socks in the hallway, made his way to the windows, where he closed the blackout curtains, and turned on the light. He opened a can of tomato soup in the little kitchen and put it on the gas. Then he telephoned the Cremer house.

Cremer came to the phone and sounded determinedly jolly. He had obviously already been informed of De Witt's visit with the police president. De Witt might want to join them for dinner, he suggested, and at the same time see the house and grounds.

"I can come over now," De Witt answered, "but I cannot stay long. I have to be somewhere else later."

"As you wish. Let me send my chauffeur over then to pick you up."

"No, no, that won't be necessary."

De Witt had passed the Cremer house on dozens of walks; it was just a few blocks and then a bridge away from him. But across that bridge another world began: only three or four villas per block, each one hidden behind walls and extensive gardens. The Cremer house was almost invisible from the road, screened by a double row of poplars. When De Witt tried the gate, he found it locked. He pressed a bell and immediately a man in chauffeur's uniform came down the path, carrying a huge electric torch, and unlocked the gate for him. He was led into a library where an open coal fire was burning and where Cremer was sitting with an evening paper, a drink in his hand. "Mr. Mayor," Cremer said. "I guess you haven't dined yet. Will you have a sherry with me?"

"Oh damn," De Witt muttered. He just remembered he had left the gas on under the tomato soup.

He accepted the glass and said, "You seem pretty safely ensconced here, Mr. Cremer."

"A kid could climb that wall. There are several back doors, French windows—"

"Have you been receiving threats?"

"Yes," Cremer said. "I'm not a nervous man. People in my walk of life attract freaks. The threats do not come from freaks."

"What were they? Letters? Can you show them to me?"

Cremer shook his head.

"You can't or you won't?"

"Neither. Look, De Witt, you're our mayor, that's to say, our head of police. General Buurman, our new police president, told me today you will cooperate with me. Will you?"

"Sure."

"Well, I don't need your help as a private detective. I can hire those myself."

"Presumably you can also hire a private bodyguard yourself."

"I don't want a private bodyguard," Cremer answered. "I want the visible protection of my country."

"Against unspecified threats?"

"General Buurman is satisfied that those threats are serious."

"Are they originating from, let's say, anti-German circles?" De Witt asked.

"And what is that supposed to mean?"

"I mean, are they perhaps meant to warn you off working too closely with the . . . with the new authorities."

"A strange question for a representative of authority," Cremer remarked.

A silence.

"Anyway," De Witt said. "Anyway. A rotating guard, just one man, twenty-four hours a day, would use up virtually our whole police force. Are you suggesting the rest of Amsteldyk should do without?"

Cremer pressed a button under the top of a side table, and it opened up; in the middle a glass cage rose up in which rows of cigars were exhibited. "Have a cigar," he said, selecting one himself.

They're all offering me cigars today. The Germans must have scooped up every cigar in the country, and they're now doling them out to their faithful. De Witt decided to take one. They're mine as much as anyone else's, he thought, picking a Monte Cristo.

"I only need a man during the day," Cremer announced. "When I'm in my office in town or at the exchange. For my wife and for the children. I'm used to taking care of myself. What I want is a visible presence. A token presence, you might say. To patrol the grounds here."

"Even one man—"

"I'm also used to making very substantial contributions to the police benefit fund. Your cigar isn't burning properly."

De Witt put another match to his Monte Cristo. "For how long? . . ." he began but then decided against that question. "Well, Cremer," he said, "I must look into the mechanics of this with my chief clerk." That did not sound very impressive. "And with General Buurman," he added.

"I will hear from you tomorrow?" Cremer asked, or rather stated.

"Eh, yes. Tomorrow."

But on the morrow Hans Willem Cremer, leading industrialist and vice-chairman of the Board of the Amsterdam Stock Exchange, would no longer need this visible protection by his country.

It was still pitch-dark when the telephone woke up De Witt and he lay motionless for a moment, listening to the plaintive ring. He saw on the little clock on his night table that it was seven. *"L'heure de Berlin,"* he said aloud. He had read those words somewhere once. Since the Germans had put all of occupied Europe on Berlin time, the sun did not rise in Amsteldyk in midwinter until nearly nine in the morning.

The smell of burned tomato soup still hung in the apartment. He picked up the phone.

"Mr. Mayor." The voice of his police sergeant. The man sounded angry.

"Yes, Koos."

"You're a sound sleeper, sir," Koos said.

"Well, not really. I couldn't get to sleep last night. Took a pill."

"Mr. Cremer has vanished."

"Oh, for God's sake. What do you mean, 'vanished'?"

"Yes sir. But Mrs. Cremer insisted I call you."

De Witt sat up in bed. It was a freezing morning. "I talked to the man last night," he told Koos. "Vanished. He may have gone anywhere, he's probably sound asleep in a nice, warm hotel room in Amsterdam—" He was about to add "with a nice —" but stopped in time.

"Yes sir. That's what I said."

"I'll call her, Koos. You just forget the whole thing."

He hung up, jumped out of bed, closed the blackout curtains, turned on the light, and jumped back under his covers. He had his hand on the phone when it rang again. It was the police president, General (or, really, ex-General) Buurman. They surely throw their weight around, these Cremers, De Witt thought. "No sir, you did not not wake me." The general was presumably being ironic now. "Yes, I was about to call Mrs. Cremer. Not that—yes, quite."

Mrs. Cremer next. Her line was busy. Then, finally, a housekeeper answered the phone. She would try and have Mrs. Cremer come to the telephone.

It took Mrs. Cremer a very long time, but then her tone of voice stopped De Witt from producing the scathing comment he had ready. "My husband . . ." she said. "My husband . . . Mr. Cremer has been found. He was found in the back of the garden, under the hedge. He is badly hurt." The line went dead.

When De Witt reached the Cremer house, the gate stood open. He recognized the two police bicycles leaning against the gatepost. He walked around the house and into the back garden, where the sergeant and one of his policemen were standing in the brown winter grass, flapping their arms to keep warm. It was beginning to get light; a murky dawn descended from the entire sky and dyed the men's faces gray.

"Seems we were wrong," Sergeant Koos said. "Wrong to—"

"Yes."

"We're waiting for the expert from Amsterdam. We've roped off the area."

Stringed off, rather. White string had been wound from tree to tree, delineating some hundred square feet. It looked like kite string, De Witt thought. Did Cremer have a son? "Found in the back of the garden." He realized he hadn't thought about it further; he had simply gotten dressed in a haze, shaved with cold water, and come over.

"What happened?" he asked.

"They had already carried him inside when we got here."

"And?"

"That's all we know. The lady asked me to stay here."

Did she now? De Witt made for the garden door but it was locked, and there was no response to his knocking. He went around and rang the front door bell, where a manservant in an apron let him in. The man asked him to wait, but De Witt heard a voice behind a door, opened it, and looked into a brightly lit room. He saw light beige and off-white rugs and furniture, a breakfast table set for two near a window. A white tablecloth, cut carnations even, toast in a china rack. In an easy chair, a pale woman in a housecoat, obviously Mrs. Cremer. Across from her a dapper, gray-haired man with a medical satchel at his feet. De Witt entered and closed the door behind him.

"I'm Jerome de Witt," he said softly.

The lady looked at him and did not answer. The man stood up and, taking him by his arm, led him to a far window. "I'm Dr. van Weyhe," he said. "With e-y-h-e."

"Yes, we've met."

"Hans Cremer is dead. Do you want to see him?"

De Witt nodded and the doctor, still holding him by his arm, led him out of the room by another door. De Witt tried some kind of bow toward Mrs. Cremer but she stared past him.

"I've given her something," the doctor said in the hallway. "He looked terrible."

The doctor opened another door. It was dark in there, the curtains were closed, and he turned on a light. On a couch a man's outline was visible under a sheet and blanket. The doctor went over, gently folded these down, and made a gesture for De Witt to come closer.

The head of the man on the couch had been bandaged almost down to his eyebrows. The face below the white looked so different from the man with whom De Witt had talked the night before, it took him a moment to see this was indeed the same Cremer lying there. The color had gone from the skin, the cheeks were sunken. He had aged twenty years in dying. Involuntarily, De Witt stepped back.

"He was alive when I got here," the doctor said. "This was the nearest place to put him down."

"And?"

"He died a few minutes after. But there wasn't a chance."

"Shot through the head," De Witt said.

"No. They—whoever they are—broke his skull."

"A police expert from Amsterdam is on his way," De Witt told him.

"No doubt. One or two very heavy blows. Possibly as long ago as the middle of the night. Blows so heavy that they. . . ." He looked at De Witt and did not finish his sentence. "Yes, several hours ago," he said.

4

It was Saturday late afternoon, end of a wretched week. De Witt was lying on his bed, his hands behind his head, staring out of the window where clouds raced across a light green sky. Holland is the next windiest place on earth after Patagonia. My head is full of such useless facts, he thought. But it sure always blows here. It's the climate that makes us into Calvinists—think of sitting on some beach now, an azure sea, a girl with long tanned legs like that one in that *Esquire* ad. . . .

It was warm in the room. After spending half an hour trying to split his coal ration in equal parts to last the rest of the month, he had suddenly filled the round iron stove to the rim. There was a lovely red glow now behind the mica window. If only he had a cigarette.

A vile week. The Cremer murder was being investigated by the Amsterdam police, not by Sergeant Koos with his one police officer, three adjuncts, and Piet, the part-time aspiring officer. But twice De Witt had been summoned to the city, the second time to face not only General Buurman but the secretary general of the Justice Department. De Witt had pointed out that Cremer's request had been for a daytime policeman; even if he had immediately had his way, it would not have prevented this night attack. He must have received a late visitor; he seemed to have walked out with him or them into the garden and—

Here the secretary general had interrupted. "Are you a trained detective, Mr. de Witt?"

"No, I'm the mayor of a small town. Or maybe, *was* the mayor. You can have my resignation."

"Let us not err in haste," General Buurman had said and gone into a muffled conference with his superior. They hadn't lost faith in him, they had told him, and didn't want his resignation. But the murder looked to have been a local deed, if only because of the 11 P.M. to 6 A.M. curfew in force every night. They wanted his cooperation (not as a detective, the general had interjected with a little smile, which could actually be seen as a dig at his boss). De Witt knew the local personalities and the local tensions. "This is a deed of local tensions and passions, Mr. de Witt," the secretary general had announced. "Let us keep sight of that. Let us not see it as a political crime. A political crime would bring the German police in. Most undesirable from my point of view, and obviously also from the point of view of Amsteldyk."

("But I'm certain it is a political crime, or perhaps a political deed," De Witt had wanted to say, but thought better of it.)

Yes, surely it was desirable to keep the Germans out of it. He could imagine those green-uniformed *Polizei Fuehrer*, or whatever they were called, going over his files, searching for "Reds and Jews," having people beaten up in some basement —they weren't supposed to do those things in Holland but they were sure to do just that. Yet De Witt's alternative was to help the Dutch police find the murderer or murderers.

Cremer's head had been broken with an iron bar—that's what the police report said—but was that any worse than a gentlemanly bullet from a pistol such as the German officers so neatly wore? Wasn't Cremer, hadn't Cremer been a traitor? Then he thought of the pale ghost of a woman, his widow, with whom he had had two miserable interviews; of the children, seen in pictures only; they had been sent away somewhere.

Surprisingly, the Germans had done nothing to keep the matter hushed up.

De Witt couldn't remember a single crime that had made it into the newspapers since the German takeover, except of course for the jealous-husband–knives–rival type. And here they were playing this up with headlines, pictures of the murdered man and the bereaved family. Even the little Amsteldyk weekly, the Friday *Courant,* had had front-page photographs of Cremer as a student, as a skater in St. Moritz on a Swiss vacation, and as a dead man. De Witt had called the editor and asked how he had got hold of that last one. "They sent it to me," the editor had said. "With a notice on the back, 'Carry in the next issue over two columns.' " It was strange that the Germans were broadcasting a fate that could well await any other of their friends and collaborators.

Darkness was falling. The window was now only a gray oblong. He should get up, close the blackout curtains, turn on the light. He had reports to write. In a while.

Voices rose from the sidewalk, boys and girls. That did make him get up and go to the window. Three couples, teenagers, were standing on the near corner, holding their bicycles, their flashlights making dancing lines in front of them on the pavement. They were arguing about where to go. Amsteldyk had several bars and cafés. They were shouting and laughing as if there was no war. Of course, it was Saturday night; why should they rob themselves of their Saturday nights? How many are there in one lifetime before you are too old? Say, twenty-five years worth, twenty-five times fifty-two . . . that's what, about thirteen hundred, not that many, thirteen hundred in all eternity. . . .

He thought of his own Saturday nights when he had been a law student in Amsterdam, and of the excitement of that first year in another city, away from his mother, a grown-up, drinking gin in that bar on the corner of Leyden Street, what was its name, something English or French, the Dutch always liked foreign names better, there had been a pianist there, a young man not much older than he, he had thought that was the job he'd like to have, sleep till noon, amble through town, play in a bar till early morning, go home in the first light with a girl. . . . It seemed very much more appealing than studying law and being a lawyer.

Some Saturdays he'd go to the Walletjes, the old canal streets behind Dam Square, where the local whores sit behind their windows or, the cheapest ones, stand on the stoops. Afterward he'd always worry about syphilis, a subject he must have been lectured on at least a dozen times since he was sixteen, and he'd run home and wash endlessly. But that was afterward. Then he had met Lydia. God, those tussles. "I want you to use one of those things." "What things?" That made her furious; she didn't want to say the words. And then his mother had died, Lydia had told him she didn't want to run around any longer "with a student," and he had dropped out of law school. They had ended up marrying, years later, when they had become thoroughly tired of each other, and even knew it, and all that what was left was a frenzied kind of lovemaking. . . . How could he have been such a fool?

The kids were no longer at the corner. It was deadly still in the street and in the room. He closed the curtains and put on the lights. Reports. And a dinner of bouillon and tomato-paste sandwiches, which was all that was left from his rations of the week. He did his own shopping, and not too well. The rationing system was hardest on people living alone. And, as he was their mayor, neither the butcher nor the grocer ever suggested some black-market item on the side to him.

5

On Monday morning Jerome de Witt entered the town hall right behind the mailman, who dumped a large pile of yellow envelopes on the desk of his chief clerk, most of them marked *Official* or *From the Office of the Secretary General.*

"More directives," Smit, the clerk, said. "They're sure putting things in order in this country."

"Yes, I wonder how we ever got on without them," De Witt answered. He walked over to the stove, on which a blue enamel coffee pot was heating, and poured himself a mug. The coffee was boiling hot; good old Terpstar must have put it there first thing. De Witt noticed his chief clerk was watching him as he took a sip.

"This is awful," De Witt muttered.

The clerk smiled. "No more official coffee ration, Mr. Mayor."

"What is this stuff?"

"Caramel and carotene, it says on the package."

"I can't start the day on that," De Witt said. "Anna! Anna!"

The cleaning woman stuck her head around the door.

"Anna, can you lay your hands on some real coffee for us?"

She did not answer but held her head sideways like a bird and winked.

"Then please do. I'll pay for it," De Witt told her.

He went into his own office, leaving the door open (it was numbingly cold in there), and sat down behind his desk with his coat still on. Soon his clerk would come in and drop all those badly mimeographed announcements and orders in front of him: new maximum prices for things that weren't to be found anyway; new hours for this; no more this, no more that; "you are herewith enjoined from . . ."; "let us have a complete list of . . ."—all of it by order of the *Reichskommissar fuer die besetzten Niederlanden . . .* and all on top of caramel and carotene coffee.

He jumped up. "I'll be back in a couple of hours," he said to the surprised Smit. "I'll be at the stock exchange. I'm going to their board office."

"Eh—"

"Cremer's case, you know," De Witt added.

Outside, he breathed deeply. Somehow it felt less cold in the street than in his office. The day looked better, there was some blue in the sky, and for once the wind wasn't actually trying to knock you over. To top it off, *the* taxi, the only one still functioning in Amsteldyk, slowly drove by just then and De Witt recklessly hailed it. To hell with the money, I can't face that frigging bus today. Maybe if I handle the Cremer case cleverly, they'll restore my gasoline allowance. (His car was on blocks in the municipal garage.) "Official emergency," he told the driver, who wouldn't be allowed to take him otherwise.

But do I want to handle it cleverly? Cremer—his yellow face —an iron bar breaking bone. Then he had an image of some young boys, students maybe, standing against a wall, trying to start singing the national anthem as a squad of green-uniformed German police lifted their rifles and fired—or maybe they just hanged people. . . .

The bus they passed—and, once they were in Amsterdam, every streetcar—was bulging with passengers, the sidewalks were crowded with men and women going to work on foot, but the roadways were almost empty except for bicycles and the German army trucks with their black and white license plates and swastikas. Civilian car traffic had already become very rare. In less than twenty minutes the taxi pulled up at the stock exchange, just behind Dam Square. He had never been in there. It was just a block or two away from the Walletjes with the red-light ladies. Very convenient for the stockbrokers, he told himself.

When he said who he was he was immediately received by a Mr. William Scheltema, who was "not quite a member of the board" but fully informed on everything De Witt might want to know. Scheltema was an old-looking young man, elegantly attired in a three-piece charcoal suit with a dove-gray tie. His office was warm, too, and on his desk was also a box of cigars.

"William?" De Witt asked, "not Willem?"

"Yes. My mother was an anglophile."

What specifically did Mr. de Witt have in mind? "I would like to get a clearer idea of the late Mr. Cremer's work," De Witt answered. "What does a vice-chairman do? This is a mysterious place to an outsider."

Scheltema looked pleased at that. "I can see it would seem so," he said, "and yet it is basically simple. Mr. Cremer, our late VP, was a much respected member of the exchange. Do you realize it took only two months—two months and five days," Scheltema corrected himself with a little smile, "to reopen the exchange? We closed on May 10, 1940, the day the war started; we reopened on Monday, July 15. All things considered, that was a minor miracle, you must admit."

"Yes. Indeed."

"It was Cremer who did that. Almost single-handedly."

"Was it a good thing?" De Witt asked.

"I don't follow you."

"I mean . . . I could imagine an attitude that it would be in our interest to leave the place closed under the German occupation."

"Do you think the bakeries should have stayed closed?" Scheltema asked with a slight frown.

"I see your point," De Witt said.

There was a pause. Scheltema put his hand on the cigar box, withdrew it again, and got up. "Let me show you the exchange floor," he said. "Trading hasn't begun yet, of course."

When they had just gone out of the door, the desk phone rang and Scheltema excused himself and went back in to pick it up. Meanwhile De Witt slowly paced up and down the marble corridor. He heard Scheltema's voice, sharp now; then the man came out of his office, said "excuse me" as he went by De Witt, and vanished around the corner. De Witt contemplated a huge photograph behind glass, in sepia and yellowed white, in which a group of very satisfied-looking Dutch planters, all with large mustaches and riding crops, had had themselves gathered in rattan chairs under palm trees. Around them an array of Indonesian natives was standing, those close to the chairs in ceremonial costumes, those at the edge half naked. Everyone, white and native, was staring at the camera with obsessive intensity, as if immortality was now within their grasp. How depressing, he thought. "1868" was written in brown ink in the corner. Seventy-two years ago. Everyone of them dead by now, except maybe those two little boys whose heads were just discernable, peaking around a palm tree in the background.

Scheltema reappeared. He entered his office and held the door open for De Witt.

"Problems?" De Witt asked.

"The *Beauftragte* for the Netherlands Bank was on the phone," Scheltema said with a shrug. "One of our directors was to meet him and didn't show up. The Beauftragte is a rather unpleasant man when he's kept waiting. He even threatened to stop the trading for today."

"Beauftragte?"

Scheltema shrugged again. "The German liaison man, watchdog if you will, with our state bank. He has a veto and all that, but he's really rather decent if you don't rub him the wrong way."

"Oh."

"I'd better stay with my phone for the moment," Scheltema said.

"Tell me, Mr. Scheltema, Mr. Cremer couldn't have been in some kind of financial trouble or crisis, could he?"

A genuine smile now showed on Scheltema's face. "Mr. Cremer was," he began with a certain relish, "Mr. Cremer was a, or the, major stockholder in"—he ticked them off on his fingers with animation—"Royal Sumatra Tobacco, Bandung Tea, Batavian Petroleum, Moluccas Quinine Company, Sumatra Independent Rubber, Banka Tin and Zinc. . . . He was one of the wealthiest men in Holland and, in fact, in Europe. Before the war, in 1938, the American magazine *Forbes* put the worth of just the Batavian subsidiaries—refineries, that is—at thirty million dollars—with the dollar at about two guilders, eh, one guilder 84 cents to be exact. Mr. Cremer's net worth, as a very rough estimate, mind you, would be in the neighborhood of . . . no, I shouldn't even try to guess."

"Oh," De Witt said again.

That afternoon back in his office, where it was now perceptibly less cold, De Witt got a telephone call from Police President General Buurman. Another board member of the stock exchange, the man who had missed his appointment with the Beaufragte that morning, was dead. Jonkheer Johan de Bock had been shot dead in his Amsterdam apartment.

Jonkheer is a Dutch title, something between the knights and the baronets of the British. The Carlton Hotel apartment where De Bock had been found around midday had been his Amsterdam *pied à terre:* he had lived on a country estate twenty-five miles from the city, alone but with a considerable staff of servants. Like Cremer, he had been an extremely rich man.

At the end of that day Jerome de Witt found himself standing on the sidewalk and thinking that he couldn't possibly face his empty, cold apartment. Not just yet.

De Witt used to have many friends in Amsteldyk and in Amsterdam: in the Dutch manner, they often met in cafés after work. Then, later, the De Witts started giving dinner parties or they all went to movies and restaurants in the city. But most of that had ended with his divorce, when their friends all seemed to feel they had to choose, and to his surprise chose Lydia. (He had always thought they sort of wondered why he had married her.) Now the war had put a final stop to whatever was left of that life for him. He felt there was something indecent about going out at night in this defeated country with all those German officers and soldiers sitting around everywhere, not to mention the German uniformed women who seemed to be a cross between an auxiliary army and *Reich* army prostitutes, "the gray mice," as the people of Amsterdam called them, for they were forever scurrying around buying things. Others in Amsteldyk felt the same about staying home evenings, but they were mostly the older people; the younger ones packed the cafés and bars and stood in line for the German movies, which were the only ones still shown.

One couple, the Geelkerkens, had stuck with De Witt instead of with Lydia, but theirs had become a stilted friendship: in the first week of each month, he went and had dinner with them, and never saw them otherwise. He would have liked to reciprocate and cook for them, but they always reacted to that suggestion with a smile. Clearly a man alone could not cook anything they'd want to eat. Thus, De Witt kept things balanced by showing up to his dinner each month with a more and more expensive, hard-to-find box of candies or bunch of flowers. This day was not a Geelkerken day, however.

His chief clerk had told him that one of Amsteldyk's cafés had been declared out of bounds by the Germans to their own military personnel. This was becoming common practice in poor areas (and, in Amsterdam, in the streets around the zoo, where a majority of the population was Jewish), but it was a first for Amsteldyk. As he was hesitating in front of the town hall, wondering where he could go instead of going home, he saw Smit appear, double-lock the front door, and quickly walk away. De Witt hurried after him and caught up at the edge of the square. "Say, Smit," he asked, "where exactly is that place we got the German out-of-bounds notice for today?"

Smit stood still. "Eduard's Café."

"Oh yes, but I forgot where it is."

"Across from the paint factory. A dinky little bar."

"Oh. Right. Do you—come, I'll buy you a drink there."

"At Eduard's Café?" the clerk asked. "You can't go there, sir."

"I'm not a member of the German army."

Smit smiled uncertainly. "It's a very dirty place."

"Come on. The gin will kill the germs."

"Very kind of you," Smit said. "But you see, my wife is waiting dinner."

"Oh, right you are. See you tomorrow then."

Smit did not move yet. "It's a long way," he said, "all the way across town."

"I need the exercise. I need airing out."

It was not a pleasant walk. In the gloom of the unlit evening, men and women hurried home like shadows. These were the streets where De Witt did his shopping, but most stores were closed. Having little to sell, they locked up before dark. And in case the boxes and tins in their windows would tempt any burglar, they all carried signs announcing that the window displays were empty. One greengrocer was still open; the twilight showed a couple of sacks of potatoes on the shop floor. Some twenty or thirty people were silently standing in line. "Came this afternoon," the last man in line told De Witt. "He's selling two pounds to a customer." Almost automatically De Witt took his place behind him, but then he thought to hell with it, and quickly walked on.

Once beyond the level crossing of the Amsterdam-Utrecht railroad, the streets lay abandoned, walled by shuttered and boarded-up workshops and factories; some closed since the Depression, others since the May 1940 war days. In the quickly thickening dark it was hard not to stumble over all sorts of debris lying around. A gang of grown boys ran by, banging on the shutters with sticks, and he was so startled by the sudden racket that he jumped and twisted his foot. When he finally got to the bar, his mood had sunk another two or three notches. But he could see it would be crowded inside, for stacks of bicycles were piled against the wall and from behind the blacked-out windows came the din of many voices. In the last light he could just distinguish the sign in the window, with its black Gothic lettering: *Nicht fuer Wehrmachtsangehoerigen*, "out of bounds to German soldiers." He opened the door and closed it behind him, pushed aside the oily blackout curtain touching his face, and entered.

The place was indeed packed, warm and smoky, all men as far as he could see. A few of them looked up, one or two who looked familiar gave him a nod. No one paid further attention to him. He made his way to the bar and asked for a Dutch gin. An evening paper was lying on top of some coats that had been piled up at the end of the counter, and he saw that De Bock's death, like Cremer's before, made a fat headline. The owner noticed De Witt staring at it while he poured his drink; he reached for the paper and handed it to him. "They've got rid of another one," he said.

The news report said nothing he did not know, except for an announcement within a heavy frame: The board of the stock exchange was offering a five-thousand-guilder reward for information leading to the arrest of the killer or killers, and another five thousand had been added to the award by that same Beauftragte for the Netherlands Bank.

What a repulsive business, thought De Witt, not knowing if he meant the two murders or the two murdered men themselves who, until their deaths, had so calmly continued their prospering affairs in a beaten nation. Perhaps most repulsive was that you could not even be clear anymore about where right and wrong lay. But he was out of it now. General Buurman had agreed with him that, since the case had gone beyond the borders of little Amsteldyk and its mayor's competence, it should be left to the police. "The Dutch police," Buurman had said, "or so I still hope."

"Another one," De Witt asked, holding out his empty glass.

Eduard (if that was the man's name) made a face. "Only one to a customer," he answered. "I can draw you a beer."

De Witt hesitated: the glasses of beer looked stale and had a very dubious color. His neighbor spoke up. "You're right," he said, "it's cat's piss." And then to the café owner, "What's the matter with you, Eddie? Don't you know that's our mayor? Give the man another gin."

Eddie looked annoyed rather than impressed with that news, but he refilled De Witt's glass. "Thanks," De Witt said to his neighbor.

26

"That's all right. He has to be skimpy. His quota is only fifteen liters a week."

"Of course. I see."

"Maybe you could do something about that," the man continued.

De Witt looked doubtful. "Those rules come from The Hague, you know."

"Yeah. The Hague."

"The Hague indeed. I feel the same about them. You know," he went on, "actually, I don't even like gin."

"You're kidding me."

"No, I'm serious. What I mean is I don't like geneva, Dutch gin. Never have. They used to needle me about it when I was a student."

"You're kidding me," the man repeated.

"Now English gin, you know, with ice and tonic, that used to be lovely stuff. . . . Or whiskey. . . . Of course, now geneva is the only thing left. I mean it's at least real alcohol, right?"

"Yes, well . . . whiskey . . ." his neighbor muttered, staring into the smoky distance of the bar.

It seemed, though, that De Witt had now somehow broken through Eddie's liquor barrier, and when he had emptied his glass, the man filled it again without waiting to be asked.

After a while De Witt began to feel completely different. What a sad sack he was, little mayor of a little town, standing there in his suit and tie and almost clean shirt. Those men around him were on the side of honesty. They had always been the underdog and they still were, only their masters now had a new set of German super-masters. What did they care? But he, people like him, what frauds they had been, playing the student, the lawyer, the judge, the mayor; thinking they were in control of a world; leaders, setting the standards, holding forth on God and country. But their whole edifice had not been based on history and morality, had it? In reality it hadn't been based on anything but the ramshackle Dutch draftees army with its two and a half tanks. When that collapsed, everything collapsed, and the judges and mayors were left standing

27

in their underpants, their laws and theories meaning less than a hand grenade in the belt of some German private who until this war had never set foot on a paved street and who had been taught that democracy and culture were Jewish tricks. What's to be done? "Before the war . . ." he said to his neighbor.

"Yeah?"

"Before the war, we had no community, no commonwealth. That's what was wrong. People were isolated from people."

"You may be right," his neighbor muttered without conviction.

Much later, back out on the street, De Witt realized that he had to hurry to beat the curfew. The wet wind hit him in his face, but once he had rounded the corner it pushed him from behind and he was loping along. A pale, drained light shone through the clouds, as in old lithographs. Not a soul on the street. He remembered that he had explained to a number of people in the bar why he was a fraud, and that he had given his tie (his best one, too) to the café owner, had insisted on the man's taking it; he also had the uneasy feeling that he had promised Eduard—or, better, Eddie—to do something about increasing his liquor quota from the government bureau in The Hague. He wasn't really drunk, he knew that; more in a state of dizziness, neither unhappy nor happy, feeling that things didn't matter that much, that dying wasn't that difficult or terrible and that therefore nothing else was either.

Then he suddenly felt sorry for himself and had to swallow back actual tears. A girl, he thought, a woman, a softness in this gruesome landscape of iron and barbed wire and stone and foreign soldiers in caps planting their black and white signposts in our landscape.

7

Tuesday started quietly under a monotonously gray sky, the light on all day in his office. The paperwork was a new routine, the listing of German "Payment Certificates" received in the town. It was what the Germans used for money with the local population, and all amounts under two thousand guilders had to be reimbursed by the town hall; larger claims went to The Hague. The case of Johan de Bock—"the police are probing all possible leads"—loomed large, on page two in the morning newspapers. In the right-hand corner of the front page the papers all carried the same item: civil servants of Jewish origin were to be fired. "Of Jewish origin" was defined as having or having had two or more grandparents of Jewish religion. When Smit gave him the official questionnaire from The Hague, which came in the second delivery, he threw it away. Lost in the mail. At quarter to five he told Smit, "Let's call it a day," and without really thinking about it, walked again in the opposite direction of his apartment, to Eddie's bar.

But at that hour, the regulars hadn't yet arrived; the place was empty and behind a half-closed curtain he saw the owner and his family having their dinner in the back room. Eddie got up and poured him a drink, then went back to his meal. This time the gin didn't help, and the café didn't look the same. It was, after all, just a shabby and rather pathetic room where poor men could get warm and cheerful for a couple of hours through some kind of chemical reaction between their blood and Dutch gin. He put his fifty cents on the counter, held up a hand by way of good-bye, and went back into the twilight. He decided to eat out, not an easy enterprise: the little Amsteldyk hotel, Rozenboom, served dinner only to those who had meat ration coupons. Without such coupons all you could get was a plate of potatoes mixed with spinach or kale, and gravy made from a tablet. If they knew you and you paid extra, you could get the real dinner without giving the coupons, but of course a mayor couldn't get mixed up in such hanky-panky.

The dining room was badly lit and cold; De Witt kept his coat on and muttered that he'd have "the vegetarian entrée."

"We still have some half bottles of wine," the waiter then said unexpectedly. He was an old man in a yellowing suit of evening clothes, an incongruous remnant of prewar luxury in that gloomy place.

"Really?" De Witt asked, "French wine?"

"Bordeaux, sir."

So the waiter came back with a battered silver-plated tureen of kale hotchpotch, a bottle, and a crystal wineglass. I'm becoming an alcoholic, De Witt thought, emptying his glass in one gulp and smiling to himself. He looked up and saw that a woman across the dining room had caught his smile and almost imperceptibly smiled back. She was young. At her table, with her back toward him, sat an older, gray-haired woman in black. The girl was dark blond, in a red dress; he thought she was splendid, even or maybe especially in the dreary setting. There was something bright and glamorous about her, he thought. Just her sitting there took some of the curse off things.

Throughout his dish of kale and his Bordeaux he every now and again looked in her direction. I must get to talk to her, but how? If only the old lady would turn around; perhaps I know her. When the waiter came with his check, De Witt asked softly, "Who are those two ladies over there?" The waiter followed his eyes. "Oh damn," De Witt said. The table was empty. They had gone.

"I'll inquire," the waiter said, but De Witt hastily asked him not to. Just as well. Saved from making a fool of myself.

When he turned the corner of his street, he saw against the shimmer of light in the sky (an almost full moon behind the clouds) a man standing with a bicycle in front of his door. As he went closer, he recognized him as one of the policemen. The man had seen him and hurried toward him. "You're to come immediately, sir," he said. "To the Cremer house."

"Now what's happened?"

"I don't know. The sergeant sent me here. He called the station house."

"I'm exhausted," De Witt said. "Can I borrow your bicycle?"

The policeman hesitated, then answered, "I guess so. I'll follow."

8

Evelyn Cremer, widow of the murdered vice-chairman of the stock exchange, had herself been killed.

De Witt stood once more in that same beige and white breakfast room and with the police sergeant looked down upon Mrs. Cremer. She was lying on the large rug, facedown. The rug was off-white and a fan shape of black stains spread out on it, while her black hair was streaked with white stains. He was not quite certain what it was, but he turned away.

"Where are the children?" he asked.

"Thank God, sir, they hadn't come back yet. She was found by the housekeeper. The doctor is with the housekeeper now. He didn't touch her" (pointing toward Mrs. Cremer). "He said, 'She's dead all right.' We phoned Amsterdam, but we didn't get through until fifteen minutes ago. There seems to be no one else in the house."

At the edge of the rug lay a black iron handle, one of its ends gleaming as if wet, but black rather than red. Was that blood? He looked at Koos. "Is that a crowbar?" he asked.

"A tire iron, sir. She was hit with what is called its lug wrench end."

In the silence that followed they heard a door slam somewhere upstairs in the house, then the put-put of an old automobile approaching.

"That's Amsterdam's Citroën," the sergeant said.

"I'll go." De Witt went to the front door and saw two men coming up the path.

"I'm Jerome de Witt, the mayor of this town."

"Police HQ Amsterdam," one of the men said, holding an identity card in front of De Witt's face. "You'd better close the door. Blackout, you know."

De Witt did as he was told. "That way," he said, pointing to the door of the breakfast room. Then he left the house.

That night De Witt sat at the desk in his apartment, trying to draft a personal report to General Buurman. When he thought of Evelyn Cremer as she had looked during those two talks he had had with her, it seemed to him as if she had already been dead then, if her pale forehead had been traced with blood. He felt, literally, overcome with horror. In the middle of a great war, worldwide calamities, this one death seemed an outrage beyond acceptance. He remembered her quavering voice when she had started talking about how she'd raise the children by herself, and how neither she nor her husband ever had had enemies . . . Evelyn Cremer had put her hand on his arm when he stood up; she had muttered something about how perhaps, one day, he should meet and talk with the oldest boy. He had hastily answered that yes, of course, he was available. They can't do this, he thought.

He stated in his report that, under the circumstances, he wanted to be informed of anything they found out in Amsterdam; he would devote the best efforts of the Amsteldyk administration toward assisting them. Then he lay down on his bed and fell into a heavy sleep.

When he woke up, it was light; the German soldiers in the basketball court were already at their singing. He shuffled over to the window. They were just shadows in the half light and their voices, metallic, not cheerful, were very loud. "Denn heute gehoert uns Deutschland, und morgen die ganze Welt," they sang. "Today Germany belongs to us, and tomorrow the whole world."

He opened his window. "Sure thing!" he shouted.

The next day after work, as he was sipping his first gin at Eddie's, he recognized the man in mechanic's overalls standing next to him at the bar. "I'm Jerome de Witt, I'm the mayor of Amsteldyk," he said to him.

"I know. I've seen you."

"I've been breaking my head the last few days about who to go and see," De Witt told him. "And here you are. For my purposes you're the most reliable man in our little community."

"Who do you think I am then?"

"You're Titus van Collem, right?"

"Right. Not so very long ago I spent a month in the little jail of our little community."

"I know. That was very long ago. That was in another geological era. That was before the war."

In the late thirties, during a demonstration staged by men on the dole, Titus van Collem had been arrested and then jailed.

"I also know you were a member of the Socialist-Anarchist League," De Witt told him, "until it was banned by the Germans."

Van Collem seemed about to answer but decided against it.

"In short. . . ." De Witt hesitated. "Can we go sit over there for a moment?" He pointed to a table in the far corner.

Van Collem looked as if he were going to refuse, but then he picked up his drink and went to sit down. De Witt followed him. It was an old iron table with a hole in the middle for a garden umbrella, a table that once must have been standing under a sunny sky, maybe at a beach, De Witt thought. Once, people around this table. . . .

"Shoot," Van Collem said.

"I realize," De Witt said under his breath, "from what I know of you, from things I hear in my work, that you are a likely man to have contacts in the Dutch underground."

Van Collem laughed briefly. He looked genuinely amused. "The Dutch underground?" he asked without bothering to lower his voice. "But Your Honor, there's no such thing. If there is, I've never heard of it. How would they do it? Our soil is too muddy for anyone to go underground."

"You know what I mean," De Witt said softly. This is the wrong place, he thought, but he wouldn't have come with me anywhere else. No one is near, no one is listening.

"Frankly, I don't know what you mean," Van Collem answered.

"Well, if there was such a thing, I would want to talk to someone there. Under whatever circumstances, with whatever guarantees they'd want."

"Why?"

De Witt constructed a careful answer. "I have to find out more about the deaths of the Cremers. If they were killed for political reasons, I have to know why."

"Why?" Van Collem asked again in a flat voice.

"I'm involved. I don't know where it will lead me. I'm sure you know I'm no collaborator with the Germans. But killing a woman like Evelyn Cremer. . . ." His voice trailed off.

"You mean you want them to produce a murderer for you."

"No. Of course not. I know, or let's say I assume, that the people in the . . . in the opposition are responsible men. And women."

"Why do you assume that?"

"I've seen their pamphlets. What I mean is, if someone got out of hand, his arrest could endanger others. I assume the different groups know about each other. This is a small town. They . . . they could do something about it themselves. I don't want to have anything to do with endangering honest men. Do I sound confused?"

"Yes."

"I need their help. They need my warning."

Van Collem studied De Witt's face and shrugged. "I don't understand what you're saying. And I don't know of any un - der - ground."

De Witt sighed and stood up. "If you don't," he asked, "then why did you want to know my reasons?"

The other man grinned. "I'm always fascinated by glimpses of the official mind. They never fail to amaze me."

Chief clerk Smit stuck his head around De Witt's door. "Germans," he said.

The two of them went to the window. A black Mercedes-Benz had stopped in front of the town hall. A chauffeur in the uniform of an army private had opened the back door and was standing at attention. Two men were getting out. They looked around and marched up the steps. They wore loden coats and had felt hats with feathers in the bands.

"Would you believe it?" De Witt said. "Keep 'em waiting a bit."

He closed his door behind Smit, put his coffee cup in a drawer, an armful of files on his desk, and sat down.

Steps, then Smit's voice in his execrable German, "I will see if the mayor—." He did not get any further. De Witt's door opened and one of the men came in. De Witt tried to look up with a mixture of surprise and anger, but the man who had entered paid no attention to this. He went over to the desk and held out his hand. *"Herr Buergermeister!"* he cried.

De Witt stood up and stared; the man grabbed De Witt's hand and shook it.

"Captain Gottlob. SD, *Sicherheitsdienst.*"

"How do you do?" De Witt said. This Gottlob looked like the orchestra conductor in the first and last movie he had gone to see since they had become all German, a Viennese musical.

"We, the Security Service, and you, will work together," Gottlob announced. "You have had two murders in this peaceful, cozy community." He waved toward the window as if inviting De Witt to have a look at it. Just then, a hard and sudden rain squall started hitting the glass.

"Yes, but Herr General Buurman—," De Witt began.

"We have strong reason to believe they were political crimes. And local crimes."

"How would you know?"

"All at the proper time," Gottlob said, admonishing De Witt with a finger. "The Marxist virus. Degenerate elements. You and I will find them. You doubt this?"

"Eh—no. Surely."

"Such elements would sabotage the good understanding between our two peoples. You and I must show them otherwise."

"Eh—yes."

I'm not being very forceful, De Witt thought. But who

would have thought that my first official German would look like that? "I must say—," he began.

Gottlob did not so much interrupt as not listen. "You speak excellent German, Herr Buergermeister," he said. And then he opened the door and called, "Buber!"

An older man came in, with a belly, and a dull expression on his face. "My assistant, Buber," the captain announced. Buber clicked his heels and bowed toward De Witt. The two men appeared to be waiting for De Witt to say or do something.

"Would you like some coffee?" he finally asked. He jumped up. "Just a moment."

He went out and found Anna in the main office, whispering with Smit.

"The Greens," De Witt said to them in an undertone. That was a Dutch name for the SD in their green uniforms.

"They're the worst," Anna whispered.

"Anna, let's all have coffee."

"The real stuff?"

"Are you joking? The caramel."

Smit said, "The Cremer case, right?"

De Witt nodded.

"What do they want?"

"I don't know yet. To find degenerate elements."

"They don't look very dangerous," Smit remarked.

"Maybe they're just members of the SD oompah band," De Witt said and returned to his office.

The captain and his helper had taken chairs. De Witt sat down with a kind of little smile.

"We will begin with a look at all your communists and socialists and Jews," Gottlob said cheerfully. "You have them listed?"

"Well, not really."

"We will use the names from the membership rolls of the political parties you allowed here, before 1940. We find them very useful. For the Jews, you have the J-cards list, of course?"

A personal identity card for everyone in Holland had been

made obligatory by the Germans. A J was stamped on those held by Jews.

Gottlob was looking at him, waiting for an answer, and De Witt said, "The Jewish citizens of Amsteldyk do not tend to violence, I think."

Gottlob frowned at the expression "Jewish citizens." For a moment he looked less jolly. "You'd be surprised, Mr. Mayor," he said. "We have more experience than you."

"Yes. No doubt."

Anna came in with the caramel coffees and winked at the mayor. They both looked at Captain Gottlob.

"Excellent!" the captain cried, having tasted carefully. He put his cup on the edge of the desk and asked, "Buber?"

The assistant opened a briefcase and handed the captain a list.

"We have some forty names here," the captain told De Witt. "Our first *Auslese*. And very sour grapes they will be."

Buber had clearly heard this joke before but he laughed heartily. De Witt produced a smile.

"We will go over them one by one," the captain said.

That evening De Witt stayed in his office after everyone else had gone. He had asked Smit to give him the key.

Thus far, he had managed to have Titus van Collem's name, which had been on Gottlob's list, scratched out. It had been only too easy: the captain seemed convinced that he and the mayor saw eye to eye in the matter at hand. De Witt also had had the captain add a name, that of an aggressive building constructor who was the only official Dutch Nazi in Amsteldyk. But this was a short-lived and childish game. As for Titus, it was gratifying to be able to protect someone, but did not this very protection imply he was throwing others to the wolves? What was the morality of playing Providence as the partner of an SD captain? Here was the easy alibi, "I'm staying on in my post to prevent worse," but in the end it was a cowardly alibi.

What an amazing experience it had been. He realized now that for months he had braced himself for this: the day that his country's subservience to the German occupation powers would take concrete shape, the day Germans would enter his office. A showdown of willpower he could only lose, as it already had been lost for him by the Dutch and the French armies. Still, a confrontation. Barked orders. Maybe his arrest on the spot. Who could have guessed it would take the shape of a police captain who appeared to love his brother Aryan Dutch, him, his clerk, his caramel coffee?

De Witt walked over to Smit's desk and put a sheet of paper with the municipal seal into the typewriter, with two carbons. "To the Secretary-General of the Department of Justice, The Hague," he typed, and continued, "I am herewith tending my resignation, effective February 1." That was the Saturday of the following week. Smit, poor devil, needed time to get himself ready for his successor. Smit couldn't quit, not with a wife and all those children of his. Smit presumably wouldn't think of such a move anyway, war or no war; Smit lived in an orderly universe. For that matter, what was he, De Witt, going to do? Who'd give him another job? He had just three hundred guilders in his post office savings account. Would they even let him keep the apartment?

But I can't get cold feet now.

He had a hard time with the letter, for whenever he had to erase a mistake on the copies (one was for General Buurman), the paper shifted, but he managed a nice paragraph about a mayor's duty to his citizenry. When he had finished, he typed the two envelopes, then sat at the desk and stared into space. It would be the end of a long period of his life.

Maybe I'm a fool. Lydia would surely think so—if she ever even heard about it. Maybe they would force him right away to join the war labor service in Germany, where the unemployed of Holland were sent. He would vanish like a pebble in a pond.

Gottlob, with his Oompah bandleader's face, was a member of the German SD. He worked under the orders of a man called Reinhard Heydrich, the number four of five in the Berlin hierarchy, or maybe really number two, Goering and Hess didn't look quite serious, too vague, too corrupt. De Witt had stared once for a long time at a photograph in the German magazine *Signal*, he remembered the occasion precisely, the magazine had been left on a seat, a train journey to Rotterdam. He had stared at Heydrich's frozen face, the narrow skull with the plastered-down hair, the black uniform with the atavistic, barbaric, rune insignia.

He had thought that here was a being from another time and place, a time and place that had never before existed. This man was no Attila the Hun; he looked clean, ascetic, young; he probably had been to the university. Yet here, De Witt had thought, was the true terror, the terror of the twentieth century.

Gottlob had seemed convinced that he would find the people he was after and that the murders had been political. "Political" meant they had been directed against his Germany, against his upper boss, SS General Reinhard Heydrich. The momentousness of that realization had struck De Witt. It had been early afternoon. It had been getting dark in his office and he had been about to get up and turn on the light, when he stopped himself, thinking don't do anything to help this Gottlob. And the idea of that bloody tire iron, gruesome as it was, being but a pathetic weapon in this enormous, continuing war had blurred the image of poor Evelyn Cremer's broken head. He did not believe in the men who had wielded the tire iron but he couldn't sit by and watch them fall into the hands of jolly Captain Gottlob.

He sealed the envelopes, locked up, and went to drop his two letters in the mailbox at the corner of the town hall square.

10

De Witt had the habit of visualizing the events he expected. He had seen himself in his job during its final days, facing the indignant Germans, Smit at a loss but admiring him. It turned out quite differently. Without explanation, the Germans did not come back to continue their search. Smit, when told of the resignation, didn't show much of a reaction. That was a bit of a shock. Had the man only pretended to like him all those years? Anna reacted as foreseen: she was sad.

On Saturday morning, when the office was open until noon, a governmental messenger appeared with a letter. In it, the secretary general informed him that his resignation was not parallel to or concomittant with the interests of the service and would make an unfortunate impression on "our German colleagues." De Witt had three working days to reconsider, and in his own interest (underlined) he was adviced to do just that.

"Our German colleagues." Colleagues my ass. How serious was the threat encapsuled in those tortuous sentences? And where was Captain Gottlob anyway? Three working days—until Thursday. Then only two and a half more days during which he could avoid any phone calls or visits if it came to that, and he'd be free. Free to dodge official moves, that was. Not, he thought, that there was likely to be any. He mustn't start exaggerating. In another week the former mayor of Amsteldyk would be forgotten by all those gentlemen.

That same Saturday, at four in the afternoon, De Witt was at the Victoria Hotel in Amsterdam, where a reception and dinner were scheduled by the Port Authority of the city. (Because of the nightly curfew, everything started earlier than it once would have.) Since the May war he had stayed away from such occasions but, with his mayoral days numbered, it seemed somehow all right to go now. And the idea of well-heated rooms, maybe even some prewar liquor, was suddenly irresistable. An occasion to forget His Excellency the Secretary General, and the jolly captain, and the whole damn mess.

An icy wind was whistling down from the harbor, which faces the Victoria Hotel. Even nature is on their side. He pulled up his collar as he hurried from the streetcar stop to the entrance. He had to squeeze between the cars—some people were still being driven in limousines; he saw several cars with

German license plates—and entered through the revolving door. The warm air of the lobby enveloped him, and he caught sight of himself in the mirrors. God, he looked pathetic, that red nose, a cut from his month-old razor blade, his raincoat with a stain up front. He hastily took it off and gave it to the old lady at the checkroom counter, the very same one who had taken his coat on his first visit to this hotel, as a boy, when his mother had brought him here for tea after school, a super-special birthday outing. He smiled at the attendant and she smiled back.

The huge reception room was packed with people standing about, a sea of faces. Along the walls were rows of little tables, mostly empty; he saw the adjunct-mayor of Amsterdam at one, in earnest conversation with an elderly gentleman who had a tiny swastika in his buttonhole. Those two seemed to be drinking real cocktails; on their table stood a prewar soda siphon. De Witt intercepted a waiter with a tray. "Are those whiskeys?" he asked, pointing at glasses full of a tea-colored liquid.

"Oh no, sir. That's Wimpo."

"Wimpo?"

"It's a, a cordial-type refreshment. A substitute, you might say. Something new."

"Oh." He took a glass of Dutch gin from the tray and after a moment's hesitation, another one, and steered across the room with them as if heading for a friend somewhere. He sat down at a table by himself and drank them both down. With that, he felt a bit better.

Look, he thought, everyone seems in the best of moods. White, starched shirts, as if you still just open a tap and get hot water out of it. Ladies smiling as their cigarettes are lit. Don't they know there's a war on? Am I the one who's crazy? My mother always said I took things too hard.

The same waiter appeared in front of him and put a full glass on his table.

"I brought you some whiskey, sir. Haig."

"You're kidding."

The man winked. "It's really for——" and he made a move with his head toward the rear of the room.

"Well, thank you." De Witt started searching his pockets for a tip.

"That's all right, sir," the waiter said. "They shouldn't drink enemy liquor anyway, should they now."

De Witt slowly lifted his glass and took a deep sniff. Ah. . . . He tasted it, took a swallow to get rid of the gin taste still in his mouth, and then sipped. A warmth different from the gin warmth filled him. An Anglo-Saxon warmth, he said to himself. A prewar warmth. A very un-German, un-Gottloby warmth. This was a double or a triple. Bless that waiter. There was a decent fellow. The ordinary people, the people of Amsterdam, they were all right; it was all those damn bigwigs, smiling, kowtowing. "The more I see of the upper classes, the better I understand the guillotine," Bernard Shaw had written somewhere. Here's to Amsterdammers.

A neat man, youngish, had taken a seat at his table and seemed to give him a look of recognition.

"Nice party," De Witt said.

"Mr. Mayor—," the man began, rather coldly.

"Well, yes and no."

"You don't recognize me. I'm Scheltema, of the stock exchange."

"Of course. Sorry, Mr. Scheltema. It's been a confusing day. Or even week. How are you?"

Scheltema did not answer. He's scrutinizing me, De Witt thought. And he looks different. That's why I didn't recognize him; he's lost that polished look; it's not his clothes, they're as gorgeous as ever; it's his face.

"Well, Scheltema, old fellow," he said. "The port of Amsterdam seems to be flourishing again. You can't keep the Dutch down."

"All during our war with Spain, Amsterdam did a roaring trade with the enemy," Scheltema answered. His somber voice sounded like a teacher talking in a classroom.

The unexpected answer and, even more, the man's tone of

voice disturbed De Witt's mood of hazy peace. He sat up straight. "That was three hundred years ago," he said.

"You can't change human nature."

"No, I suppose not."

Scheltema stood up. "It has been nice talking to you," he said. "We must continue this conversation."

"Absolutely."

"Tomorrow?" Scheltema asked.

"Tomorrow?" De Witt repeated, very surprised.

"I'll telephone first," Scheltema said, and he disappeared into the crowd.

In the freezing darkness, De Witt was walking along the harbor quay. At the last moment, just when a guest had asked him, "What's the number of your table? I'm Corver, non-ferrous metals," he had decided to skip the Port Authority dinner.

The temperature must have dropped twenty degrees, he thought. I haven't been really warm for about half a year now. Who'd have thought that war would translate as chill blains, boredom, and the runs? He turned into Zeedyk, a street of bars and nightclubs, and pushed a door behind which a pale, blueish light was just discernable. An old man with tattoos on his bare arms was laying out a game of solitaire on the bar. At its far end, a girl was staring into space. She was clearly a professional from the Walletjes around the corner, but she had a nice, fresh face.

"A gin," De Witt said to the tattooed man. "No, beer. No, a coffee." He had to get back home. There was no point in more drinking. And what had that fellow Scheltema been about?

"Coffee?" the bar o, ner asked. "Tida ada."

De Witt smiled at him. Those words were sailor's Malayan for "there isn't any." "I've had too much to drink," he explained, "and nothing to eat. My stomach's upset."

"A drop of gin with a lot of bitters will do you as much good," the owner said, getting up. From the end of the bar, the girl looked at them. "Offer her something too," De Witt said. "And can I use your toilet?"

"Sure. But there's no light."

When he came back, the girl had got herself a glass of what looked like lemonade and had come over with it, next to De Witt.

"Cheers," she said, and then, "Do you want to?"

"It's ten guilders," she added after a pause.

De Witt now focused on her. Poor devil, he thought. In this cold. What lives we lead in this year of grace nineteen hundred and forty-one.

She misunderstood his silence. "You look okay," she said. "I'll take five. My name is Marlene."

He found himself saying, "Okay, Marlene. You're on."

De Witt got to his apartment just as the bells of the New Reformed Church of Amsteldyk tolled the curfew hour, eleven. On the floor inside his front door lay a piece of paper with a message written on it in pencil, "I was waiting for you. The metro was not involved." It was signed, "Titus at his desk."

11

De Witt looked up Titus van Collem's address in the town register and that Sunday went to see him; he turned out to live above a tobacco shop with, as the entry in the register had said, "the woman Vrede, calling herself Van Collem." There was no doorbell, so he climbed up the steep staircase next to the shop door and knocked. A girl opened and a warm smell of cooking enveloped him.

"He'll be home soon," she told him. It was a narrow room, neat and crowded, with a bed against the back wall. The girl was cleaning vegetables and dropping them into a pot of boiling water on a little iron stove. Steps were heard on the staircase, and Titus came in. He hugged the girl, dropped a parcel wrapped in newspaper on the table, went over to De Witt, and shook hands with him without a word. Then he started to peel off the various scarves and sweaters he was wearing instead of an overcoat. He pointed to the parcel. "Sausage," he announced. "Of sorts."

He went back out to the landing where De Witt had seen a toilet. They heard the flush, he reappeared, washed his hands at the sink, and sat down opposite De Witt. "There's really nothing else to say," he immediately said. " 'The Metro' means—"

"Yes, I understand," De Witt hastily answered. "Not that you'd get much security from it, if that's a code."

"No code. I was just being funny."

"And how can you be sure, about the underground not being involved, I mean?"

The girl interjected, "When Titus says something, he is always sure."

De Witt looked at her and then asked, "And 'Titus at his desk,' did that mean anything special?"

Titus was surprised. "But De Witt, don't you know? It's the name of a painting, a very fine painting."

"Rembrandt," the girl added.

"Oh. Of course. I wasn't thinking along those lines."

"Would you like to eat with us?" the girl asked.

"I can't," De Witt said. "I've another appointment." The moment he had spoken he was sorry, but he hadn't wanted to eat from their rations. He had no appointment; he had nothing to go back to, only his lonely Sunday night apartment where another can of tomato paste and maybe—he wasn't sure—a last can of something called herring-meal paté was awaiting him.

"I wonder who had an interest, then, in killing those people," he said.

"They were still collaborators with the Germans," Titus told them. "Someone from their past, an old enemy, or even just a clerk—someone could have felt justified by that.

Some old plan of revenge, who knows."

"I used to read a lot of criminology," De Witt said, "when I studied law. I never heard of a case where first a man and then several days later his wife are murdered."

"We've been thrown back into the past, into old and violent times," Titus announced, more to himself, it sounded. "The little dream of middle-class peace is over."

"I don't know why peace would be middle-class," the girl answered him. She started to ladle out her soup. "You're sure now?" she asked De Witt.

"Yes, I'll be on my way." What a lovely smell. He stood up and put on his coat.

"A tire iron—that's a weapon of impulse," Titus said.

"Or of a brute," from the girl.

At the door, De Witt asked, "Why did you decide to help me, after all?"

Titus, who had been blowing on his soup, held his spoon in mid-air and half smiled. "Well, you're no longer our mayor, are you?"

"How do you know? . . ." De Witt began, but let it go at that. In the doorway, he turned again and asked, "And how do we actually know the Cremers were collaborators?"

They looked surprised at him. "Did you ever see the cigars he smoked?" Titus asked.

The following morning he was at his desk at eight. His telephone directory listed three W. Scheltemas in Amsterdam, but only one lived at an address where he could imagine the elegant stock exchange man. He called and got his Scheltema.

"Hope I'm not interrupting," De Witt said.

"No, no. But, as a matter of fact, I'm in a bit of a hurry to get out of here. A big board meeting at nine."

His voice sounded odd. "I was waiting all Sunday for your call," De Witt told him. " 'Tomorrow' you had said."

"What? Oh, that. I *am* sorry. I didn't mean anything—I wasn't quite myself at that reception, you know. I'm usually not a drinking man. Didn't realize you were taking that seriously."

"Oh. No harm done."

In the middle of the morning, the jolly Captain Gottlob showed up, alone, and with a new list of names. "Urgent business elsewhere, Herr Buergermeister. You will prepare notes on each of these, very confidentially, please. We will make some arrests soon."

"I can't," De Witt answered. "I—"

But the captain had already left; De Witt heard him outside, shouting at his chauffeur, who had just started crossing the square toward the shops at the other side.

There were only six names on the list; those he recognized were of men who had worked for the old Dutch Labor Party. He wrote beside the names, "All Amsteldyk citizens of unsullied reputation," and took it to Smit. "Do we have an address for Captain Gottlob's office?" he asked.

"Yes."

"Well, let's just send this back without any accompanying letter."

He telephoned the Amsterdam police and after much waiting and "what's this in reference to?"'s, he got the main laboratory.

Did they think both Cremers had been killed with the same weapon, he asked.

He had assumed the question would surprise them, but the immediate answer was, yes, sure. The edges of the skull wounds were alike. Cremer and his wife had had different blood groups; both groups were on the tire iron.

"How much does such a thing weigh?" he asked.

He heard the man at the other end shout, "Hey, Jan, this joker wants to know how much the Cremer tire iron weighs!"

The answer came. "About eight pounds. Why, sir?"

"It's strange that people would walk around with such a

weapon for days. It's one thing to pick it up in a fight, but to carry it and use it days later—"

"Well, you know, it's the kind of tool you throw in a tool kit of a car or a truck."

"Why would they have left it behind, then, the second time?"

"They were disturbed by the housekeeper. They were in a hurry. The first murder was in the middle of the night, everything quiet."

"Okay. But then—," De Witt began.

The lab man interrupted him by clearing his throat. "Hold it a moment, sir."

De Witt heard voices at the other end, a little conference. Another voice came on, a sharp, university, The Hague voice. "Mr. de Witt? I'm Heldring, head of the lab. I think when we asked for your help, we were thinking in terms of your familiarity with the local scene, family feuds, undesirable elements, that sort of thing. Blood groups and fingerprints and all that we're quite good at ourselves."

De Witt tried to come up with a rejoinder, but all he could think of was, "I'm trying to get a complete picture."

"Quite. But, Mr. de Witt, I've been given to understand you will presently return to the status of a member of the public. You must forgive our reticence to speak to the public."

12

Around four o'clock he stood posted outside the member entrance of the stock exchange. A doorman kept looking at him, but he had decided not to go in, not to have himself announced. He wanted to take Scheltema by surprise as he came out.

The cold had stuck. How glad we would have been once with such weather, he thought, schools closing, skating on the canals. The sky and the air itself were gray, and every now and then little ice crystals seemed to materialize out of nowhere and slowly descended on him.

A chauffeured car pulled up the very second a gentleman in a fur-collared coat came out, and scooped him up. Then what had to be one of the last taxis of Amsterdam rolled to the entrance. The doorman opened its door, and a similar gentleman came out of the building and got in. They don't get cold, those folks, De Witt thought. Damn, maybe Scheltema will drive off, too.

Two men emerged: an older one with a walking stick, and Scheltema. They set off together toward Dam Square. So far, so good. He started to follow them at a considerable distance. On the square, the man with the cane got on a streetcar. Scheltema recrossed the street and entered a café near the corner, on Damrak. I'm good at this, De Witt told himself as he entered the café in his turn.

Scheltema was sitting at the long table where newspapers and magazines were provided for the customers. A waiter was already bringing him his coffee.

De Witt sat down across from him and said, picking up a tattered hotel trade publication, "It's not much of a selection anymore, Mr. Scheltema. No more *Esquire*s."

Scheltema looked thoughtfully at him. "I noticed you when I came out of the exchange," he answered, "but as you looked away—"

De Witt felt himself reddening. "I didn't want to intrude."

"Quite."

A silence. Scheltema had kept one eye on another customer who had just finished with an evening paper, and when the man put it down Scheltema reached over and took it.

De Witt ordered coffee too. It came immediately and was a terrible imitation, not even hot. "Our Amsteldyk carrot coffee is better than that," he said, but Scheltema did not look up from his paper.

"I'm here because you wanted to tell me something about the Cremers," De Witt said to the paper.

Scheltema gave him a brief look. "The Cremers were honorable people."

A silence.

"Who is managing the estate?" De Witt asked.

Scheltema put his paper down. "The court will appoint a trustee. First there has to be a criminal investigation."

"Did he have enemies at the stock exchange?" De Witt asked. "Mortal enemies, that is?"

"Look, Mr. de Witt, let me assure you there is nothing in the various probes you are, eh, probing. No scandal, no squabbles. And our top exchange men never break rank, never break their solidarity. They are men from the same background, the same families even."

"There must be something that set Cremer, and his wife, and Johan de Bock apart," De Witt said.

Scheltema stared at him and picked up his paper again.

De Witt finished his coffee in one gulp and put forty cents beside the cup.

"Well, but what were you thinking of, then, at the Victoria Hotel, Scheltema?" he asked softly, standing up.

Scheltema eyed him along the top edge of his paper, which he did not lower. Finally he said, "There are some very strange movements in the market. Very strange. But I have satisfied myself there is no connection."

"Then why would you want to talk about it with me?"

"A whim." Now Scheltema produced a little smile. "I'm sorry I stirred your curiosity. I realized afterward the matter is of no interest to an outsider." And he ducked back behind his paper.

13

Although he had taken one of his knockout sleeping pills, he slept badly, half awakening several times; he heard shouts, the screaming of car tires, very far away, perhaps in his dream only. But at seven, Police Sergeant Koos phoned and informed him in a curiously dead tone of voice that a number of Amsteldyk citizens had been arrested by the Germans that night between two and three. Seven or eight people, he could not get confirmation on that.

De Witt dressed, shaved with a shaky hand, and hurried to the town hall. The lights were on; everyone else was already there. In the front room men and women were standing around, relatives of the arrested. They had been all men, ten of them. The arresting force had been the German "Green Police," the SD.

"Did you make a list?" he asked Smit. Yes, Smit had, and he handed it over.

The first telephone call De Witt made was to General Buurman, to his home on Apollo Avenue in Amsterdam. A woman's voice announced that the general was not available and would he please call him at his office after nine-thirty. De Witt then tried to get the home listing of the secretary general in The Hague, but the operator assured him the number was secret and that she herself had no access to it.

De Witt put the phone down and wondered what to try next. He wasn't going to spend the next two hours waiting for Buurman to get to his damn office. He could hear the voices of the relatives outside, arguing. Smit had asked them to wait at home, but it didn't sound as if any had left. He went over to Smit and asked if he knew where the SD had its headquarters. "We have Captain Gottlob's office," Smit told him.

"I know. Where is it?"

"It's in what he called their *Aussenstelle*, something like their public bureau, I guess. It's in the girls' high school on Euterpe Street, near where the Gestapo is too."

"I'm going there," De Witt said. "The list makes no sense, not even in their terms. They picked ten names out of a hat."

The requisitioned school with the SD in it was a nice building in Art Deco style. Around the entrance were sculptures in low relief showing Minerva holding up a laurel wreath to a group of maidens in togas. Above this, a huge red and white swastika flag flapped in the always strong wind. It had taken De Witt an hour to get there, but he had no trouble getting past the sentry and to a receptionist. Then there was another hour's wait. Finally, a policeman in the typical green uniform led him to a small office.

"Halber," the man behind the desk said. He was in civilian clothes, heavy, reddish hair. He read the form they had made De Witt fill out. "You are . . . the mayor of Amsteldyk?"

"In the course of last night, without prior notification of the town authorities, ten of my inhabitants were taken from their beds."

"And?"

"That was a police action. I am, as mayor, head of the Amsteldyk police. Captain Gottlob and I had worked together on the case."

"Which case?"

"The Cremers. The Cremer murders."

"I don't know the case, but—"

"May I see Captain Gottlob?" De Witt interrupted.

"But I can enlighten you on procedure."

"Can I see Gottlob?"

"Captain Gottlob is occupied. Now then, the SD is an independent executive police, reporting directly to SS Obergruppenfuehrer Rauter. We do not even, we do not even except as a matter of convenience or courtesy, report to the Reichskommissar. We do not report to the mayor of Amsteldyk."

"There's no rhyme or reason to the list of arrests," De Witt said.

"I don't know the case, but I'd be surprised, Mr. Mayor. We make very few mistakes. Now you'll excuse me."

General Buurman was hardly more helpful. The first thing he said was, "Did you withdraw your resignation, De Witt? If not, you should not be in my office."

Oh goddammit, fuckit, damn damn damn, De Witt said to himself. "Yes, I withdrew it," he answered loudly.

"Well now . . . that had been an overly hasty move, hadn't it?"

"Yes sir. To get back to those arrests."

Buurman swiveled his chair around and gave De Witt a look at his back. He seemed to be contemplating the view. "If we had found the culprits ourselves," he said, turning around again, "the Germans wouldn't have had to get involved."

"Sir, those aren't any culprits. Ten murderers? They're names plucked out of a hat. One of them is an accountant, one a foreman at the lumber yard, one—"

Buurman held up his hand to stop him. "I have the list on my desk," he said, waving a sheet of paper at De Witt. "They're not exactly names out of a hat. These ten men are on record as egregious elements in your community."

"Egregious elements?" De Witt asked in a rising voice.

The general blinked in annoyance. "Pray don't repeat my words in that tone. They are men who are obstructing a proper relationship between Germany and our country."

"Which makes them murderers?"

"They have not been accused or convicted yet, have they?" the general asked sharply and loudly. "I have been informed that their arrest, at this stage, is no more than a signal to your community and to the country at large."

"Are you satisfied with that, sir?" He looked beyond the general and noticed that the pastel of the water lilies had been replaced by a large group photograph of men in uniform, Dutch and German. It looked like something from pre–World War I maneuvers. Had Buurman hung up this comrade-at-arms stuff to polish up his new bosses? De Witt tried to distinguish the faces.

Buurman cleared his throat like a pistol shot to get De Witt's attention. "Yes, I'm satisfied," he said.

"And if we find the real murderers?"

"Then they will doubtlessly be released. The Germans are nothing if not correct. I will keep you posted."

De Witt stood up.

"De Witt."

"Sir."

"You had better go directly from here to the General Post Office. Do it in person. Send a wire to The Hague, withdrawing that resignation. I wouldn't like to think that you were willfully misleading me."

When, tired and in a vile temper, he got back to the town hall, he saw to his dismay that even more friends or relatives of the arrested were waiting around. "We're trying, we're trying," he said.

"Do you know where they took them?" someone asked.

"No. But I think they're safe for the time being."

"Why?" "How do you know?"

"We don't think the Germans themselves think they're guilty, we think they're holding them until the real murderers are found."

"Well, let's find them!" a lady cried, jumping up from a chair. "Why should my husband be jailed for some miscreants! Let us form an auxiliary police. Let us help them."

De Witt did not answer her. "Let us get back to our work here. You're much better off waiting at home."

"That comes from having a pinko mayor," he heard one of the people say as he went into his own office, where Smit was waiting for him. De Witt told him he had withdrawn his resignation. He was about to explain why he had resigned, that he had thought he'd be helping track down members of the Dutch underground if he didn't, but then decided, no, let's keep Smit out of all that.

"I'm going to get Gottlob on the phone if it kills me," he said. "Excuse me." He closed the door behind Smit, took a deep breath, and started—beginning with the Kommandantur, the general German HQ—to try and get Gottlob's number. Half an hour later, when he heard Gottlob's voice on the phone, the sweat was running down his back, although his office was as ice-cold as ever.

The jolly captain was unjolly. No more "Herr Buergermeister" either. "Weren't you told this morning that I was busy?" he snapped.

"Yes, Captain, but ten lives—"

"Ten lives! We are fighting a war for our existence!"

De Witt decided to change tactics. "You and I were conducting an investigation together. I simply think we got off course."

"Those arrests were a signal to your cozy little community, De Witt."

A signal. General Buurman had used the same word.

"But captain," De Witt persisted, "none of those men could possibly have—"

"Are you ready to take their place, to stand guarantee for them with your own life?" Gottlob asked.

De Witt, taken aback, did not answer.

"Well, there you are! What more is to be said?" He seemed about to hang up.

"Yes," De Witt said quickly. "Yes, sure. I will do that."

Now the captain was silent. "Don't talk nonsense, De Witt," he finally said. "Some people will not fit into our new order; that is all that is to be said. Don't waste our time with your superannuated liberalisms. Shed them while you can. Goodbye."

At ten the next morning, Police Sergeant Koos came into De Witt's office with a lopsided grin on his face and said, "Guess what?"

"What?"

"They're out! They're free. They're back. All ten of them. They just got off an Amsterdam police bus."

"No kidding! What do you know!"

He dialed General Buurman.

"I told you, De Witt, the Germans are correct. You'll make a fine mayor yet, but you must learn to be less hasty."

"Did you achieve this, sir?"

"Eh . . . not directly. A word here, a word there. You know. There's more than one way to skin a cat. And now we ourselves better find the killers. Do what you can, De Witt!"

De Witt decided to call Gottlob and thank him. It was farfetched to thank someone for not keeping innocent people under arrest, but he had to think of the future of Amsteldyk. When he got through to the proper office, though, and to the same assistant who had connected him with the captain the day before, he was told that Captain Gottlob had been recalled for duty in the Reich.

14

"It makes no sense, Titus."

Titus shrugged. "Someone decided they had made a mistake, a tactical mistake. And with true German efficiency they rectified it and let them go."

"Losing face all over the place. It makes no sense," De Witt said.

"They don't give a damn what kind of face they save or lose with us."

"You're joking. All the talk was about *signals*. Those arrests were a *signal* to Amsteldyk to behave. They were going to shoot those men, Titus. I am sure of it. If this were Poland, they would have shot them on the spot, in the town hall square."

Titus van Collem and Jerome de Witt were sitting at the table against the back wall of Eduard's Café, the iron table with the hole in the middle for a garden umbrella. It was becoming a habit: After work, De Witt would walk across Amsteldyk to the little bar and drink Dutch gin with Titus. This was very unorthodox behavior for a mayor, even for a little mayor. Amsteldyk had always observed the proprieties; in Amsteldyk everyone knew his or her place. And here De Witt was drinking in a working man's dump with the town's ex-anarchist, now its municipal gas fitter. He liked Titus's company and Eddie's place was the first bar where, in this occupied country, he felt comfortable. You couldn't visualize a war profiteer or a German entering through its dirty door (even if it hadn't been out of bounds). Anyway, since he had gone through his resignation flip-flop, De Witt felt different about his post. He would never again take it as seriously as before. It was a civil-service job, a little better paid but neither nobler nor with more real power than delivering the mail.

"You're still absolutely sure about that . . . eh . . . metro business?" he asked.

"Yes. Yes. They were not involved. When I heard of the arrests," Titus said, "I figured the Germans were using the murders as a pretext for some widespread roundups. And then a bigwig must have decided, no, they'd stick with the tack of a good relationship with their brother Aryans a bit longer. So the ten poor brother Aryans were set free, and Gottlob, who had made the actual mistake, was transferred to East Pomerania."

"Hmm. It was a signal, and then your bigwig decided it was the wrong signal."

"Let's have another. We haven't drunk our quota," Titus suggested.

"I don't really like this stuff, you know," De Witt said.

"Well, there's a war on. What've you got in there?"

"My shopping. When I get to it, all they always seem to have left is tomato paste. On my meat coupons the man gave me blood sausage. But I found razor blades. Made in Bulgaria."

"Blood sausage?"

"He said it was all there was this week."

"He was lying. Maybe Vrede can do something with it. You'd better come eat with us tonight."

When Eddie brought them their drinks, he also carried an evening newspaper. "The paper, Mr. Mayor?" he asked. He had, belatedly, become impressed with his new customer.

De Witt opened it. "Now look, Titus, look here. Page three, and over two columns. 'No Clues in the Case of the Stock Exchange Murders. Amsterdam police chief: "We are facing a blank wall." ' Now consider that."

"What about it? Had you expected an item about ten false arrests by the SD?"

"No! That's not it. It doesn't fit, don't you see?"

"Fit where?" Titus asked. "It's all a pack of lies, lesser lies and bigger lies."

"Fit in the paper! Look at all the rest. Food situation improving. Preparations for the spring invasion of England said to be in final stage. A new German war plane. The Fuehrer congratulates. . . . Don't you see? It's all quote positive unquote. This is the only item in the whole damn paper, I bet you, where Authority, where German Law and Order, are 'facing a blank wall.' "

De Witt drank his gin down and he did not taste it this time. For a split second he had the feeling that he understood the mystery behind this—as when you meet someone and have his name on the tip of your tongue but you can't remember it quite yet. The solution to the puzzle was at his fingertips, if he would just use his head, use logic. Nothing else was needed. He could solve the whole thing right here in Eduard's Café. Then the feeling faded and he felt as baffled as before.

15

He decided to go and have a talk with the Cremer housekeeper, but when he telephoned, the operator came on the line to say that the Cremer number had been disconnected. At midday he went for a walk past the house: it lay closed, the front gate padlocked. He stood there a while, staring through the bars of the gate; he could just make out one window with closed shutters. On the lawn, patches of snow alternated with islands of dead, brown grass. He thought of that first evening he had been there, the lights, the open fire, Cremer with his sherries; and then of the evening when the house had been still, Evelyn Cremer dead, only the housekeeper and the doctor in an upstairs room. Now it was as if the house itself had died too.

After that, he made an expedition to the Carlton Hotel, in the center of Amsterdam. The hotel staff didn't seem any happier with his visit than the SD had been, but in the end the manager was brought forth. De Witt explained to him who he was. "I'd like to see the apartment where Johan de Bock was —" he could see the manager wince and ended "—where he lived."

The man remained motionless behind the counter of the reception desk. "The Cremers were your people," he said. "But Jonkheer de Bock and Mr. Cremer were not close at all. I don't remember ever seeing them together."

"The connection is in their work. Surely it can't have been a coincidence."

The manager sighed. "However that may be, the apartment has already been redecorated and rented. There is a great shortage these days."

"Oh. Didn't the police seal it?"

"Only for a couple of days. Nothing had been disturbed in it."

"Except Mr. de Bock."

"Yes."

"Then why redecorate it?"

A shrug. "I'm using the word loosely. The redecoration was more for emotional reasons. People don't like to live in a place where—"

"Quite." De Witt had begun to find that a useful word. "Nothing was really changed then?"

"Curtains . . . cleaning. . . ." The manager looked at an assistant who had been listening in. "John?"

"We repainted a wall, sir. Stubborn blood smudges. And the new guests didn't like three blue walls and one white one, anyway. That had been Jonkheer de Bock's idea."

The manager smiled wistfully. "Yes, he was a funny man. Decorator colors, he said. He had gotten used to them in New York. You never knew with him if he was being ironic or serious."

"Blood smudges?" De Witt asked the assistant.

The manager closed his eyes a moment in resignation. "The police know all about it. You really should get together and spare us all this. Jonkheer de Bock had hurt his hand; the palm

of his hand was badly cut. Presumably in a fight with the—.
When he fell, his hand struck that same wall we had painted
white for him that summer he came back from America."

"And no one heard anything?"

"As I showed the police, our apartments are large. Our doors
and walls are soundproofed."

"May I see the place?"

The manager turned to look at the key racks. "Not really,
Mr. de Witt. They're in. And even if they weren't . . . I assure
you, there is nothing to be seen."

He's right, De Witt thought, what do I expect to find? That
feeling in Eduard's Café, that I alone almost know what it's all
about, that set me on this track——But I'm no detective, and
the solution is not in blood smudges and hidden clues.

"And his possessions?" he asked.

"Well, obviously, after the investigation they must have
been returned to the family estate in Baarn."

"Oh yes, of course."

The early morning train to Baarn, dirty and unheated, took
an hour over the twenty-five miles, and he was the only passenger to get off there. The icy, ever-present wind blew along the
station platform. Everything was closed; posters advertising
local holiday pleasures of a prewar past waved their tattered
edges at him. God knows what I'm doing here. It's better than
sitting in my freezing office in that damn town hall of mine.

The square in front of the station was deserted, too. In its
middle an oval lawn, fenced off by a low railing, lay under old
snow. He started walking and came to a tobacco shop that was
open.

"No cigarettes," the tobacconist said before De Witt was
even inside the door.

"I just need some information, how to get to the De Bock
estate."

"You just missed the bus," the man told him with visible
pleasure. "The next one goes at two in the afternoon."

"I'll walk. How far is it?"

"A mile, a mile and a half. You can't miss it. Follow the road to Amersfoort."

The De Bock estate turned out to be a small eighteenth-century castle facing the road from behind a dry moat. It was an elegant place and in fine condition. De Witt had not phoned before because he had been sure he'd get the brush-off, but, standing at its smart entrance, he realized he looked far from impressive. However, the servant in red-and-white-striped waistcoat who opened the front door appeared to find nothing unusual in his showing up there.

He was let into the hall and told, "The family is not here. No one is, only staff."

"I'm De Witt, the mayor of Amsteldyk. I have been involved in the tragic circumstances of those deaths. . . ." He let his voice die out.

"It's all up in the air," the man said. "The Jonkheer's brother, the heir, is in Batavia. Or was in Batavia. In the Dutch East Indies. We've been informed he is on his way home now, but that's going to be a very long journey, what with the war."

"I am sorry. I should have telephoned first."

"We don't have a phone in the castle. Jonkheer de Bock didn't like them. When he came out here, he wanted—"

"Peace and quiet."

"Well, no, I wouldn't say that. Lots of friends, you know, sir, lots of parties. That was before the war, of course. People just showed up, just like you now. But in cars, of course. No, what I was going to say was he wanted no business calls out here. They were always trying to reach him for things. Telegrams. He wouldn't open them. He loved the country. He was a fine sportsman, you know. You realize he won the last Concours Hippique before the war, the B division? Look there," and he pointed at a glass cabinet filled with trophies.

"How old was he then?" De Witt asked.

"Thirty-five I would say, thirty-five, thirty-six. Yes, the Jonkheer was thirty-five or thirty-six."

Going back to the railroad station in the bus, which had

mercifully stopped almost in front of him, he stared at the melancholy trees lining the road, under a watery sun that made the hoarfrost melt and drip from the branches. He had thought of De Bock as much older; the word "widower" in the news reports must have created that impression. There had been no pictures of him, little personal stuff as far as he remembered. But here is something to set him apart from the Cremers, he told himself: De Bock was young and in fine shape. That explained why he had been shot while the Cremers had been beaten to death. He could see the scene, a murderer coming at De Bock with that same iron, but he had intercepted it. And had wounded his hand on it. And only then, when things threatened to go wrong for him, had the murderer shot De Bock. But what kind of murderer, armed with a pistol or a revolver, would try to kill a man by breaking his skull with an iron bar? A psychopath, a sadist?

16

It was by fluke that De Witt discovered another stockbroker in Amsteldyk, one of Cremer's fellow board members on the stock exchange. This man was called Jonas Schutte and he had recently bought a large villa on the northern edge of town, near the main road to Amsterdam South, screened from the traffic by a lake and a park. He had been brought to De Witt's attention when he had demanded a lower appraisal of the property and Smit had put the appeal on the mayor's desk. "Profession: stockbroker. Board member, Amsterdam Stock Exchange."

De Witt immediately tried to call the man but his number was unlisted. Then he sent Terpstar over with a note, asking for a meeting. No answer came. Finally he went over himself, at eight in the evening, feeling he was now justified in doing so. Actually, he preferred just dropping in on people, a habit carried over perhaps from his early years in Houten, a tiny village near Utrecht; he disliked appointments and formal calls. A maid opened the door and let him wait in a drawing room. The house was large but the rooms very plain.

Nothing could be further removed from the Cremer style, he thought: instead of a chauffeur and all those other servants, a housemaid–farmer's daughter who'd earn six guilders a week and board; instead of the indirect light, the crystal, and the inlaid woods, a table, lamp, and chairs from Vroom and Dreesman, the big, cheap department store of Amsterdam. Schutter was clearly one of those sober old Calvinists. De Witt was reminded of the luncheon he had once been invited to, long ago, by a fellow student, son of Amsterdam's leading shipowner: The boy's mother had cut a thin slice of chipped beef in two and put half of it on his sandwich, and the other half on that of her son.

"You've every right to be annoyed," De Witt said hastily, standing up, as a pale, angry man entered the room. "But you see, you didn't give an answer to my messenger, and I'm here on behalf of a dead colleague of yours, Hans Cremer."

Schutte stared silently at him.

"You may be able to help us," De Witt plodded on. "An insider's view."

Schutte said, "Being our mayor does not give you the right to enter people's homes uninvited."

"No, of course not," De Witt answered with a smile aimed at breaking through this crusty fellow's reserve. "Still, we're a small community, and you know what it says about being our brother's keeper and all that."

"Please leave."

"I'm sorry," De Witt muttered. He knew he was reddening. He walked past Schutte without looking at him. The maid was at the front door, holding it open, and he could hear Schutte behind him as if to make sure he'd really go out the door.

He shook his head as he went down the path to the road. I'd better stop all this. I don't know what I'm doing, just making a fool of myself all over the place. What an unpleasant old bastard!

But then, as he conjured up Schutte's face, he wondered. It hadn't been the face of a curmudgeon resenting intruders. Not a bit. Schutte had looked afraid.

Why? Again he felt he didn't need to go trapsing around for more facts; he just needed to think. Think, damn it, he said to himself.

If Schutte is afraid, it means he is involved in some way or other with the deaths of his colleagues. How could that be? The Free Market Forces, as my old economics teacher used to call them with capital letters, don't include bumping off folks. At least not directly by hitting them on the head.

Is someone blackmailing the board members of the Amsterdam Stock Exchange? But blackmailers get killed, they don't do the killing. Has someone, have some men, set up some grand revenge scheme against the stock exchange or members thereof? Because the stock market reopened under German tutelage? But that takes us back to underground politics, and Titus is sure. . . . And wouldn't the underground be more likely, say, to kidnap one of these men, or indeed even shoot him, but not a woman surely, and not using tire irons? If I'm honest with myself I must admit it looks more than anything like a criminal plot, on a bigger scale than we're used to here in Holland, but then everything is these days; and if it is that, it isn't any of my damn business and I'd better get back to the ration coupons, and paper army marks, and property taxes. But there's still the mystery of all that newspaper publicity. . . .

17

General Buurman had agreed to a conference, with him and the Amsterdam police both sitting in. I'll give it one more try, De Witt had thought, and told the general he had some new ideas about the murders.

The meeting started well. "I have begun to see the Cremers and Mr. de Bock in a different light," De Witt told the general, who gave De Witt a benevolent look. He probably thinks I've begun to approve of collaboration with the Germans, De Witt thought, which is not what I mean. "That is to say, sir," he went on, "I no longer believe they were killed by, eh, anti-German elements. I think we must look—" But here the general interrupted.

"Yes, Mr. De Witt, duty," the general said. "When all our gods fail, what we have left is duty. Good for you, De Witt."

One of the Amsterdam detectives, after a nod from the general, now read his report out loud. It was about autopsies, fingerprints, the blood smears on the wall at the Carlton, the caliber of the pistol that had killed De Bock (.32), the tire iron (sold through the Tabak Garages in Amsterdam; there were hundreds like it). Beyond that, nothing. "We have our little informers," the detective said. "They always dig up something, some gossip, some rumor. After all, murder—it's not our daily fare in Holland. But nothing this time, nothing at all. Silence."

"Isn't old Tabak a Dutch Nazi?" De Witt suddenly asked.

"Yeah, I think so," the detective answered, and added with an unexpected touch of humor, "but the tools he sells aren't, they're neutral."

"All right, Mr. de Witt," the general said. "You've talked to local people? Our Amsteldyk mayor has a fresh slant," he told the detectives.

They all three looked at him, and De Witt felt a sudden chill, a hunch that he should keep quiet. How could he explain the idea to them that the coverage of the murders seemed the only piece of unadorned truth in newspapers that were now German propaganda sheets, and that there must be a reason for that? Buurman, and presumably these policemen too, were all committed to "honest collaboration," "fitting into the new European order," and all that stuff. All they'd understand from it would be that he was some kind of troublemaker.

"Well," he said, "First of all, I think I have found a good explanation of why De Bock was shot rather than beaten to death," and he gave his theory of a struggle between De Bock and his attacker.

"I didn't know about that wounded hand of Jonkheer de

Bock," the General said with a deep frown, looking at the detectives.

"It didn't seem a particularly useful clue, sir. He could just as easily have hurt his hand struggling for the pistol. We assume it was a Belgian .32 Browning. Now laymen wouldn't know this, but those pistols have a little steel point on the barrel. It's part of the sight."

"And if you tried to grab one, it could cut your hand?"

"Exactly, sir. The Cremers lived on a suburban avenue, where a murderer could drive up in a truck or a car and grab a tool. He wouldn't walk into an Amsterdam hotel with a big tire iron."

"Hmm," the general said.

"Anyway, sir, why would he or they go out of their way to establish a link between the Cremer killings and De Bock—with that iron, I mean?"

"Of course the stock exchange was already the link, for all to see."

"I don't know about that," the detective answered, and his colleague said, "It could just be, here are about the three richest people in the country. It could be a big gangland money conspiracy."

"Gangland, gangland," Buurman said. "Where did you get that? This is just Amsterdam."

"That's the right track, though," De Witt began, but the detective hadn't finished. "We know nothing was stolen," he went on, "in the sense of silver or paintings, but it could have been peculation, couldn't it? Larceny, involving their real money. We won't know for weeks or months. We have to wait for the report from the financial expert. Such affairs are tangled."

"De Witt?" the general asked.

"I saw another stock exchange man, a man called Jonas Schutte, who also lives in Amsteldyk."

"Yes?"

"General, he was afraid."

"What of?"

"I don't know. He refused to talk to me. But—"

But, the general seemed to have stopped listening. Maybe he was running out of steam, De Witt thought. In the harsh daylight coming in from under the bleak winter sky, he looked very old.

The detectives paid no attention to De Witt; they were softly talking to each other.

Thus the meeting petered out.

18

On Wednesday, February 12, the same Mercedes-Benz or one just like it stopped in front of the town hall. Cars being the rarity they were, De Witt noticed the sound of the brakes and went to his window. He saw a man in the back seat, but the chauffeur, who had jumped out, did not open the back door; he accepted a document through the window and went inside with it. Half a minute later he was back and the car drove off.

De Witt hurried to the hallway, where Smit handed him the document with a pained face. Under the SD letterhead, it informed him that twelve Amsteldyk citizens were to be taken into custody that day, "for questioning in the case of the murders of Hans Willem Cremer and Evelyn Cremer." Smit, who had looked at it with him, said, "The same ten they took last time! Plus Felleman, the doctor, and his wife."

"Who are Jewish."

"Yes."

"Let's go, Smit. Let's go and see these people and warn them. Who's nearest? Waldemar. Quick."

"Me too?"

"Yes, yes, we'll split the list. Come with me to Waldemar first."

Smit hesitated, but only a second. They took their coats and went on a quick march to the Waldemar house. "Waldemar is a friend of yours, isn't he?" Smit asked.

"Yes. Was a friend," De Witt answered.

Since the episode of the first arrests, Smit had for some reason of his own ceased calling him "sir" or "Mr. Mayor" (which was fine with De Witt).

As they rounded the corner of Waldemar's street, they saw a group of people standing near his stoop, talking. "Damnation," De Witt said.

"Gone, Mr. Mayor," a man said. "Very quick and smoothly, too. The Green Police again."

"He'll be back again tomorrow, Waldemar will," someone else said.

After three more addresses, De Witt and Smit gave up. The letter had obviously been delivered after the arrests were completed. "At least this time they tell you," Smit said to De Witt.

"What on earth do they think they're doing?"

He phoned Buurman. "General, we'll find the murderer or murderers ourselves. Please tell them to lay off."

"I'll see what I can find out, De Witt. I'll call you back. Stay near your phone."

It was a long wait. De Witt sat at his desk with his feet up, then stood at his window to stare out over the muddy town hall square, where housewives in kerchiefs walked by, carrying their shopping bags and nets, some improvised out of what looked like pillow cases, one a prewar specimen with gold lettering, "Dicker and Thys," which used to be the finest gourmet shop in Amsterdam. For a moment he started thinking of smoked eel and salmon cut very, very thin, of those rough patés they used to sell there and the black lobsters with their claws tied together, crawling over each other in the window, doomed to be boiled alive, which he had always studied with a mixture of guilt and greed. Coming back to the present reality, he shivered. "Anna!" he shouted.

"Yes!" her voice came to him from somewhere.

"Tell Terpstar to put some more coal on the stoves!"

At these words, Smit stuck his head around the door. "We're beyond our ration as it is," he said.

"Oh, go to hell, Smit," De Witt answered and was immediately sorry for his words.

Twelve people, a drop in the ocean if you thought of the soldiers facing each other across the Channel, the RAF crews flying over blacked-out Europe through the winter nights. But still—

The phone rang. "General Buurman for you."

"De Witt, Buurman here."

He could tell from Buurman's voice that the general had failed and, having failed, had jumped across the fence, had joined his opponents to hide his defeat, even from himself perhaps.

"De Witt, you were mistaken. Or perhaps I should in all fairness say we were both mistaken. Those German police, you must hand it to them, they seem to know what they're doing."

"But—"

"Let's keep our hands off for a while. Let them handle it. I mean that, literally. No more interviews with anyone, nothing. Just run your town. It's their baby now."

"But that is precisely what you wanted to avoid."

"Well, perhaps I did. Anyway, there it is." And the general hung up.

De Witt banged his receiver on the hook and cursed so loudly that Smit once more looked around the door.

"He's telling us to lay off," De Witt informed him.

Half an hour later De Witt was told that Terpstar was outside and wanted to see him.

"They're putting posters up, sir," Terpstar said.

"Who are 'they'?"

"Police. They're Dutch, I think, but they're in German uniforms. They gave me one." Terpstar started to unbutton his various layers of clothing and brought out a folded sheet of heavy white paper.

De Witt spread it out on a table. It was about two by three feet, in two languages, German left, Dutch right. The names of the twelve arrested people were in heavy print. "Marxist and Jewish elements in the community of Amsteldyk, themselves part of the conspiracy, who will be summarily shot in seventy-two hours unless the perpetrators of the cowardly murders of

Hans Willem and Evelyn Cremer come forward and present themselves to the German authorities. The term ends Saturday, February 15, 1941, at 8 A.M." Signed, "H.A. Rauter, Hoehere SS and Polizei Fuehrer fuer die besetzten Niederlanden."

No one spoke. Anna had appeared, the junior clerk, and the errand boy. They all read it again; it was the first time they had seen such a thing.

De Witt picked up his phone and called Buurman back. There was a long wait before he got him.

"Yes?" the general asked in a highly irritated voice.

"Sir, I have to read you something. It is important." And he started reading the entire text into the phone.

A silence.

"General?"

"Yes, De Witt, I heard you. It comes as no surprise."

"Now surely you'll let us try everything we can to prove that those people are totally blameless and to find—"

"Mr. de Witt, I want no such thing."

"General, I have reason to think that I can—"

"De Witt. Didn't I tell you an hour ago to lay off?"

"Yes, but that was before this."

"The ruling stands. Lay off."

19

Seventy-two hours.

In the early morning of the second day, a detective from Amsterdam telephoned with the rumor that a Greek, or anyway a foreigner, had given himself up and had been arrested as the murderer. "Don't say anything yet," he added, but as Smit, who took the call, had repeated what he had heard sentence by sentence, the request came too late. Several relatives of the arrested, who had once more begun a vigil in the front hall, let out a ragged cheer. But they remained uneasy, it hadn't sounded right, and only half an hour later another call came with word that the Greek had nothing to do with Amsteldyk; he had been arrested for an act of sabotage in Rotterdam harbor.

Silence descended on the group of relatives. The town hall staff tried to get on with their chores. Anna brought everyone coffee—or hot whatever-it-was. There weren't enough cups, and so she had to wash them and do two shifts.

De Witt was at his desk with the morning papers, the four left in existence at that time by the Germans. They all had the same fat front-page headline: "Tin, zinc, bronze, brass, iron, called in." The population was ordered to bring in all metals except those that formed essential parts of buildings or machines, and some few certified antiques. Failure to comply would lead to jail in a camp in Germany. Collection points would be set up in schools and, in small communities, in the town halls.

The phone rang. It was the mayor of Breukelen. "Did you see the terrible news?" he asked.

"Yeah, all kinds. Which do you mean?"

"De Witt! The metals, of course! We have to collect it! Think of the mess! How are we going to handle it? And how are we going to be responsible? I called the Ortskommandantur already and asked if it included the bells in the tower of our castle, very old bells, mind you, and they said 'of course' and hung up."

"Well, I think it's the best news in a long time," De Witt said.

"What *do* you mean?"

"It shows they themselves don't believe they can invade England this spring. It shows they're now planning for a hard and long war."

"And that is good news?"

"Yes," De Witt said.

The mayor of Breukelen sighed. "Yes, maybe you're right. . . . Still, I can't see myself sitting here surrounded by bells and pots and garden fences."

"We'll get used to it."

"Of course, you have your murders, poor fellow. Is there any news on that?"

De Witt decided not to talk about the hostages. "No, nothing."

"Yes, I gathered as much. I see the papers have dropped it."

They had, hadn't they? Every day, morning and evening, there had been articles, even when there was nothing to say. "No leads," "Police baffled," and on and on. And then, suddenly, nothing. Nothing since—he checked through the pile behind his chair—nothing since Monday, February 10, when they all had big spreads. The day before the arrests, on Tuesday, February 11, "the stock exchange murders," as the papers had called them, had been dropped like hot potatoes.

For the tenth time that morning, De Witt dialed General Buurman. "The general is out of town. We will notify him of your call upon his return."

Let me think clearly now. All that publicity showed that they wanted those murders made known. Never mind the new German law and order, the public was to know that brutal murders had been committed and that the murderers had not left a single trace. More important still: the victims were among the powerful, or were friends of the powerful.

Then a reversal. Ten arrests. They no longer wanted to instill public fear of the murderers, but of them, the Germans.

Another reversal. It has all been a mistake. Back to stage one.

Then, on the morning of February 12, yet another reversal. Fear of the Germans to be inspired in all of us but *not* in the murderers, for when you take hostages and issue an ultimatum you make it very clear that you've no idea where to find the real culprits.

In the morning papers of February 11, the publicity had stopped. Thus, on Monday afternoon, or on Monday night at the latest, someone had given the word to do just that, to drop it. And the next day they decided on the arrests. On Monday late in the day they decided the chase was hopeless, or pointless. On Tuesday they decided on the arrests to save face.

What could have happened on Monday to bring about this change?

He picked up his telephone again. "Scheltema? De Witt. Sorry to interrupt, but do you remember telling me about those quote weird movements unquote in the stock market?"

Scheltema, apparently his original self again, was unhoped-for friendly.

"Yes, of course," he said. "In fact, I may publish something about it. I found a monograph in our library, 'Speculations by Amsterdam Merchants Between the Years 1605 and 1609,' and it is astonishing. As we said, human nature does not seem to change."

"Well, in a few words, what was it all about?"

"In a few words?" A little laugh. "You'll have to wait for my publication."

"Tell me this then, is it still going on?"

"No. Actually, it stopped as suddenly as it had started."

"When?"

"Last Monday, just before the market closed."

"Monday the tenth?" De Witt asked.

"That's right. It is all back to normal. Listless, in fact."

"Do *you* understand it all?"

"No. No one would. But, when all the factors are in, and that includes of course all the rumors and fears of these times, it will all make eminent sense. As it did during our war against Spain."

"Thanks, Scheltema, thanks. I have to ring off." De Witt hung up and grabbed his coat. "Smit," he yelled, "call the taxi!"

But the taxi did not answer, and he hurried out, having to push his way through the ever thickening cluster of waiting relatives and friends. No bus. He started walking. Time is very short. A German military truck coming up from behind. He stepped into the road and waved his arms. The truck stopped and an anxious face, a corporal, leaned out. "*Ja?*"

"An emergency, official business. I have to be at police HQ in Amsterdam. Our car is out of order. I need a lift."

The corporal pondered this. "Climb in the back," he then said.

At police headquarters De Witt looked so determined and breathless that no one tried to stop him. He marched straight up to General Buurman's door and opened it. The general, as he had assumed, was there, sitting at his desk, leaning back with his eyes closed. For a moment De Witt thought he was asleep. He entered.

"De Witt! You were told—"

"General, please. It's a matter of life and death, of twelve lives. I think I have a serious lead."

The general rubbed his face. "A lead?" he then asked in a low voice.

"There is a connection between those deaths and the Amsterdam stock market." He held up a hand as the general was about to interrupt him. "I'm certain now, sir. A connection between the vast holdings of those dead and a wild movement in certain stocks or shares. Some gigantic fraud, as that detective suggested. The dates show it."

"Which dates?"

"This plot or fraud or whatever was completed on the tenth. And on the tenth the Germans also realized it was too late to catch the murderers, and so they canceled the publicity about the murders, which would have backfired if the murderers remained free, and decided on the hostage method."

"Let me understand you, De Witt. While this fraud, as you call it, was still in progress, the Germans thought they'd catch the murderers, and then, when it was completed, they gave up and went back to their original idea of setting an example with hostages?"

"Sir, I don't quite understand the details. Not yet. But I know now that this is a criminal fraud and not a plot against the Germans. What we need is time. There are less than twenty hours left in their ultimatum. Promise them that, if they give you an extension, you'll give them results. You *must* get an extension."

"I mustn't—," the general began, but then he changed his

mind. He picked up the phone. "Please wait outside, De Witt."

De Witt stood outside the oak door, but he tried to get as close to it as he could, until his ear touched the wood. "Sir!" the secretary cried indignantly.

He stayed a second longer, but all he heard was the murmur of the general's voice.

He walked away from the door.

After some ten minutes he saw the light go out on the secretary's desk phone. She answered a buzzer and listened. "You can go in now, *sir*," she then told De Witt, in a tone of heavy irony.

He opened the door and stood still. The general looked at him and only slowly shook his head.

The following day, a Saturday, dawned slowly under a threatening sky. At half past eight, Hulser, one of the Amsterdam detectives De Witt had met in the general's office, telephoned. "The twelve have been shot." The man hung up immediately.

Toward noon, two men in the green SD uniform started posting announcements on the walls of Amsteldyk. These were printed in red, in German and Dutch. They listed the twelve names again, and said, "As the fellow conspirators in the cowardly murders of Hans Willem Cremer and Evelyn Cremer have failed to give themselves up within the time set by German authority, the above listed twelve people, Marxist and Jewish elements, were shot at 8 A.M., February 15, 1941. The Reich reserves the right to take future measures of a similar nature until the perpetrators have been brought to justice. By order, H.A. Rauter, Hoehere SS und Polizei Fuehrer fuer die besetzten Niederlanden." This time "SS" was written.

The policemen were still at it, carefully covering the back of each bulletin with starch, when it started to snow, wet, heavy flakes.

20

It snowed for two days, a white pall descending on the little town.

When De Witt woke up on Sunday, bright light filled his room. I should leave the blackout curtains closed at night, he thought fuzzily; it'll help keep the heat in. Then he felt the unusual warmth beside him and saw the head of the girl next to him in the bed. She had crept over to the edge, and it was hard to understand why she didn't fall out. Her left shoulder was bared; she was so thin that her collarbone seemed about to pierce the skin. She was the girl from the Zeedyk bar, Marlene, and she looked terrible in her streaked makeup on her white little face. She was sleeping with her mouth open.

He slipped out of bed, put on his bathrobe and socks, and went to the window. Hesitantly, blankets of snowflakes—separate horizontal layers of them, it seemed—descended on his town. The school with the German troops, and beyond that the bare fields, the row of stunted trees, all were hidden in the veil of snow. Total silence reigned.

He stood there for a long time. Twelve people, eleven men, one woman. He felt that in this stillness everything was different, everything was possible. A man was as strong as he wanted to be. A crazy idea, he thought, but in a world without sound, armies would lose their power, which flowed from barking voices, screaming dive bombers, explosions. Dammit, it's cold. He crawled back into bed and pushed his feet against those of the girl. She turned over and gave him a sweet smile, which completely changed her face. He put his arms around her and turned until he lay on top, and, with her left hand she quickly and professionally guided him inside her. The evening before it had been dark in the room, and it had been hasty, just using her whole body to masturbate instead of his own hand, he had thought. Now he saw that she looked hard at him while he was

76

in her, and when he came she had that little smile again.

"You look about fifteen," he said. "I hope you aren't."

"I am twenty-one."

"Good. You're a nice girl, Marlene."

"Marlene is my professional name."

"I see."

"My name is Geertje. Geertje Zondervan."

Poor devil. That was a name for a fisherman's wife in some nice green village in Friesland, not for an Amsterdam whore.

"Can I stay here today?" she asked. And when he did not answer, she added, "I'll go before curfew. I'll get home by myself."

"Oh—well, yes, why not."

"I'll make breakfast," she said, jumping out of bed.

"You won't find much to make."

When they were sitting at the table, he was curious to see how she'd react if he told her what had happened. Like Smit's I-don't-want-to-have-anything-to-do-with-it? Or would she say something defiant? I simply want to know how it will sound, he thought. I must dare to speak aloud of the executions, of Waldemar, of the doctor's wife.

She did not even stop chewing the imitation French toast she had made. "We're all going to get it, and sooner, not later," she said with a shrug. "Maybe they were lucky." Then, when she saw his pained expression, she added, "Never mind me."

"It's sure quiet here," she said after a while.

"Yes. Normally not as quiet as this."

"You're very angry, aren't you?" she then asked. "Still, there's nothing you can do about it now."

"I wonder, should I pursue it?" he said half aloud. "What's the point, you may well ask."

"You mean, pursue who really killed those millionaires?"

"Yes."

"Were they the good guys or the bad guys?"

"I wish I knew."

On Monday morning, another communication from the SD was received at the town hall. It listed, once more, the twelve people, but this time there was nothing about Marxists or Jews; they were listed neutrally and impersonally, like things. The notice stated that next of kin, upon proof of identification, could claim them at the freight depot of Muiderpoort railroad station. A charge of twenty-five guilders for a pine coffin would have to be paid before each body could be taken away.

21

The *Journal of Trade and Commerce*, which still published a fairly complete stock-market report, showed little lines instead of figures in the columns for most Dutch East Indies stock since the second half of January. De Witt had got himself the copies of the past month from the public library. From among the names of Cremer's companies enumerated by Scheltema, the only one De Witt remembered with certainty was Batavian Petroleum. It was quoted on January 24 at 300, and on February 12 at 298. All the dates in between had only those little lines in the corresponding columns. On February 13 and 14, it was unchanged, 298.

He had his hand on the telephone to call Scheltema. No, someone different—why not try the editor of this paper? That proved simple: the man answered his own phone and immediately told De Witt that the funds would not have been quoted on days when they had moved more than twenty-five percent from their permitted level.

"More than twenty-five percent? Isn't that strange?"

"They're strange times," the editor answered.

"Were they too high or too low?"

"I would assume, too high. There's no way of being sure. There are a million rules and regulations from the Germans. It's all restricted; it all takes place in private these days. Rumor had it, much too high."

"And what would that indicate?"

"I've told you all I know myself," the editor said.

Which other companies had Scheltema ticked off so voluptuously on his fingers? De Witt went over the listing in the paper again. Tin—yes, that would have been one of them, Banka Tin and Zinc. Banka Tin and Zinc was unquoted too for those same days. On January 24, it was at 90, and on February 12, 13, and 14, at 86.

Next he called Hulser, the detective he knew. "Mr. Hulser, this is De Witt. About the investigation of—"

"That file has been closed," Hulser interrupted. "Or better, turned over to the German police. After the tragic events of last Saturday."

"Yes. Quite."

"And so?"

"I just need the name of that government financial agent you mentioned, the one who is going over the estates."

"Why?"

Why. "We have to send him the papers for the Cremer house in Amsteldyk," De Witt improvised. "Taxes. We want to close the file too."

"Oh, I see." A bit less inimical now. "Hold on. Right. Here he is. Dom, Dr. J.H. A doctor of monies. Government Accountancy, The Hague."

"You don't have the address?"

"That will get it there, just that."

"But—"

"It's that blue stone building, on Twent Street, don't you know it? But 'Government Accountancy' will get it there."

"Okay, thanks. And, eh, good luck."

"Yeah."

"Their lemon sole is still excellent," Dr. Dom said. "I recommend it."

They were in the little dining room on the second floor of the Old Dutch, a restaurant in The Hague looking out on Buitenhof, once a famous little town square and, De Witt had to admit, not visibly changed. Even the snow wasn't dirty here but white, the hedges dark green, the entire scene miraculously free of the black and white German road signs and public notices.

"Sole?"

"They know me here," the financial expert said with an emphatic wink.

And thus, during a strangely suspended hour and a half, De Witt sat at a table of white linens, ate a sole in the best tradition of Dutch cuisine, sipped a wine that had been brought after much whispering between Dr. Dom and the waiter, and looked out on a square where prewar ladies in prewar fur coats walked by. And through it all Dr. Dom chatted: anecdotes about "the dear old finance minister" (De Witt wasn't sure whether they were placed in 1920, 1930, or 1940), with the present making its appearance in stories about the odd practices emanating from "our neighbors to the east," as Dom called the Germans.

"But about the Cremer estate, and the De Bock estate . . ." De Witt asked for the third or fourth time, when a change of plates created a silence.

"Yes, yes," said Dr. Dom with a sober look, "I know that is the reason behind our little feast. But frankly, my dear man, there is not much to say. You see, the Beauftragte sent his team over, and they play those things close to the chest."

"Is that proper?"

"Oh, you know, *A la guerre*, etcetera. They've assigned me the handling of all the private obligations and incomes of the estates, and there is very much work in just that—you wouldn't believe how much. Luckily, another De Bock seems to be on his way home from Java. But they say that what they call "the public wealth," the holdings in public companies, must stay under their jurisdiction. Of course, I have an idea what they're doing, but they don't really consult me, you know."

"Well, what are they doing?"

Dr. Dom sighed. "You're not a financial man, Jerome, are you? The Cremer and Bock estates are among the largest in The Netherlands. They are very similar in structure, they consist of holdings in the five or six top colonial companies. Dutch East Indies. If those shares were freely put on the market in these uncertain times, to raise money to cover the inheritance taxes, say—and they will be enormous—or speculatively, nobody knows what would happen. Chaos would result. I can see how the German Beauftragte wants to avoid that, for political reasons of course. I think he's decreed some kind of private moratorium, frozen the portfolios, so to speak. Not strictly according to the rules, but then what is, these days? Between you and me. . . ." Dr. Dom looked around the small room. In one corner an elderly German officer was drinking little glasses of liqueur with a lady of whom only the mink-coated back was visible. In another corner, two heavy gentlemen, looking like rich provincial cattle dealers, were talking, their heads together, while their waiter was heating some kind of dessert for them on a chafing dish. The other tables were empty.

Dr. Dom seemed satisfied that he was not being overheard. "Between you and me," he repeated, "the other day I told my broker to buy me some Batavian Petroleum. Just to test the waters, you see. They're cheap, taking inflation and all that into account."

"Yes, 298," De Witt said.

"Aha! You're not as innocent as you look!" Dr. Dom wagged his finger at him.

"And what happened?"

"You wouldn't believe this, but . . . there weren't any!"

"And how could that be?"

"I don't know. I can't find out, either. Not from here, anyway. The members of the exchange are like an Italian family. They stick together like glue."

"And how," De Witt asked, "could that situation be to anyone's advantage?"

"Advantage? Why would it be?"

"Well, someone or some folks have created that situation— by murdering the holders of those portfolios."

Dr. Dom looked stricken.

"You mean you hadn't realized?" De Witt asked.

"Of course, of course. One tends to repress unpleasant facts. I really don't see a connection. There is no imaginable stock-market angle to those murders. Family intrigues, international intrigues, politics. Anything but that. A rich man can be robbed. People as wealthy as the Cremers and the De Bocks are above such hazards. To put it succinctly: The financial consequences of those deaths will not have been the reasons behind them. You see the distinction?—No, here, I am taking care of that. We have an account here, you know, all old friends. My father used to have lunch here every day. I wonder, though, how much longer they'll be able to call themselves 'the Old Dutch.' Wouldn't be surprised if it had to be changed to 'Das Alte Holland,' ha, ha."

22

De Witt got from the restaurant to the The Hague railroad station just a few minutes before the three o'clock train to Amsterdam was to leave. He squeezed into a second-class compartment in which several people were already standing between the two benches. No one spoke; they were all waiting for the whistle of the station master. Nothing happened. At twenty past three the train started up with a heavy jolt, which made De Witt step on a seated lady's toes. "Hurrah!" someone cried. The train left the station, gained speed, then slowed down again. Finally it came to a stop in the middle of snow-covered fields. "Amsterdam, everyone off," the same man said who had cried "hurrah" before.

"Goddammit," De Witt muttered. He began to feel slightly sick, standing there. All the eating and drinking. God knows what the bill had come to. He used to dream of prewar meals and here, when he miraculously had been given one, he felt as if he were going to throw it up. The train moved jerkily another half mile or so and came to another stop. A man in a corner seat lowered the window and looked out.

"Do you see anything?" he was asked.

"No. Yes—here's someone running. A train guard."

The guard came closer. "Air alarm!" he called. "Everyone out! Air alarm! Air raid!"

The passengers pushed the door open and in a scramble jumped down onto the cinder track. Some started to wade down the slope, halfway up to their knees in the snow; others crouched beside the train. De Witt was about to jump off when a lady who was still in her seat held him by his sleeve. "Please, sir, get my suitcase down for me. There's a month's food for my family in it."

He was too surprised to refuse and lugged the lead-heavy case down and put it in the doorway. She squeezed past, pulling it toward her. It almost knocked her over, and then she started dragging it away.

In the sudden silence, the high drone of a plane engine was audible. Now De Witt hesitated. He looked out of the window.

The guard came running back. "Everyone out! Enemy planes!" he cried.

De Witt pulled his head back and sat down, propping his legs up on the other seat. They're not my enemies, he said to himself. I'm staying right here. Room at last.

In the continued silence, the sound of far-off explosions was heard, or perhaps it was anti-aircraft fire. Then nothing. After a long time, the guard again, "All clear! Everyone aboard!"

One by one the passengers climbed back into the compartment, brushing off the snow and mud. The lady with the suitcase plaintively asked for help, which was given by a young man who then informed De Witt he was sitting in his place.

"Finders keepers," De Witt said.

"But you can't do that."

"But I did. Cram yourself in here if you must. I'm not getting up. Risked my life for this seat."

The man gave him a strange look but did not answer.

The train started up. It was now getting dark and the little blue ceiling light threw a ghostly gleam on the faces of the passengers.

De Witt felt, of a sudden, that this had been a profound experience, something that had shown him how to act. Not getting off that train had been a private victory, it had been a choice. And giving yourself the chance to choose was the big thing. That was what kept you going, made you feel a man. Or a woman, as the case may be. To choose instead of ducking, and instead of trying to live in the past. It wouldn't be enough, after this war, to go back to the past.

When he came out of Amsterdam's Central Station, it was dark, it was sleeting, and it was past six o'clock. But, instead of going home, he went in a quick march to police HQ, which was only a few minutes away, and asked for General Buurman.

"General, we must retain our self-respect, our freedom of choice."

Buurman stared at him. Unexpectedly, De Witt had been admitted right away. At that hour the place was almost deserted; employees in hats and coats were hurrying down the dark corridors to get out and to get home.

"I was in an air alarm on a train," De Witt went on. " 'Enemy planes,' they told us. But of course they weren't, they were English. I'm not a German."

"Their bombs won't know the difference," Buurman said with a ghost of a smile. "Is that what you've come to tell me?"

"Sir, I want your okay to continue the investigation."

"Oh, for God's sake. You're a mayor. You're not a policeman."

"Before, you *asked* me to investigate."

The general did not answer. He leaned back and, with the curtains drawn and only the lamp on his desk lit, his face became quite indistinguishable.

"If I don't, I'll have twelve citizens of my town on my conscience, forever," De Witt said.

"What? How do you figure that?" the general asked with sudden anger. But continued, "Never mind—I don't want to hear it. You have to return to your regular duties. Let us all just hope that this drama will remain the exception to the rule. An anormality. Let us hope for normal relations."

"Normal relations?"

"I'm not talking about morality," the general said. "I sort of like you, De Witt. You've got . . . you've got a way about you. Do I really have to spell it out for you? A high political morality, that was our little luxury here in the West when we were running things. And it was something for the underdogs in the rest of the world to look up to. It was their opium, you might say—like that business about religion being the opium of the people? Quite clever that, actually. But when our very existence is at stake! . . . Am I getting across to you?"

"Eh—yes."

"And?"

"And nothing."

"It's do or die, De Witt. Don't you understand? Either we're their junior partners, or we are nothing, subhuman, *Untermenschen*, and we'll go down the drain with the Jews and the Reds."

A silence.

"Sir, let me ask you just one thing then. Let me go see the Beauftragte to the Netherlands Bank."

"The Beauftragte? Why on earth would *he* want to see *you?*"

"He would if you introduced me."

"And what would you say to him?"

"I'm not sure yet. I'd feel out the situation. I still think that if a stock market fraud eh, lies hidden behind the murders, he can't like it either, and—"

De Witt stopped when the general leaned forward and his face became visible.

"I see, De Witt. I'm to call the Finanzkommissar who is holding the economic existence of this country in the palm of his hand, and tell him the mayor of Amsteldyk, population two hundred, wants to feel him out."

"Four thousand. Not two hundred."

"De Witt, listen carefully. If you raise this subject with me again, I'll request your dismissal from the secretary general. Now leave me alone."

When he had closed the general's door behind him, De Witt

saw that the secretaries had gone, only one light had been left burning. The room lay empty. He quickly opened a desk drawer, then another. Stationery. "Office of the Police President." He grabbed a handful of sheets and envelopes and hastened away.

23

It wasn't that simple. He'd type a letter to the office of that Beauftragte to the Netherlands Bank on the Police President's stationery, ask for an appointment for himself, sign Buurman's name. But then what? The letter couldn't suggest that they call the mayor of Amsteldyk directly in reply. Big fish don't call little fish. He could send Terpstar in his old beadle uniform with the letter and have him wait for an answer. The essential thing to avoid would be that someone at the bank telephone Buurman about the matter.

De Witt was in luck with the streetcar and the bus: it was only around eight in the evening when he got back to his apartment. He was starving. Going up the stairs, he tried to remember what was left in the cupboard. He should have asked for a doggie bag at the Old Dutch.

As he put his key in the front door, he realized there was a light on inside. He slowly opened the door. The table was set, and in his only comfortable chair the Zeedyk girl was sitting, her feet tucked up under her, reading one of his books. "For God's sake," he said.

She looked at him nervously. "I hope you don't mind. My stove was broken, its door came off. And—"

"But I do mind. How did you get in?"

She reddened and muttered, "The door wasn't locked."

"Try again, Geertje."

"On Sunday I found a key in the kitchen drawer. I kept it, just in case you—"

De Witt sighed. "You're a nice girl, but I can't have you

here. Sorry. Put your coat on. I'll walk you to the bus."

"You don't have to," she said, standing up.

"I want to."

"All right then. Do you . . . do you want to do it first?"

"Well, no, not really. I'm sort of preoccupied. And worn out. And cold."

"Okay."

He walked her to the bus stop. The sky had cleared, but it wasn't as cold as it had been. He waited beside her at the stop, he tried to think of something to say. Then the narrow gleam of the screened headlights of the bus appeared. "There you are," he said. And he put a folded ten-guilder note in her hand.

"No, you don't have to do that."

"Keep it. Good night, Geertje."

"Good night, Jerome," she said quickly, and got on.

Jerome? She must have read my mail, too. Oh well. When he was back in his room, he was sorry for a moment. The table looked nice and in the kitchen he found she'd prepared a kind of casserole of tomato paste and heaven knows what else. It tasted terrible, but she must have been so disappointed. Poor devil. Do you want to do it? In his bathroom he pulled up his shirt and looked at his naked body. God, not very appealing. You could count the ribs.

He saw the answer to the appointment problem now. He sat at his desk and drafted a careful letter, with General Buurman introducing De Witt as "a special aide," making it clear that De Witt himself was supposed to take the letter directly to the Beauftragte. "Matters of a possibly urgent nature." He found his high-school German dictionary and weeded out the errors. He'd type it on the best machine in the town hall, under the general's letterhead, and he would present it at ten in the morning at the Netherlands Bank and then just wait. If necessary, he'd come back again the next morning.

It did not seem likely that, before seeing him, they would phone the general about it. In the daily course of events, Buurman had nothing to do with the state bank or its German supervisor; there was no established channel.

At his first try, after a half hour's wait, De Witt was shown into the office of the Beauftragte to the Netherlands Bank, Reich Finanzkommissar Fischbein.

24

It was clearly the former office of the bank president. On one side of the huge room was a desk with chairs, while on the other stood a low table with a couch and more chairs. Above the couch hung a portrait of the Fuehrer, with an inscription. Wide windows, framed in red draperies, looked out over Rokin Street.

De Witt took all this in before he looked at the man behind the desk. It happened to be a nice day, the first one this winter, he had thought during his streetcar ride. There was little wind and a bright sun sparkled on the metal of the German army trucks parked in a row outside and on a desk ashtray made out of a highly polished cannon shell. To the side of the desk, in a straight chair, a man in a dark civilian suit was seated, holding a pencil, a notepad in his lap.

Behind the desk, the Beauftragte, nodding at him, "Herr"— a look at the letter—"Herr de Witt." He was a middle-aged man. He was wearing a black uniform with gleaming insignia. These, too, caught the sun. The man's short hair was slicked down sideways over his skull. He was wearing rimless glasses. The moment their eyes met, De Witt thought of Heydrich. Here was Heydrich twenty years later, no longer interested in the German outdoors or in hunting but with that selfsame aura of being beyond human sensations. Yet, on longer look, you saw wrinkles, intelligence, the face of a man who had read books, who had studied, the face of a German professor. Perhaps they've always been that way, De Witt thought. Perhaps some of us are that way. It's simply that Hitler has set them free. What had Scheltema said? "A decent fellow if you don't cross him." But this man was neither decent nor not decent.

De Witt made a little bow. The assistant was not introduced.

"Ah yes, the old General Buurman," the Beauftragte said. "Well, let us start. We have fifteen minutes. I will be in The Hague at twelve. Sit down."

"Herr Finanzkommissar," De Witt began. "We—as an aside, one might say, to the tragic murders of Mr. and Mrs. Cremer, and of Mr. De Bock—we have come upon irregularities on the Amsterdam Stock Exchange. Which is why we wanted to consult your office. We know that the SD, the German authorities, think those murders were committed by political, by opposition, elements. That is how those hostages. . . ." His sentence faded out.

"Quite so," the Beauftragte said.

"Well, if we can demonstrate that the motive was not political, that we have here a case of criminal fraud, it would be of great significance for us. Very great significance. It would safeguard our citizens from further, eh, measures. There has been a threat of further measures."

The Beauftragte stared at him, or past him, with half-closed eyes. He is not listening, De Witt thought. The man won't help, not against his own police he won't, not unless I can reach his interest in the smooth economic machine he wants to run here. That's his only emotion available to me.

The Beauftragte looked at his watch. "Continue, please. What signs of fraud did you find?"

"We don't have access to the records of the estates. Your men do, of course. We understand you may have frozen the portfolios. Nevertheless . . . huge transactions have taken place in Dutch East Indies shares. A vast illegal profit must have been made, outside the trading on the floor."

"A vast profit," the Beauftragte repeated.

"As you know, very large sums of money are involved here. A hidden blow must have been delivered to our entire economy, for private gain. The frustrating thing is that your police must have suspected something, been on a definite trail, when they dropped it and made the fatal decision to arrest hostages."

"And what makes you think that?"

"The way the police handled the publicity, I mean the way they publicized the crimes," De Witt began and then stopped. How could he go far enough to make the German suspicious of his own police, and not accuse the Germans in so many words of filling the newspapers with lies? He had to be very agile.

But the Beauftragte did not wait for De Witt to complete his answer. "You aren't suggesting that our higher police authorities were involved in stock market speculation while on war duty in occupied territory, are you, Herr de Wit?"

"Eh . . . no."

"It would cost a man his head." The Beauftragte bent two fingers of his right hand and made a little twisting gesture with them. Turning an electric switch? Tightening a garrote screw? That strange little movement destroyed De Witt's train of thought.

The Beauftragte picked up his telephone, asked for an extension, and began a conversation about committee meetings, which had no connections with De Witt's visit. While speaking he did not take his eyes off De Witt's face.

In that moment De Witt could feel drops of sweat popping up on his forehead. He clutched the briefcase he was holding in an effort not to start shaking.

He had made a deadly mistake.

While speaking, he had for one-tenth of a second seen a kind of twitch descend that smooth, immobile face, a twitch traveling from the pale eyes to the corner of the mouth.

And like a flash of lightning, the realization now came to him that Finanzkommissar Fischbein knew all about the fraud. And Fischbein would therefore be aware, too, that twelve Dutch hostages had been shot as a maneuver to cover up some German error or, indeed, complicity.

And now De Witt had served notice that he was on to the scheme; he had been advertising his own cleverness, begging to be the thirteenth victim of this cover-up.

"By all means," Fischbein was saying, as De Witt stared at the man's left hand, which was stroking his cannon shell ashtray.

"Are you unwell?" the assistant asked, bending over toward De Witt.

"No . . . my stomach—I have to go to the toilet for a minute. Excuse me."

The man laid his pad on the desk. "I will show you the way."

De Witt put his briefcase in his chair, made a kind of apologetic gesture toward the Beauftragte, clutching his stomach with the other hand, and followed the assistant. Outside the office, on the left, a narrow door showed a little white "Free" sign.

"In there," the assistant said.

De Witt went in, locked the door, and turned on a tap. He stood and listened, staring at his face in the porcelain glare, until he thought he heard the steps of the assistant moving away. He forced himself to count to ten and then on to twenty. He opened the door and walked away from the office.

"The other direction, sir," a secretary said, a Dutch lady, and she pointed with a smile.

"A paper, I forgot a paper," De Witt mumbled, heading down the wide staircase.

He walked fast, got lost, found himself in a long narrow corridor without carpeting. Stone steps down. A half-open door came out on a bicycle shack. No one was around. He lifted a man's bicycle off a ceiling hook and wheeled it toward the exit. An old Amsterdam policeman was posted there and touched his cap as De Witt passed him.

He was out on the street. He swung his leg over and cycled toward Dam Square, waving past the row of army trucks, trying not to seem in too much of a hurry.

25

De Witt often enacted escapes in his mind. He liked to conjure up the idea of police knocking on his door, and how he would manage to climb out, drop to the ground and hide in the bushes, make his way to an all-day cinema, smuggle himself aboard a freighter, and end up in Africa or South America, possessing nothing, hunted but free and with the whole world to hide in. In those daydreams he didn't dwell on the reasons for his being hunted, though it was understood that these were not banal.

The presence was different, but surprisingly not terribly different. Once he was out of sight of the bank, he was not very afraid any more. Just as in his fantasies, he felt exhilaration at being cut off from the routine round of things; he did not think for a moment he could go back to his old life. That's why I feel pleased with myself, he thought. I was real quick in making that decision.

There must always be that very brief moment, before matters have crystallized, when you can escape. People wait too long. I was a mayor but I could have made a good criminal. If I had stayed in the bank, I'd never have set foot in the street again. But the Beauftragte, stroking his cannon shell and talking on his phone, never suspected I already knew that. He only saw this dumb Dutch civilian who had to run to the toilet.

I wonder if I still have time to be De Witt, not to go to my apartment for sure, but to get to the post office and take my money out. He couldn't possibly have sent an alarm reaching down to postal savings clerks.

He got off his bicycle and pushed it, for otherwise he'd have to go around with the one-way traffic on Dam Square. People gave him dirty looks because they had to sidestep the bicycle, or were they looking because he was the only person on the street without a coat? His hat and coat were still in a closet at the bank, where the secretary had put them when he arrived. At the post office he put the bicycle in the outside rack. It would be sensible to leave it there; no point in steering clear of the SD only to run into the bank clerk to whom it belonged.

There was a line for postal savings accounts, and when his turn came the woman at the window made him fill out a form for withdrawals without passbooks. "Two hundred seventy-five guilders, please," he said. "And I'm in a terrible hurry, I have to get back to work."

"Sorry, but this has to be checked against the register," the clerk told him. He watched her walk to the back and leaf endlessly through a ledger. Didn't she know the alphabet? Then she went over to a man working at a table and started talking to him. They both seemed to peer in his direction.

At this, his feeling of calm suddenly evaporated, he turned, bumping into the man behind him in line, and rushed out of the building. He jumped on the rear platform of a passing streetcar making the turn in front of the post office and heard a traffic cop shout, "That's forbidden!" He went inside the car, sat down, and opened his wallet. His hands were shaking. Goddammit, seven, eight guilders, that was all. What a damn fool I was there. They were discussing the meat rationing, I bet you. Make a good criminal indeed. I'd better shape up fast.

He stayed in the streetcar, which was, amazingly, half empty, and ended up in West Amsterdam, a part of town he hardly knew. He got off near the end of the line and entered a small café. It was like being in the country already—sand on the floor and everyone nodding at him as he sat down. He read the prices on a blackboard and ordered beer and the cheapest sandwich. It was just twelve noon, hardly more than an hour since he had walked out of the bank.

Adriaan, he thought. He's my best bet; he'll help. He's right next to police headquarters, however. I must wait till dark. He studied himself in the tarnished mirror behind the counter. It can't be that hard to make yourself look different. Of course I never recognize people anyway.

Then, remembering his panic in the post office, he suddenly wondered if anything at all had happened—except in his own imagination. Suppose that Beauftragte was at this very moment eating his lunch in some requisitioned palace or ministry in The Hague, without a thought about a little official who had run off in the middle of an interview because he had diarrhea?

Those twelve hostages. Had they been tied to posts as in that movie where, who was it, Mata Hari, Greta Garbo, had refused the blindfold? Or did they make them sit down on kitchen chairs and shoot them in the neck? Doomed without reason, without motivation, they must have been so frightened; maybe they had to be dragged out. . . . And then he saw very clearly again that aged Heydrich face in the sunlit bank office. And the twitch descending on it, a miniscule surface manifestation of great anger. Not the anger you feel toward an opponent, but contempt—a kind of irritated, deadly, resentment—the inverse of that other German trait, the desire to be loved, he thought. No, I don't think I am wrong about the Beauftragte, he said to himself.

Although it was lunch hour, the café remained quiet. By two o'clock, and after two more watery beers, De Witt was alone with the man behind the counter and the old waiter who fussed around and seemed to be waiting for him to leave. Then a heavy-set man came in with a fox terrier on a leash. He elaborately took off his coat and told them all, looking at each person in turn, that it was getting quite cold again. The waiter brought a bowl of water for the dog, and his owner drank beer, standing at the counter. De Witt avoided his eyes, for he knew the man would start chatting with him; he beckoned the waiter and paid, counting out a tip of forty cents. As he stood up, the dog owner told his dog to sit, passed him with a little smile, and went into the toilet. The waiter had gone to the kitchen and the man behind the counter had his back to him. Without further thought, De Witt walked to the door, grabbing the dog man's coat on the way, and was out in the street. But even before the door had fallen shut behind him, he heard a loud, indignant shout from the waiter, and he dropped the coat to the ground and started to run, without looking back, running as if his life depended on it.

26

Maybe it did depend on it. And what was the matter with him, anyway, stealing bicycles and coats from poor devils who'd have to suffer for his heroics? No more of that. He had a lot to learn.

He had slowed down in an alley, stepping over garbage, an old mattress, and piles of dog shit. He was panting.

He walked along canals, past warehouses (with beautiful tropical names on the fronts, "Paramaribo," "Cayenne," "Ternate & Tidore," now looking shabby and abandoned), then through busy, poor streets, careful not to double back on himself. He had one coffee in another café and sat with it as long as possible. Finally the sun, which had seemed so friendly that morning and had remained motionless that endless afternoon, set behind the houses. Darkness fell. He took a streetcar back to the center of town. It was freezing now, and he hurried along, his collar up, to the university gateway and into the secondhand-book courtyard. Thank heaven, Adriaan was there. He was already closing up shop, lowering the wooden top on a crate of books.

De Witt touched his arm and Adriaan looked around. "Jerome." He seemed to sound less jolly than usual. "Aren't you wearing a coat?"

"I lost it."

"Lost it?"

"It was stolen in a café."

"Do you have any textile ration points left?"

De Witt shook his head.

"I can send you to a place where they'll sell you a good one without."

Standing there in the dark, cold yard, De Witt had a feeling of anti-climax. During the past hours, he had thought the whole city was staring at him, and here was Adriaan, continuing his packing up and more or less ignoring him. Maybe he knew and was afraid to get involved.

"Did you see the evening paper?" De Witt asked.

"Yes, sure," Adriaan said without turning toward him. "Same old news. Why?"

"Oh, nothing."

Adriaan was finished. "I have to run," he said. "I'm meeting someone in the Gerstekorrel Bar. I'd ask you to come along, but it's a business deal."

"Sure. Fine."

"Maybe we'll have a beer tomorrow." He held out his hand to De Witt, who hesitated.

"I wonder . . ." De Witt said.

At last Adriaan focused on him. "Anything wrong?"

"I wonder if I could borrow your key. I want to get off the street and I can't go home right now."

Adriaan opened his mouth, presumably to ask why, but thought better of it. He pulled out a key ring, took off a brass key, and gave it to De Witt. "Turn it clockwise," was all he said.

"Thanks." De Witt hurried out into the street, where the little flashes of pocket lights carried by the passers-by only accentuated the total darkness.

27

Adriaan came home after curfew and looked unhappy upon finding De Witt, who was reading in the ice-cold room, wrapped in a blanket.

"I didn't think I should put coal on your stove," De Witt said. "I didn't know how you were fixed for rations."

"Oh, rations. I'm on to bigger things." Adriaan poked up the fire. "Have you eaten?"

His tone of voice made De Witt answer, "Yes," although he was starving.

"Well, let's go to sleep. I'll get you a pillow and another blanket. Are you all set for tomorrow?"

"Yes."

Adriaan hesitated in the doorway and then said, "I won't ask you what you're lying low for. In such matters it pays to be discreet."

"Very sensible." And, as Adriaan still seemed to wait for something, De Witt asked, "And you—have you become a black-market big shot?"

"Black market? Let's say I'm moving from dealing within a loser's economy to dealing within a winner's economy."

"That's nice."

"It makes more sense."

De Witt tossed and turned for a long time on the couch, not because he was six feet and the couch five, but because thoughts kept racing through his head. A friendship, of sorts, but still it had been many years. How strange that it could so easily evaporate. "It pays to be discreet." He should have given him a punch in the nose and walked out, but whereto, and after curfew at that? A terrible feeling, to be dependent on someone you dislike. Well, tomorrow morning first thing, I'm off.

He lay staring at the little red window of the coal stove and at last toward morning, when the fire had died down, he fell into an uneasy sleep filled with dreams. When he woke, sweaty in the shirt he had slept in, the room was cold again and dark, with the blackout curtain still down. Adriaan wasn't there. A note on the kitchen sink said, "Had to leave early. Just pull the door shut behind you." And underneath that, "Have some breakfast."

De Witt opened a cupboard and faced a solid wall of prewar cans: cans of fruit, soup, meat; bins of flour; packets of tea. He felt dizzy with hunger. He chose a large can of spaghetti and meatballs, but, no matter how long he rummaged through all the drawers, he could not find a can opener. Finally he used a shoe brush to hammer a table knife into the top of the can.

The knife point broke off and the brush got dented; he cut his finger; sauce splashed on the wall. But he managed to make a jagged opening large enough to get a spoon in, and he ate the whole can cold. Then he pushed can and broken knife down to the bottom of the garbage can, below papers and other stuff. Next, he shaved with Adriaan's razor. This isn't being dependent, he told himself. It's not giving a damn, just as he doesn't give a damn.

It was half past nine. He raised the blackout curtain. The snow had completely vanished, even from the roofs, and Dam Street lay black and gleaming far below. Rain was falling, drawing patterns on the green water of the Voorburgwal canal, which cut across Dam Street some fifty feet away from the house. The road was empty; on the sidewalks umbrellas made black circles. A cart appeared on the bridge over the Voorburgwal canal, pulled by a man who had put a sack over his head against the rain.

De Witt went to have a look in Adriaan's hall closet. A short coat of dark blue wool—the kind called an ass tickler by Amsterdammers—and a gabardine raincoat. Several hats. He put on the raincoat and picked a hat, then put the hat back. At the bottom of the note in the kitchen he wrote, "Borrowed a coat. Will return it a.s.a.p." He'd be too conspicuous without one in the rain.

He hurried down the five flights of stairs, afraid he would run into Adriaan. Next to Adriaan's house was a stationery shop that carried newspapers and had a public telephone. He would phone Smit; there was no risk in that.

"I want to phone Amsteldyk," he told the man in the shop.

"Just a second, I have to look that up. That will be, sixty cents."

A lady was using the phone and he looked through the morning paper. On page two, a short one-column item in the semi-anonymous Dutch newspaper tradition: "Mayor fired. The mayor of the community of A. near Amsterdam has been relieved of his appointment by the secretary general in the Justice Department, after having been reported missing from his post. Rumors of financial malfeasance could not be confirmed, but we hear a criminal investigation is in progress."

Well, it was actually a relief, now he no longer had to brood over whether it had all been his imagination.

"You—sir. The phone is free now."

Hmm. Smit. Smit's thin voice.

"Eh, thanks. I changed my mind," De Witt answered the shopkeeper.

28

The rain was a bit of luck: it made people less observant, it made them flit by. As he walked north on Voorburgwal, his lips were moving as if he were praying; he was reciting half-aloud all the names of friends and former friends and acquaintances he could think of. He was trying to come up with someone he could turn to but knew already there wasn't anyone. Titus? Yes, but Titus himself was a suspected character and, anyway, how could he help with his one room and no money? There was an uncle alive in the village of Houten and another up north in Groningen, but they would at best be a last resort. He had not come this far only to go to ground in the countryside.

Now more than ever, he had to get on with it. Why, he didn't entirely know. Perhaps because of Fischbein, the humiliation of that interview. He realized now that it was Fischbein who had played the major role in those miserable dreams he had had on Adriaan's couch.

He found himself on Zeedyk. A familiar bend in the street, although it looked very different by day. It was the bar of Marlene-Geertje. Jesus, did I come here on purpose, am I really saying that after half a lifetime she's the only person I know who might help? No, he had simply walked away from the Dam Square area with its offices and police headquarters and people who might recognize him.

The window of the bar was blocked by a black curtain with a bowl of artificial fruit standing in front of it, but its door was wide open. Inside, chairs were on tables, and the old ex-sailor with the tattooed arms was swabbing the floor.

He looked up as De Witt stopped in the doorway. The mixture of rosy light from the little wall lamps and the gray daylight coming in through the door made it seem as if he were smiling. But he wasn't. "Closed," he said and continued his cleaning.

De Witt didn't move. Still it's odd, he thought, that I've come here. But it's like Eduard's Café. A place where you feel people are on your side. No, on no one's side. They're not on the make, they are not after anything, and that is why you can trust them.

The ex-sailor must have been aware of De Witt still standing there. "Well?" he asked, without looking around.

"Tida ada rumah," De Witt said. That was ship's Malayan for "I've nowhere to go."

Now the man turned and straightened up, leaning with both hands on his broom. "Oh, it's you," he said. And went on, "Don't tell me you're a sailor."

De Witt's deprecating smile came natural: he felt defensive about the white-collar job he had held on shipboard, the year he had dropped out of law school. "In a fashion," he answered. "The Lloyd had me as an assistant purser. Not for very long."

The man made no comment. He dipped his broom in the bucket of water.

"On the old *Prinsendam*," De Witt added. "The one that burned out in the Red Sea five years ago."

"I can serve you a cup of coffee this time," the man said. "Bought some last night from a German navy cook. Go sit in the back, where the floor has dried."

29

The tattooed man told De Witt that his name was Jopie.

"And this bar?"

He shrugged. "Same name."

"You mean, 'Jopie's Bar'?"

"No, just 'Jopie.' " And, indeed, "Jopie is locked," he heard a man say after trying the front door.

That day their conversation did not go much further. When Jopie had completed a very thorough cleaning job, he went into the kitchen. After a while he served De Witt a plate of bread and cheese, real cheese, and a large glass of gin. But he didn't sit with him and he disappeared again behind his kitchen door. Dutch gin at noon wasn't De Witt's idea of lunchtime pleasure but, sitting in the back of that barroom, a paralyzing depression descended on him and sipping the stuff helped, he thought. Jopie had turned off the pink wall lights, opened the blackout curtain, and locked the door. It was still raining, water was running down the window and through that wet veil and the irregular glass the passers-by made a distorted procession of shadows. The daylight hardly reached his table; he could just make out the print in the newspaper, which he read several times, down to the classified ads. These amazed him; he had not been aware of that strange half-world that had sprung up at the edge of the German occupation after less than a year, in which a used tea kettle or one typewriter ribbon or a fountain pen "not in working order" were offered for sale and "retired gentlemen" made themselves available for standing in line at movie houses or holding seats in trains waiting in Central Station at rates of from fifty to eighty cents an hour.

Around two o'clock Jopie reappeared. "That was nice," De Witt said. "How much do I owe you?"

"Four guilders."

He had five guilders left in his wallet and he put them on the table.

"I'm going to open," Jopie said. "Why don't you go upstairs, two flights, and sit in the back room. You'll find some books there too."

"Okay." It now came easy to De Witt not to ask questions.

He climbed the steep stairs and found himself in a narrow room, with near its window an old easy chair, a table covered with black sailcloth, and a cabinet bulging with books, photographs, and various odds and ends. He spent the rest of the afternoon at the window, some unopened books on the floor beside him, looking out on the roofs and the chimney pots, the dripping and leaking gutters, and once, a cat dashing from one sheltered spot to another. He did not stir.

It was dark when Jopie came in. He closed the blackout curtain, muttering something about helplessness, and turned on the light. He put two small bottles on the table. "From a friend of yours."

One bottle was hair dye, color "Raven Tresses," the other label said, "Sportsman's Skin Tonic. That Desirable Outdoor Effect."

"From Geertje," Jopie told him.

"Geertje? Did you tell her—can she be trusted?"

That annoyed the man. "Can we trust you?" he asked sharply.

"Eh—I see what you mean. Sorry."

"I'll get you a sleeping bag in here," Jopie said. "Can you afford ten guilders a week for this room?"

"Well, yes. Sure. I'll have to get the money. It may be a couple of days."

"Oh. That'll be all right, I guess. Food—do you have your ration cards?" De Witt shook his head. "Your ID card?" De Witt shook his head again.

Jopie started whistling a little tune. "Those are hard to get hold of, expensive."

"Well—"

"Use that stuff, on your hair and face. There's a toilet one flight down. Tomorrow we'll take a picture. You'll need some clothes too."

De Witt did not answer. Jesus, what a disastrous mess. Did he want to go through with all this, and how could he manage it? He felt so lost that he asked, "Is Geertje downstairs now?"

"Yes."

"Can she come upstairs unnoticed? Would she?"

"I'll ask her," Jopie said in his unchanging, detached voice. "You can't do it in here, though."

"What?" De Witt even reddened. "I just want to talk to her, I wouldn't—"

"You see, I'd lose my license," Jopie interrupted. "The Dutch cops are very keen about that kind of thing. I often think there's nothing in the world that worries them more. If Geertje does it in her room, it's private enterprise, if you do it in here, it's a brothel."

She did not come up, which was just as well, De Witt thought, with him feeling sorry for himself, an apology planned for that evening when he had sent her home—it would have sounded pathetic and phoney.

The next day Jopie showed up with a small, silent man who carried a reflex camera and hung up a sheet for background, but when it appeared that De Witt did not have the fifty guilders handy he wanted in advance, he packed up again. "He'll pay tomorrow," Jopie said. "Then I'll take the picture tomorrow," the man answered.

"Just as well," Jopie commented when the photographer had gone. "You didn't use that stuff right. You're spotty, like a dog."

"I'll go borrow money from a friend tonight. But you'll have to lend me a few guilders for car fare and bus fare."

Jopie sat down on the sailcloth-covered table. "I never lend money. Doesn't work in my business. I feed folks on credit. Even pour them gin. Lending money, no."

"I know I owe you food coupons," De Witt said. "That cheese yesterday, that must have been a month's ration. I hope you're not sorry you got into this. I'll pay you back all right. Don't worry."

"I don't." Now Jopie grinned. "It's sure funny, when you consider. Holland, and you can't buy yourself a chunk of cheese."

"Not funny ha-ha. The Germans have dragged everything away."

Jopie shrugged. "The fat cats always drag everything away. It's just that guys like you feel it for the first time."

"You mean you don't mind the Germans?"

At these words Jopie jumped off the table. He put a hand in his pocket, and for a moment De Witt thought he was going to pull a knife on him. "Sorry," he said.

"I shipped out on a German freighter once. Just one voyage. It felt bad from the start. Germans don't belong on the sea. I'm used to singing when I work, it sets the rhythm if you know what I mean. The mate used to tell me, 'Joppy, the cat gets the bird that sings too soon.'"

"I see."

"Do you? Some people and some countries think everyone's against them. They're now set to make the rest of us feel the same."

That evening at six, De Witt left the bar for the first time. He took the streetcar and the bus to Amsteldyk. Just before six, Jopie had come up to his room with five guilders.

30

His destination was once more Jonas Schutte, the stock exchange man who had been so afraid. Admittedly, not a brilliant new idea, but the only simple action he had been able to think up. He had to do something. Schutte, scared into not talking, could also be scared or bamboozled into talking. Perhaps he could be made to believe that he, De Witt, was in contact with the Dutch government in London. Perhaps he would even loan him a few hundred guilders, against his savings account maybe.

In the meantime, De Witt did not have an ID card or any other card on himself and he was still wearing Adriaan's raincoat which should have been returned. He had given his face and hands another application of Sportsman's Skin Tonic and looked sort of leathery now, although the effect was more of a skin disease than of the Desirable Outdoors. Nevertheless, it was marvelous to be out on the street again, and his depression vanished immediately. I've gotten tougher, he thought. I'm free in a way. I want to be a bit like that Jopie. He must be in his sixties but he's hard, he doesn't talk unnecessarily, he's gentle but you know he wouldn't take any crap from anybody.

He caught the streetcar at Central Station, and then the bus to Amsteldyk. It was strange getting on that bus, but he was going against the traffic of any of his fellow citizens out for an evening in the city. Anyway, it was almost dark now.

Hard to believe he'd been away only two days. To his relief it started raining again as he got off at the first Amsteldyk stop, well before the town hall. He stayed back at the bus shelter, tying his shoes, until the other passengers who had gotten off with him had vanished into the darkness.

Using his flashlight sparingly, he set out for Schutte's villa. Two days ago there had been a new moon. Soon there wouldn't be a glimmer of light left in the sky; as of old, he thought, we are once more aware of the phases of the moon when we travel.

It was half past seven when he came to the Schutte driveway. He could just make out the edge of the roof against the sky. His heart was beating fast; he remembered from his first visit that there had been no dog, no barking. There still wasn't. He could hear the pebbles crunch under his feet and maneuvered until he felt grass. The walls of the house became visible and in them, just barely, the blacked-out windows. Mr. Schutte was a thorough man: There wasn't a gap in any curtain. De Witt hadn't anticipated this; he had planned to sneak up, study the man in his dining room or at his desk, and wait till the maid and his wife, if he had one (he didn't remember), had left him alone. He stepped back now, as water from the drain pipe hit his neck, then turned around to the front door and rang the bell.

"Who is it?" a voice asked from behind the closed door.

"De Witt for Mr. Schutte."

An older woman, not the maid from last time, opened the door a crack, leaving the chain on, and had a quick look. "I'll call him," she said. "I have to close the door again, for the light."

A long wait this time; he listened at the door and heard steps, voices. Then the woman opened the door an even narrower crack and said, "He'll be with you," and just before the door was shut once more, he heard a click in the hallway, which registered right away: it was a telephone receiver being replaced, stealthily.

He half ran across the grass to where he knew the gate to be, but when he got to it he bumped full-force into a bicycle propped up against the fence and fell in the mud. A fierce pain shot up his leg as he scrambled to his feet and hobbled to the road. When he had reached the highway T-junction, he saw a slit of strong blue light approaching very fast; he turned, ran a few steps in the opposite direction, and ducked behind a tree. It was a German police or army car, a camouflage-color Opel, as he could see in the wet road's reflection of its blue lamps, and it tore into Schutte's driveway.

He started running. Fuck this, he thought, that old bastard has twenty-four-hour police protection at his beck and call. God, what a mess. I'm the most stupid amateur at this. I am getting on-the-job training, though. Provided I live long enough.

The asphalt changed to stones; he knew exactly where he was now. He had run toward the center and was not more than five minutes from the town hall square. He shone his flashlight on himself for a second and saw he was covered in mud; blood was dripping down from inside his trouser leg onto his left shoe.

31

As he limped on in a kind of quick march, keeping the trees between himself and the road, stumbling over roots, he could feel his key chain jump around within the deep pocket of Adriaan's raincoat. The town hall key was still on that chain and it just might save the day. "Nil desperandum," he said under his breath. I'd better get on with it, though. Guys with thumbscrews in their pockets are driving around looking for me.

He came to the end of the street that led to the town hall square. In that open space light, a mere suggestion of light, hovered. It could only be starlight from behind the clouds, he thought, for the houses around the square lay in total darkness. No steps, no flashlights, not a sound. The rain was ending with some halfhearted drops. He limped across the little park and up the stoop of the town hall. If only Smit—he was already hating the man for having changed the lock, put on another bolt, God knows what, when the door opened smoothly and soundlessly on his first try. "Bless you, Smit," he muttered, slipping inside and closing the door gently. He stood there motionless, trying to catch his breath and keep the weight off his left leg. Then he heard the German car again and even saw the blue light of its taped-up headlights reflected on the ceiling. It went around the square once and vanished.

First the bathroom, he thought. How good it felt to be on really familiar ground. A home match against the SD. Just at that instant, he hit his leg—of course, the sore one—with a numbing crash against something metal. The surprise was as bad as the pain; it was as if the air had suddenly solidified. "What the hell!" he screamed.

His flashlight showed him a pile of pots, anvils, andirons, bronze bells—the scrap metal collection. He turned off the light; "Goddammit," he kept repeating as he made his way to the bathroom. Once inside, he felt for the blackout curtain; it was down. He turned his light back on and placed it on the sink, took off his shoes and his trousers. A long, deep scratch from his knee to his ankle, from Schutte's damn bicycle, intersected a wide, shallow cut from the scrap metal. No towel, of course. He washed his handkerchief under the cold water and wiped his leg clean; the bleeding now was minor. Then he washed the mud off his shoes and finally off his trousers. Clutching all these wet things, the flashlight in his mouth, he made for his old office. The stove was completely cold. He rung out the trousers and spread them over a chair, and he dried his shoes with papers from the desk and then stuffed them with more paper. Only then did he take off his wet coat, drape it over a lamp, and sit down in his chair. He opened the middle drawer of the desk and there, as he had left it an eternity ago, was a crumpled pack of Chief Whip with one cigarette still in it. The curtains were down. The matches were right in their place in the drawer. He put his stockinged feet on his desk, lit his cigarette, and felt good.

Here I am at the scene of the financial malfeasance, he thought. What could be better than to make it come true, not only won't the papers have been lying, they'd have been true ahead of time. When he had got the last puff out of his cigarette, he padded over, in his socks and underpants, to the little room where the municipal safe stood.

Now if only. . . . For a moment he thought he had forgotten the combination, but he hadn't of course: 14-39-13. The thin key—bless Smit, bless them all—was where it always was, under the saucer of the dying geranium. And the safe opened as nicely as ever.

"Holy Moses," De Witt muttered. It was two days before payment certificates day! On March 1, claims on the German Wehrmacht under two thousand guilders were to be paid at the town hall. There were stacks of notes: tens, twenty-fives, even hundreds, a fortune! He turned off his flashlight and danced around in his socks, on legs that weren't the least bit sore. Then he sat down. Would you believe it. And they can't accuse me of anything for they already have. There's only one problem: how to get out of here and get home.

He went back to his own office, fetched an old briefcase from his cupboard, and filled it with money, lots of it. The rest he very neatly put back in its place, shifting some papers under it to make it appear to be more. This way it'll take longer before they notice. They? Well, "they" may be poor old Smit or, more likely, some Dutch semi-nazi New Order fellow. I wonder what Buurman thinks of all this, I haven't given him a thought.

He closed the safe, put the key back, and returned to his own desk chair. There was only one way to get back to Zeedyk: not by trying to beat the curfew now, and in soaking wet clothes, but at the other end, when the curfew would be lifted at 6 A.M. At that hour it was pitch-dark but people were about. The Amsteldyk area still had plenty of early-rising farmers. He had to be sure, though, to be up and away before anyone knowing him appeared on the scene; by seven o'clock his goose would be cooked. He simply had to sit and wait and make sure not to fall asleep. It was well worth it.

He had a fine night. He wandered all over the building, checked everyone's desk, took everything out of his own drawer, and then shook enough tobacco crumbs from it to roll two cigarettes; he found a prewar peppermint at the back of Smit's pigeonhole and a private letter, unopened, addressed to himself. He read some of the official stuff that had come in during the past days and felt as pleased as a child playing hookey. He had nothing to do with it all; the bureaucratic mill of enemy occupation was not for him to help grease any longer.

He sniffed around for important documents, secret instructions—perhaps for his successor—something bearing on the murders and the hostages, but there was nothing like that. It was all about German marks and textile rations, permissions and licenses.

In a cleaning closet he found a man's umbrella. One of its ribs was broken, but it looked good enough: a perfect tool for hiding one's face.

At 6 A.M. he stood ready. His trousers were still wet, but he had made a crease by putting them under a stack of directories for a couple of hours; his shoes were brushed and just damp inside; his leg, protected from his trousers by a clean rag from Anna's box. With change for the bus and street-car in his pocket, the bulging briefcase, reinforced with string, under his arm, the umbrella in his hand, he slipped out the front door, hurried past the corner and, feeling safely away from the town hall presence, walked to the next bus stop.

No one was waiting there, but the bus arrived already packed. What he could see under the little blue ceiling light was gray faces, tired, miserable expressions. No one he knew. "Watch where you set your foot." "Screw you." Everyone was hating everyone. On the streetcar, in the first light, it was the same. "You're poking that briefcase in my back, mister." "Sorry, sorry." If they only knew.

He stayed on until Central Station because there was protection in the crowd there, and he walked safely back to Zeedyk with a mass of pedestrians entering the city. It was nearly eight when he got back to the bar.

He found that Jopie had left the front-door latch off; he locked it behind him and went into the kitchen to look for some of that coffee Jopie had bought. As he stood waiting for the water to boil, he realized that, while he was in Amsteldyk, the idea of going to look at his own apartment had never entered his head. Good, he said to himself. I'm learning my role.

The letter was from the Geelkerkens, suggesting they skip the monthly dinners until things were "more normal." I've no cause to feel resentful, they're simply backing the winners. Reason is on their side. There's a majority of Geelkerkens, and maybe they're not even thinking in terms of winners and losers. Order, rules, authority, that's what they back, no matter who's behind it; change and disorder, they'll always fear and reject. I've no cause to feel noble or martyred. No one's asking me to do the things I'm doing.

32

Jopie came upon De Witt drinking coffee in his kitchen, his sore leg up on a second chair.

"Hope you don't mind," De Witt said. "I didn't want to wake you."

"It's fine. Your pussyfooting yesterday made me nervous." He produced one of his rare, lopsided smiles. "You got your money, eh?"

"Yes. Here's your five guilders back, and ten for the room." De Witt had prepared for this by taking some notes from the briefcase.

Jopie nodded with satisfaction. "I can always tell. People tell you money isn't important to them, but I can guess how much they've got in their pockets to the last guilder, just by a good look at their faces. You sure look different."

"Well, thanks for the loan."

"Those weren't my five guilders. I told you, anything, but I never lend money."

"Whose were they then?"

"Geertje's."

"Damn. That's sort of embarrassing."

"You're kidding. Whores love to do that kind of thing."

"Whores?" De Witt didn't like that.

"What did you think she was?" Jopie asked with raised eyebrows.

"She's just some poor devil who should have stayed on the farm."

"She rents out her cunt."

"Okay, okay. Does she come here every day?"

"Yes."

"Will you ask her to come see me?"

"I asked last time. She doesn't want to go upstairs. She lives just around the corner. Didn't you go with her?"

111

"Yes, but I guess I didn't pay much attention that evening," De Witt answered.

"I'll see if we can get the photographer back here today. Better stay in for that. Yesterday they had a road block at the New Market, with identity checks, the works."

The man with the reflex camera reappeared, summoned in a mysterious way (for Jopie had no telephone and he hadn't gone out). He counted his fifty guilders and took the picture, and an hour later he brought an ID card, got another fifty, and vanished without a word spoken. Jopie scrutinized the card. "It's not too bad," he announced. "I've seen better. Of course, the thumbprint on it isn't yours."

"Screw." De Witt hadn't thought of that.

"If they look that close, you'll come unstuck anyway."

Now De Witt went to see Geertje. Jopie had explained her whereabouts to him, for indeed he did not remember. At that hour, mid-afternoon, curtains everywhere closed, it was just a quiet, middle-class canal street. There was no bell, but the front door of the building was not locked, and he now recalled her door, the first one on the right. She was ironing and she wasn't surprised to see him.

"I came to thank you," he said.

"That's okay. I've got herb tea. You want a cup of herb tea?"

"Sure. Well, you know, it was very nice of you. Especially after I chucked you out that evening."

"This is different. Sit down, Jerome."

"I'm Kees now. Kees Koster. Bookkeeper."

"Stand under the light," she said. "Lord, you look terrible. Your hair is all uneven. I'll do it. It has to be done over."

"It was very hard in Jopie's little toilet. It's got a sink the size of my hand."

He sat with his back to her sink, under a towel. As she was rubbing the cream into his hair, he began with some hesitation, "Geertje—"

She stopped and came to stand in front of him. "No, that's

not on, not for now. You can't be friends if you get laid for money."

"That's not at all what I was going to ask. I was going to ask if you'd want to do some work for me."

"Work for you?"

"Well, you see, I need someone for things, errands, and it has to be a person who isn't, I mean someone whom nobody knows I know."

She went back to the hair-dying job without answering.

"How much do you earn?" De Witt asked briskly.

"Oh, I don't know. It's different every day."

"Well, on the average. Say in a normal week."

She was doing a sum, moving her lips silently. "A hundred and fifty guilders."

"Gee, that's a lot."

"They make us fork out very much rent."

"Well, I can pay at the same rate. Tell me something if you don't mind, do you have a, you know, a protector?"

"A pimp? No. I fend for myself. Is it dicey, what you want me to do?"

"Dicey?"

"Dangerous?"

"No. If someone asks, you can just say you were hired to do an errand by a customer you don't know."

33

She had done a wonderful job. Before, his hair in blackish streaks, he had not looked different at all. She got it a shiny black and then as an afterthought cut it very short, and it changed his entire appearance. With this black bristle he looked precisely the descendant from a poor peat farmer's family in the east of the country who had come to the city and made good as a forty-guilders-a-week bookkeeper. Kees Koster, born in Assen, Drenthe. He felt very safe and didn't bother further with the skin tonic. He tried to scrub off its leathery stains but that did not work.

His first move was to send Geertje with a letter to Scheltema in the early evening. He had spent hours thinking about it and obviously, after Schutte, Scheltema was now his best and maybe only bet. He needed an opening and he was still sure that Scheltema knew things.

Working on the letter, De Witt had become aware how much all this was outside his experience. His experience was normalcy. In spite of the occupation, in spite of the fact that in principle his and everyone's lives were forfeit at the snap of some German official's fingers, he like everyone else had been living in seeming normalcy. Not in the least like dancing on a volcano, that was the wrong image altogether; it was more like those farmers he remembered in *War and Peace* who went on plowing or harvesting within sight of the great battles of Austerlitz or Borodino.

At the black-sailcloth table De Witt had also written to General Buurman. That letter he sent by mail. He told the general he had left his post and fled because he had been right: there had been fraud and the Beauftragte knew it; the twelve hostages had been killed to cover the tracks of certain Germans and their accomplices. "I think you should have supported my investigation. I think you owe it to yourself, General, and to me, to break the conspiracy of silence hanging over this. It is not a matter of policy but of honor." The general often spoke of honor. De Witt underlined the word.

He didn't believe his letter would sway Buurman, but he had nothing to lose by sending it. He could never resist the urge to explain himself.

That evening the papers carried a follow-up to the "Mayor Fired" story: the "possibility of ties" was now being investigated between the former mayor of A., J. de W., recently relieved from his post by the secretary general in the Justice Department, and the criminal elements involved in the so-called Stock Exchange Murders. The public was reminded of

the ten-thousand-guilder award made available by the Board of
the Stock Exchange and the German authorities in liaison with
the Netherlands State Bank.

34

He sat at the window of his little room with the blackout
curtain raised and without light. It was warmer there than it
used to be in his own Amsteldyk apartment; for another three
guilders a week he now had a coal fire in his stove, evenings.
He had expected Geertje to come up and tell him about her
Scheltema errand, but she hadn't.

Diffused light shone in the sky high above the rooftops. It
was a murky night. Several times he tiptoed to the little toilet
from whose window he could just see the street, but it was not
really possible to tell if she was among those who came in and
went out of the bar. When it was past curfew, he softly went
down another flight of stairs and listened for voices, but all was
still. The bar was closed. Jopie had gone to bed.

In the morning he forced himself to wait until after nine, but
then his nerves got the better of him and he hurried over to
Geertje's place. The front door was locked and he attracted
considerable attention by knocking and banging on her window. Finally she opened, her face puffy, in a housecoat. She
looked at him and crept back into bed.

"Well?" De Witt asked.

"Well what? There wasn't any answer."

"No answer? Whom did you see?"

"Mr. Scheltema, as you said. He read the letter and said, 'No
answer.'"

"I'll be damned. Are you sure you had the right place?"

She got very peeved now. "Yes, of course I'm sure. You
think I can't read?"

"Well, dammit, why didn't you come and tell me last
night?"

"There was nothing to tell, Jerome. Kees. And I was busy."

"Busy??"

"There were old clients waiting for me."

"But hell, didn't I pay you for your time?"

She sat up and looked at him with a deep frown. "It's not the money, Jerome. What would people say if I suddenly refused? What about my future?"

"Your future! Your future is in the syphilis ward of the Free Hospital, lady."

At these words, Geertje hid her head under the blankets. De Witt stared at that for a moment, then he left, banging the door behind him.

At the corner of Zeedyk stood a large, old-fashioned café, the kind with billiard tables and, he knew, a proper telephone booth with a door. He went in and called Scheltema at the stock exchange.

"Scheltema here."

"What do you mean, Scheltema, 'no answer'? And don't hang up."

"What do I mean? Did you see last night's paper?"

"Yes, William. You must know that that's just fantasy. I'm going to discover the truth about all this."

"Why?"

"Why? Because I want to get that decent Beauftragte of yours before he gets me. And because it's the only way to protect my community."

A silence.

"Are you there?" De Witt's voice was hoarse with anger.

"Yes. I'm thinking."

"I'll be at your house, tonight at eight."

"Impossible," Scheltema answered. "My wife—"

"No one can recognize me. It's okay."

"No. I'll meet you at the Bodega. That café you followed me to that day."

"It's too crowded there," De Witt said.

"At two—no, at half past two, this afternoon. There's never a soul there at that time."

35

De Witt was on Damrak at two o'clock and he walked past the café a couple of times. It had become another blustery, gray day, but it was dry and many people were out on the street. He was wearing a new shirt; he had given Jopie two hundred guilders to get him some black-market shirts and underwear and, if possible, a suit. Jopie had said he would, but all he had come up with so far was one shirt, too big but not bad. With that, and in Adriaan's raincoat, he looked respectable, De Witt felt. He passed the C&A department store, its windows almost empty: textiles were as rare as coffee beans. A lonely wooden mannequin in a greenish dress made of what looked like horsehair was staring through the emptiness. But at the glass entrance door he saw the place was jammed. There must be something to be gotten. He entered; it felt odd to be within that crowd. Mostly women, but men too, going from counter to counter, fingering fabrics, counting textile ration points. Peasants plowing during the Battle of Borodino? Plowing? They were thinking about curtains and shirts even though a great war was hanging in the balance. He stared into their faces. Do you know, madam, that our world is entering a new Dark Age? Oh, fuckit, let's just get out of here. He came to a counter where soft men's hats were sold, without ration points, hats made from the same material as the mannequin's dress in the window. They were twelve guilders and he bought himself one. With the hat, his respectability was complete.

At twenty-five past two he entered the café. Behind its glass door hung a sign, "No entry to Jews." That was new, he had not seen that before, although the papers had announced public places would be banned to persons "of Jewish descent." Scheltema had been right: there was no one except a waiter who stood leaning against the buffet, puffing on a cigarette. De Witt took a corner table at the window. He was screened from the street by the curtains. At half past two sharp Scheltema entered, looked around, then came to De Witt's table. "Well, hello," he said loudly. "Haven't seen you in a while. Mind if I sit here?"

"Please do," De Witt answered equally loud. And softly, "Did you have trouble recognizing me?"

Scheltema made a show of staring at De Witt's black hair, raised his eyebrows, and did not answer. De Witt peered past the curtain: people were walking by; no one was standing still; no one was observing the café. The waiter brought them imitation coffees.

Scheltema opened his briefcase and looked in it. Without lifting his head, he began to speak. "Dutch East Indies paper has all but disappeared. It's just not offered anymore. Yet, their quotations are stable now, obviously pegged. In an open market they'd be quoted at—who knows?—ten, twenty times par. There must be some shorting going on, trading outside the exchange, that is, but I'm told not even very much.

"The Cremers together with the De Bock family held the largest private portfolios of colonial stock. With that off the market, there was a unique opportunity to gain control by selected purchases of even just options, for the remaining shares are spread in smaller packets over a number of shareholders. Whoever did that, would have accomplished nothing less that cornering the colonial market, and with little capital outlay. 'Little,' relatively speaking, considering the enormous values at stake.

"The quiet when it was all over does not mean what you think. Once the prices were driven up by more than twenty-five percent, quotations were stopped. And once they passed thirty-five percent—and this is an unpublished rule, strictly kept within the exchange—trading became illegal. You see, this wasn't an old-fashioned bull market that had to be kept propped up. The stuff was simply priced off the market. And that's because of the German rules. Obviously they can't allow black-market prices for stock outside their domain, in the Indies; it would be like broadcasting that there are people who don't want them to win the war and who are betting with cash that indeed they won't.

"The Cremers and De Bock could have been killed to get their stock frozen and out of circulation. Or, before or after their deaths, their stock could have been stolen. You may know that with us, different from London and New York, stock certificates are made out to bearer. They're like money. You can carry them off in a suitcase, and anyone will have a tough job proving they aren't yours. Of course, the men who cornered the market were not necessarily involved in the murders. They may simply have been very, very quick to realize the opportunity created."

"Dr. Dom said—," De Witt began, but Scheltema interrupted.

"Finally, the murders may have been political. I know that Hans Cremer got letters calling him a traitor who was getting rich from the Germans robbing the country."

"Was he?"

"I thought I had made that clear a number of times to you: he didn't profit from his German contacts. And why would he need to. Which is precisely why they treated him with respect, because of his huge wealth. And he used his leverage to have them mitigate some of their economic measures. But clearly the Germans think the murders were political, and that's why they took hostages, and may again."

"And suppose it was Germans who were behind all this— say, some Sicherheitsdienst big shots?"

Scheltema finally looked De Witt in the face, and shook his head.

"Why not?"

"There'd be no point to it for them. Decree A-1."

"Which is?"

"The first decree passed by the Dutch government in exile in London, on May 24 of last year, a week after the Germans got here. A-1 states that no transfer of property from occupied territory to unoccupied territory will be recognized. Anything

119

of that kind originating here is presumed to be done under duress."

"But transfers within Holland are recognized?"

"Of course, but an SD officer is no Dutch resident. If he got hold of Dutch East Indies stock, the transfer would not be recognized in London, nor in the Indies."

"What would he care?"

"After the war—"

"Oh God, after the war. Suppose they had straw men. Suppose some generals or colonels or even your Beauftragte himself are preparing a comfortable retirement for themselves, far from the exigencies of the Fuehrer. Or maybe they are trying to finance some secret SS project. I've read that Himmler means to set up a separate SS state in eastern France."

"Yes, I've heard of that." Scheltema had dropped his didactic tone now. "And please don't call him *my* Beauftragte."

"You told me he was a decent chap."

"Did I? All I meant was, he knows the laws of the money market and tries to go according to the book."

"What?" Unintentionally, De Witt had raised his voice, and he looked around, worried. "You haven't asked me yet why I'm here, with black hair, why they're after me. Because your Beauftragte knows about these goings-on, and through my own stupidity he knows that I know and doesn't like that one bit."

"I find that hard to believe. I believe they really suspect you of having been involved in those deaths. All they see is a little town, violence, anti-German violence, and a mayor who is sort of hemming and hawing about it. I hold no brief for the Germans. But what you outsiders don't understand is that there is method to their manner. They're not savages out of the Black Forest. They have studied economics at excellent universities. The last thing Fischbein would tolerate would be chaos, private speculation, breaking of rules, anything to disturb the German war effort." He stood up. "I have to get back now."

"What about those speculations in the year 1605?" De Witt asked quickly.

"Those? Years of our war against Spain. Amsterdam merchants were buying themselves into the great trading houses of Seville and Cartagena. Prices of shares in them shot up and then stabilized when there was nothing left to buy. They covered their tracks with an artificial low, meaningless, as there were no transactions." He gave De Witt a weak smile. "The connection is a purely technical one. Supply and demand in a hidden, semi-legal, then illegal, money market. Money knows no patriotism; that's the common denominator of 1941 and 1605."

"You haven't helped me any."

"I took a risk coming here."

"*You* took a risk?"

Scheltema bent over, picked up his cup, and took a sip of the coffee he had not yet touched. "You may call me," he said. "Wait a while, though. I may have some other ideas." He put a guilder on the table and vanished from the café.

De Witt was about to follow him out when two men came in. One walked to the buffet, the other toward him.

"Amsterdam detective squad," the man said. "May I just check your identity card, please."

De Witt took the Kees Koster card from his inside pocket and held it out.

The detective studied the card, held it toward the window, started to hand it back, and then stopped. He looked closer, put his nail under the photograph, and pushed. The picture of De Witt, taken in the little room by the taciturn photographer, flipped out and slowly whirled down to the table. De Witt was so surprised that he picked it up with a little grin and held it out to the man. "Pure Aryan," he said.

The man showed him the identity card, now displaying the photograph of a stout, baldish man who was presumably the real Kees Koster and who didn't in the least correspond to De Witt's image of a bookkeeper hailing from the poor peat regions of the east. The silent photographer had simply glued De Witt's picture on top of another one.

The detective had already grabbed his right arm, and his

partner who had watched took his left arm a second later. De Witt looked at the waiter; their eyes met for an instant, and then the man looked away. "Just come quietly, sir," the first man said, and they marched De Witt out the door to where a van was parked with a uniformed Amsterdam policeman standing beside its open back door. "Up you go," the policeman said, and closed the door behind De Witt.

Inside, on wooden benches, several men and one girl were sitting. De Witt's neighbor turned toward him and asked in a low voice, "Are you Jewish?"

"What? Eh, no."

"Would you think I am?"

He tried to focus on the man. "You? Well, no. I don't know."

"That's what my wife kept telling me. But I was a fool to listen to her."

The van began moving. Its occupants bumped against each other in the curves, but not another word was spoken.

36

It was dark in his cell by the time an old Amsterdam policeman came for him and took him to an office where two local police inspectors were working at opposite desks. De Witt was told to sit down on the kitchen chair beside one of the desks. The policeman posted himself near the door.

"Name?" the inspector behind the desk asked.

"Elsschot."

"How do you spell that?"

"E-l-s-s-c-h-o-t. First name Louis."

"Born?"

"Yes."

The inspector looked up from his typewriter. "If you think it's funny, we'll ship you straight to the Germans. They've got their own jokes."

"Born, Antwerp, July 12, 1905."

"Profession?"

"Unemployed."

"All right, Louis. What's your story?"

"Well, I couldn't get an ID card because I'm from Belgium, and I didn't want to go back there. I got to talking in a café with a fellow who said he'd found an ID of someone my age and he'd sell it to me."

"And you pasted your own picture on."

"Yes."

"And how much did you pay Koster?"

"I didn't buy it from Koster. I bought it from a little dark fellow in a café. For fifty guilders. He said his name was Jan."

The inspector turned to his colleague. "Do we believe this man?"

"No. He doesn't sound Belgian."

"That's because I've lived here for years," De Witt said.

"Without papers?"

"Yes."

"Where?"

"All over the place."

"Try again, Louis. Are you a Hebrew, perchance?"

De Witt looked at the man without answering.

"Well, are you?"

"Do you think that's a proper question for a Dutch police officer to ask?"

"I'll be damned. Now he's telling us what's proper. We're doing our job, mister. *Are* you?"

"No."

"What's your current address?"

"Go to hell."

The other inspector said, "Just come clear, Louis. Where do you work?"

"I'm unemployed."

"Then how come you've got—how much?—sixty-five guilders in your pocket? How come you sit in nice cafés in the middle of the day?"

"I do some trading."

"Black market."

"I deal within a winner's economy," De Witt said, thinking of Adriaan.

The two inspectors had a consultation. "Okay, Louis, this is how it stands. Kees Koster did report his card lost. So maybe you're lying, maybe you're not. We're too busy here to go on with this game. If you're not lying, the police magistrate will deal with you. If you're lying, you go straight to the SD. Want to change your story?"

De Witt hesitated one instant but they did not seem to notice. "No."

"Okay, we'll see what the telex from Antwerp says tomorrow. Take him back to the arrest cell, Piet."

"Can I make a phone call?"

"This isn't a hotel, Louis."

"My girlfriend—she'll be worried sick."

"That's what you think," one of the inspectors said, and they both burst out laughing.

"They're stupid fellows," the old policeman said as he marched De Witt back through the long basement corridor. " 'Are you a Hebrew?' They make me ashamed of the Amsterdam police."

"My girlfriend will be worried sick. We're to get married. She's expecting."

The policeman walked on, but before they got to the stairs leading to the arrest cell, he opened a door and turned on a light. It was a narrow office without windows, with nothing in it but a table, a chair, and a calendar. "Make your call. But quickly."

Now De Witt saw there was a wall phone. He went up to it and, with his back to the door, dialed Eddie's café. He knew the number, 171, because he had looked it up the night before when he had been thinking about getting in touch with Titus. 171, with the Amsteldyk area code of 023, made a six-digit number, one more than normal for Amsterdam. He staged a coughing spell to cover the sound of the dialing. The policeman remained in the doorway, however, looking up and down the corridor.

The number rang and rang. "Come on, damn you," De Witt muttered.

"Come on, Louis," the policeman said. "Someone may be coming."

"Hello." It was Eddie.

"Eddie! Take a message, urgent. Tell Saskia that her son's friend is at the Marnix Street police station."

"Tell who? Who is this?"

"Saskia." Oh, to hell with it. With his mouth close to the receiver, he said, "Tell Titus. Titus," and hung up.

"Hang up, Louis," the policeman said.

"Okay. Done. Thanks a lot."

At seven in the morning, the men in the arrest cell were stood in line to go to the toilet and then each of them got a mug of acorn coffee and a slice of bread. De Witt had just sat down with his when a policeman came for him, a young one whose only words were, pointing at the coffee and bread, "Leave that."

In the inspectors' room, the chair had gone. De Witt stood in front of the desk, the policeman behind him. The inspector who had questioned him the day before was typing, the other man wasn't there. After a while, the inspector looked up and started shuffling around in the papers on his desk. "This will interest you."

It was a telex message with an "Antwerp Police HQ" dateline on a perforated strip of paper. After a row of numbers came the words, almost illegibly printed, "Antwerp Civil Register. Elsschot. One, Karel, born 1/1/1884. Two, Anne-Marie, born 3/4/1921. End message."

"You want to tell me who you really are?" the inspector asked.

"I'm Louis Elsschot. Their records have always been a mess. Karel was my father. He's dead."

A moment's silence. Is he going to accept it? De Witt smiled at the man. "Come on, Inspector. You know how sloppy the Belgians are. That's why I prefer living here. You can believe me."

The inspector pulled the document he had been typing out of the machine and handed it to the policeman.

"He's for the morning convoy to the SD," he said. "Make sure they put the cuffs on."

The policeman took De Witt by his wrist and pulled his arm behind his back.

"Hey, take it easy!" De Witt shouted. "Okay. You win."

"It's too late, mister."

"Listen carefully, Inspector. Pick up your phone, call Police President Buurman, and tell him that his impatient friend has to talk to him."

The inspector gave De Witt a searching look. "Wait outside," he told the policeman. He searched for a number in a small directory. "Is this the office of General Buurman? Can you connect me with his private secretary? This is Inspector Hendrik of the Marnix Street Station."

A long wait.

"Hello—Mrs.—Miss Ella? Sorry to inconvenience you, but we've got an arrest here. False papers. He says the general will talk to him. He won't give his name. 'His impatient friend,' he says. Right."

Another wait. The inspector hummed a tune and studied his nails.

"Yes . . . I see." He looked up. "Are you Jerome de Witt?"

God help me. "Yes, I am."

"Yes, Miss Ella," the inspector said into the phone. "Right you are. Thank you." And he hung up.

"What?" De Witt cried. "Wait! I want to talk to him!"

"You're going to talk to the Germans. They're waiting for you."

37

The same van, or one like it, this time with cardboard in the little windows, and he alone in the back with a Dutch policeman.

Just hold on to the idea that there's always a very brief moment of opportunity. I already missed one in that café. I should have made a run for it. I was too much taken by surprise. But now I should be ready, more ready than they are.

However, when the van came to a stop and the back door opened, he found himself in a walled courtyard. A German, an SD officer or maybe he was a sergeant, he had various leaves and crosses on his uniform but he looked sloppy, signed a paper the driver of the van held out to him from his cab. The Dutch policeman removed the handcuffs and put them back in his pocket. Then two other Germans, with rifles, daggers, the lot, walked him past a steel door into a basement and locked him in a cell which had nothing but a wooden bunk and a chamber pot with brown stains inside. After what felt like four or five hours (his watch had stayed at the Dutch police station), a trolley came by pushed by a bedraggled man in prison clothes who shoved a tin basin under the bars of De Witt's cell. It was soup with cabbage and pieces of potato. He hadn't been given a spoon, so he drank the liquid from the bowl and fished the vegetables out with his fingers, then pushed the bowl back out into the corridor.

He sat up on the bunk, his back against the wall, and fought off waves of nausea, half physical, half mental. Physical because the terrible smell and taste of the half-rotted cabbage had stuck in his mouth and nose and mixed with the smell of his own urine in the chamber pot; mental because he couldn't really believe he was where he was. He tottered on the edge of an abyss of self-pity and fear.

He tried to think of books and films about prison, the Count of Monte Cristo, Cellini, Bakunin—lots of famous people have been through this, he said to himself, real ones and story ones. They struck up friendships, fell in love with the jailer's daughter, tapped out conversations on the walls, *learned* from it. Why is this so different? How did the Germans come to be so clever at this? That fellow with the soup, he was dead, there was nothing I could have said, I could have slipped him a thousand-guilder note, and he wouldn't have looked up. Here in the heart of Amsterdam, in the basement of that Euterpe Street girls' school maybe, I am more alone and farther from everything than Monte Cristo on his rock.

He started to tremble. He remembered the tales that were told of German interrogations, Gestapo men who with their bare hands plucked out a prisoner's eye, castrated him with a loop of piano wire—he hugged himself to regain control and thought, I can never see this through, I'll do whatever they say. I don't care anymore about Evelyn Cremer nor about the Dutch East Indies nor about the war. I must protect my body.

He was half asleep, crouched on his bunk, when the cell was opened and an SD policeman told him to come out. Another one was waiting farther down the corridor. They walked up a stone staircase. Here, more lights were burning, naked bulbs. He was taken into a small office, maybe that same one, he thought, where he once went to protest the Amsteldyk arrests to, who, Huber, that was it. This was indeed that same man. Or was it? "Herr Huber," he said with a little bow.

The man behind the desk eyed him. Then he picked up a file. "Jerome de Witt? You have conspired, with others unknown to us as yet, in the murders of Hans Willem and Evelyn Cremer. You thought the Cremers were too accommodating to the German authorities. You will write a full confession and name your accomplices."

"Okay," De Witt said.

"You admit this?"

"Yes, Huber." It's not the way I thought it would be. I'm less afraid. Not out of courage, though. What a strange business.

"Very well, you save us time. Here is a notebook and a pencil. You'll be taken back to your cell to write a full statement. And my name is not Huber."

"Sorry, sorry. I know now, it's Halber."

"My name is not Halber either."

De Witt did not answer but made another little bow.

"We do not like prisoners with a sense of humor." The man stood up, took the pen and pencil set sitting at the edge of his desk, which De Witt had been staring at, and hit him across the face with it.

De Witt felt no immediate pain. He frowned. He thought, how idiotic, the crystal inkwell was dried out, I had just been thinking that set must have stood there from when this was a school. We gave one like it to our math teacher when he retired. Who could have thought? . . . His mouth filled with blood.

"Take him back," the officer said.

De Witt spit in his handkerchief. "Well, damnation," he mumbled. "I lost a tooth. Two."

"We have a humorist here," the officer said to De Witt's escort. "Teeth are small change in this place, De Witt. After your teeth come your nails and, after your nails, your eyes. Remember that. It'll help you write faster."

Back in his cell, De Witt pulled his jacket up over his head and lay down on the bunk, sideways, as closely huddled as possible. He cried and then he fell asleep. He had dropped the notebook and the pencil into the chamber pot.

It was still dark and very cold when he was awakened by a push. His mouth was coated with dry blood, and when he tried to stand up he swayed and held on to his jailer. The man shook himself loose. "Quick, quick," he said.

"I have to piss."

"Some other time."

He was led not to the right where the offices were but to the left and back out into the yard. Above the roofs was a hint of light. A car, the blue slits of the headlights facing them, was standing with the engine running. "Quick, get in," his escort said, pushing him. A soldier or policeman was already in the car. The other man got in after him. The gate was opened and they drove off.

They were in Euterpe Street, he saw now. When they had rounded a corner, the dim shadows of people waiting at a streetcar stop were visible. It was after 6 A.M. then, after curfew. They turned right again onto Apollo Avenue and stopped in the driveway of a villa.

"Quick, quick," the SD man said. They marched him into a garage where a light was burning, although the door was standing open, and pushed him into a metal garden chair.

Dawn was breaking. He could distinguish the bare trees in the garden through the half-open door. A man in uniform approached. De Witt did not recognize him as General Buurman until he had come inside; he had never seen the general in a Dutch staff uniform with a cap, he thought; in fact, he had never seen him on his feet before.

The general did not look at him. "Put his hands behind him," he said, "through the back of the chair. No, not like that; undo the handcuffs, then lock them again." He spoke German with a strong Dutch accent but in the sharp command voice of a German officer, and the SD men obeyed him as if he were one. "Leave us alone now," he told them.

De Witt let his head fall forward and closed his eyes. He could see himself as he must appear, his unshaven face caked with blood, urine stains on the front of his trousers. He sat there as if he was at the end of his rope, but he wasn't. I can deal with Buurman, he thought. No matter how big a bastard he is, he's in a different league from our eastern neighbors. No, "our neighbors to the east," as Dr. Dom would say. He giggled.

"Calm down," Buurman said. "You're in my garage. No need for hysteria here."

De Witt decided to keep his eyes closed.

"De Witt, I had you brought here because I felt no need to have you torn to threads by the SD. I assured them that all you needed was a warning. They took my word for it; I have a relationship of trust with them. Needless to say, I will not hazard it for you or anyone else."

He waited for an answer, and when none came he continued in a louder voice. "If you prove me wrong, and any false move on your part would prove me wrong, I will not save you again. I'll let them have you. And dying your hair any new color won't help. I don't know what the hell you thought you were doing, De Witt. Look at you. You got in deeper and deeper and I'm sure you were scared out of your wits yourself. That's not all bad; it means you are not a fanatic. You got carried away with yourself, boy. I say 'boy' because I once knew your father."

This so surprised De Witt that he opened his eyes and looked at the general, who was sitting in a deck chair, yawning.

"Don't worry, I will not pursue that angle," the general continued. "It was relevant because it makes me believe you are a gentleman. As among gentlemen, De Witt, I now want your word of honor that you will drop all this, that you will totally forget this whole damn business."

Here we have it, honor, De Witt thought.

"I'm afraid you can't go back to your mayoral post," Buurman said. "The Germans aren't that compliant. Your successor is already in place and indeed, as I feared, a chappie with bicycle clips on his trousers. Well, have you learned your lesson?"

"Yes."

"And I have your word of honor?"

"My word of honor."

The general got up. "I'll tell those men to unlock you and to go back to their stations. You can sit here a while and pull yourself together. Do you have money on you to get home?"

De Witt shook his head.

"I'll send my orderly out with some. And with your briefcase with your ID card, which is here. You left it behind at that, eh, that bank interview you staged."

At the garage door the General turned around. "I know you didn't conspire to kill the Cremers. What you still don't understand is that there is a *political* need for certain structures. Halftones won't serve. The Beauftragte is aware of certain irregularities. He will handle them and with an iron fist, he has told me. But he cannot tolerate the insecurity resulting from broadcasting them about. I don't even know why I explain all this to you.—I think you can call yourself damn lucky. Damn lucky."

39

For the duration of that day, De Witt agreed that, yes, he had been lucky. He kept sticking his tongue in the hole between his teeth and repeating the words, "Teeth are small change here."

He had washed in the garage and had gone straight from there to Amsteldyk. He found his apartment taken over by the new mayor; the mayor's wife opened the door, which she kept on a chain—new, this—and told him his possessions had been put in storage. "That's all I know," she said. "Mr. Smit can tell you where." She seemed to expect a scene, and behind her back he could see one of his paintings hanging at a new place in the hallway. The hell with it, he thought, and left without another word. Jopie put him up again and, when told De Witt was now legal, lowered the room price to eight guilders. Then as before, he did not ask him his name. "I got you some other clothes," he said. He also promised to find a mattress for him and a new watch.

"You didn't take away the sleeping bag, I hope?" De Witt asked. The town hall money was stuffed in the bottom of the bag.

"Why would I have done that? You look terrible. Have you eaten?"

"No, but my mouth hurts like the devil."

"I'll cook us some porridge."

"Anything in the papers about the former mayor of Amsteldyk?"

"I never read the papers, you know that," Jopie answered. "I used to read the weather reports, but as they've dropped those since the war. . . ."

They ate porridge and Jopie warmed water for him to wash properly, after which he went upstairs and crept into the sleeping bag, his feet on the money. He had hardly made it up the flights of stairs, but now he was wide awake.

Can I go back to normalcy now, he asked himself, that phoney make-believe normalcy? Find a job and avoid any quote false move unquote and show that Buurman was right and that I'm scared out of my wits? But I was. Am. I pissed in my pants, in a manner of speaking. And literally too. That's all I've learned. I'm no Dostoievsky back from the firing squad, that's for sure. If I go on with this. . . . *If.*

The following afternoon he showed up at Eddie's café. Titus was there and greeted him, but not as he had expected him to. "What's wrong?" De Witt asked.

"I don't know yet. I did get your telephone message."

"I wondered, I never thought you would. But it was a bad moment, you see. Did you do anything?"

"There wasn't anything I could do, was there?"

"No."

"It's the first time," Titus said, "that I hear of someone arrested under the Germans and then they let him phone all over the place."

De Witt gave him an angry look. "What are you trying to say? What do you mean, all over the place? I had a nice Amsterdam cop who gave me a break."

"Yeah—well, here you are out already, anyway."

A hostile silence. De Witt decided to give in. "The general got me out."

"The general? You mean the police president?"

"Yes. Don't ask me why."

"Why?"

De Witt made a face. "When all is said and done, what it comes down to is that they didn't take me as seriously as I thought they did."

Titus looked at him in a curious way. "They didn't ask you for certain promises before they let you go, did they?"

"No. . . . Well, yes, in a way. The general asked for my word of honor that I'd forget about the whole business of the murders and the hostages and the stock market."

"Which you gave."

"I crossed my fingers first," De Witt said with a smile, but Titus didn't smile back.

"Anything else you promised?" he asked.

"Such as what?"

"I don't know. You tell me."

"Just what are you leading up to, Titus?"

Titus shrugged. "When guys get out of the hands of the Germans so quickly, it usually means they've promised to play ball with them."

"Does it now?" De Witt asked. "Well, if that's what you think it means, fuck you." And he walked out of the café.

The street was as dark as a closed room. He had no flashlight and he stumbled as he tried to get off the pavement and into the middle of the road. He knew the way by heart: round the corner and straight for the railroad crossing, and then through familiar streets to the bus stop; but it was as if he were in a different town. What's wrong with me, he thought. First that fat mayor's wife who stole my pictures. And now that damn Titus. My last link with my town. "It means they've promised to play ball with the Germans." What a damn nerve.

That was his lowest ebb, that evening wandering through the pitch-dark, losing his way in his own town, feeling he was a fool who had lost the friendship or respect of everybody he had ever known. He ran smack into someone he did not even see until he hit him (the heavy overcoat and the arm felt like a man), but when he asked, "Where are we? Which way is the town hall square?" all he got in answer was a grunt. He continued and then walked full-force into a tree.

That does it. I'd better stop and think.

He stood there for a while and then turned around. Shortly he found himself without any effort back at Eddie's café. He went in and saw Titus sitting alone at the iron beach table. He sat down across from him.

"There you are again," Titus said. "Did you get another beating just now?"

"I walked into a tree."

"Oh."

De Witt asked, "Anyway, how did you know that the Germans were holding me?"

"After your call, Vrede went to the Marnix Street police station and told them you were her fiancée, and they said, 'Miss, you're minus one fiancée. The SD got him.'"

"That was nice of her to risk that, nice of both of you. Thanks. And sorry."

"Sorry for what?"

"My getting mad. It just means I'm an amateur."

"Eddie, bring us two more gins," Titus called.

"Does that mean you all of a sudden trust me now, that I didn't sell out to the Germans?"

"I guess so," Titus said. "I'm sorry too."

"Well, Titus, then that makes you another damn amateur."

40

Thus it came about that the two men decided to join forces and intercept Jonas Schutte on his way home from the stock exchange and make him tell what he knew.

"It should be easy," De Witt said. "He is a scared man. Once we get him away from his protection, he'll do as we say. In fact, you know what? Everyone must be easy, almost everyone. It is very hard to sacrifice yourself. To sacrifice one single tooth. I don't know how people do it, where they find the strength."

"It may work and it may not," Titus answered, "but please don't use the word *easy*. Please let's remember we don't really have a clue what we're about. Look at you, for instance. Or look at me. I, for one, I'm ready to man the barricades. I'm ready to blow up the Kommandantur, if you show me how. But I wouldn't know how to make myself steal the neighbor's cat."

"Well, let's stop being amateurs."

"Jerome, could you possibly cut out this amateur crap? I'm not even sure I know what you mean."

"Only that we want to be taken seriously. Just that. Now, first order, someone has to check Schutte's hours and how he gets home from his office. Could Vrede do that?"

"Not easily. She's got a job at the gas plant too now, and they're very inflexible. If she takes time off they'd only be too happy to kick her out."

"Geertje then. I have someone who'll do it. What's essential is what he does do at this end, right? It's easier to shove someone into a car on a country road than in the center of Amsterdam."

"You could argue about that. But what car are you talking about? There's no car."

"A kidnapping without a car. They wouldn't touch that in Chicago."

"Coordination," Titus said. "That's crucial. That much I know from our strikes."

"Where they put you in jail."

"Coordination. We need a neutral place with a phone. Of course, there's a phone booth in Amsteldyk. Corner of Ruysdael and Hobbema streets. One of us could be in there."

"It's out of order. I know. When I was still your mayor, I tried to get it fixed. 'After the war,' they said."

"Suppose Schutte tells us to go to hell? Suppose he starts to cry, then what? I'd be mortified."

"Yes, I guess me too." De Witt shook his head. "Well,

damnation. That's why they sing '. . . und Morgen die ganze Welt.' "

"What are you talking about now?"

"Tommorrow the whole world. That's what the soldiers sing in the basketball court across from where I live. Lived. Where your new mayor now enjoys my pictures."

"He's going to be a gem, that one. You know what? He's setting up something called the Germanic Home Arts Exhibition in our public library. We've all been asked to bring in our ancestral artifacts. Like your grandfather's spittoon? Artifacts unspoiled by the worldwide Jewish commercialization conspiracy."

41

Geertje had agreed to go back to helping De Witt. They said nothing about the scene at her place the morning of that day De Witt was arrested.

On Friday afternoon it was she who telephoned Eddie's café from Central Station to tell Titus and De Witt that Jonas Schutte had just, as he had every day that week, boarded the little train from Central Station to Watersmeer. In Watersmeer he would take a trolley line that passed within a few hundred feet of his house: a slower arrangement than the streetcar plus bus, but more comfortable and uncrowded. And Geertje had found that the trolley made a stop just for Schutte at a point opposite the back gate of his property; he tipped the motorman every day. In the other direction, going north from that stop instead of south, a municipal park began across from the trolley tracks. It held the artificial lake where, before the war, the university students used to row. A boathouse, now standing empty, sat at the edge of the course. That was where they'd take Schutte.

Titus and De Witt waited fifteen minutes after Geertje's call and then left the café. They bicycled in the direction of

Schutte's villa. It was nearly five o'clock; a hazy March sun was still quite high. They could be seen but, on the other hand, Schutte would be less watchful in full daylight.

"The days are sure lengthening," Titus said.

"L'heure de Berlin. Berlin time."

"Oh. Yeah."

They rode on in silence.

When they reached Forest Lane at the northern edge of town, they were met by a friend of Titus waiting with his bicycle, a man De Witt had never seen before. He was a hefty fellow who shook hands, but there were no introductions. He and Titus started off toward the setting sun.

"Wait, you're going in the wrong direction," De Witt called.

The lane, running parallel to the trolley line, ran east-west, but Schutte's house was to the east of where they had come out. Titus's friend continued but Titus stopped. "The trolley is due in only twenty-five minutes," he said. "My friend says we don't want to hang around near the house—not, as you told us, with a German police car patroling. We're going west for ten minutes, then east for fifteen minutes. Just follow us."

A sharp wind blew down the lane, which at this spot was without houses, and led through open countryside. De Witt's bicycle, borrowed for him by Titus, had no proper tires, only wooden rims for wheels, and bumped so much that he had trouble holding the handlebars. He was without gloves, and his hands turned red with cold. This cursed eternal wind—keep calm, he told himself, this is nothing. An aged stockbroker, a bicycle holdup. God, think, if I were an Englishman I might have to fly in a bomber over half of Germany every night. Keep calm.

Then he heard the bell, far off, of the trolley car.

"Damn, they're early!" Titus's friend shouted over his shoulder. He made a U-turn and started bicycling back very fast.

They were in sight of the high stone posts of Schutte's back gate when the trolley came around a bend in the lane and stopped. They saw Schutte get off and walk toward his entrance; he had a briefcase under his arm and carried an umbrella. But then, unexpectedly, another person got off too, just as the trolley had started rolling again, a woman in a hat and long coat.

"Who's that?" Titus asked in a low voice.

"Oh, damn. It's Geertje," De Witt said. She was supposed to have gone home after her phone call from the railroad station.

Schutte had obviously heard her steps on the cinders beside the track of the trolley; no one ever got off there but he. He turned and looked, then started in a half run toward the gate of his house, shouting, "Jan! Jan! Here!"

Almost instantly the gate opened and a man with two Dobermans on leashes came out into the road.

"Keep going," Titus's friend muttered. The three of them cycled by without looking in Schutte's direction, Titus's friend whistling the "Beer Barrel Polka." De Witt shook his head at Geertje who stood and stared. She must have imagined she looked like a suburban lady but the effect was of a child dressed up in her mother's Sunday best.

Schutte and his guard had vanished; the iron gate fell shut with a loud clang.

The following morning at nine, De Witt was at the stock exchange. Its offices were open on Saturday mornings, and he must act right away; Schutte might have recognized him on the bicycle, and any report would end up with General Buurman.

He asked to be announced to Scheltema, who came out after a few minutes, looking none too pleased, and led him to his office. "I know you're all legal and above board again," were his first words. "Still, I admit I'd like to curtail our connection a bit. Not that it wasn't interesting."

"I just wanted to see if you had learned anything new. You said—"

"I said you could call. Telephone."

"All right."

"Anyway, there is nothing new."

"Well, I won't take up any more of your time then."

"Aren't you freezing?" Scheltema asked, now obviously surprised at De Witt's mild response. "Don't you have a coat? It's still winter out."

"I live very close by now. On Zeedyk." De Witt had made his appearance in the almost new suit Jopie had bought for him, and without a coat, for a reason: he had counted on Scheltema's not taking him all the way back to the entrance of the building. And indeed, he was lucky. "You know the way," Scheltema said, staying at the door of his office.

When Scheltema's door had closed, De Witt rapidly walked away and got in the elevator. "Which floor is Schutte's again?" he asked the elevator man.

"Fourth. Room 406."

"Oh, right."

He got off and walked down the hall; no one was paying any attention to him. His luck held: His knock remained unanswered, and the door was unlocked. He stepped inside and posted himself behind one of the heavy curtains. After a moment he came out again and unplugged the desk telephone at the wall, then went back into his hiding place.

It was all up to him now, all just a matter of being convincing, of appearing to Schutte as the type of man who would not shrink from hurting or even killing him.

42

It was well after ten when Jonas Schutte came in and sat down behind his desk. He picked up his phone. De Witt thought that on not getting a dial tone, Schutte might get suspicious and even leave the room; he was about to step forward when he saw Schutte hang up without having dialed. The man picked up a pen and put it down; finally he sat still and stared straight ahead.

It was now or never; De Witt came halfway out into the

room and stood still. Remembering Jopie's gesture, he put his right hand in the pocket of his jacket.

Schutte looked up but did not say a word. Then he pulled out a trim cigar case, selected a cigar, and lit it.

Goddammit, De Witt thought, why do things never go the way I visualize them. He took another step forward. "Schutte," he said, "I don't want to hurt you, but in this pocket I have a pistol."

Schutte made a visible effort to pay attention. "Sit down, De Witt," he asked softly. "I didn't hear you come in."

De Witt did not move.

"I'm not allowed to smoke," Schutte said at last. "But it doesn't seem to make much difference now."

"Stop chatting!" De Witt cried nervously. "Listen to what I have to say to you."

Schutte didn't take his eyes off his cigar. "I might have phoned you. But here you are."

"Phoned me? Why?"

"Aren't you the man who is trying to find out about the Cremers? Didn't you come to my house that night, asking for help? And again last week? And yesterday, with two other men, on bicycles?"

"Yes! Yes. You mean you will tell me?"

There was another silence.

"I don't know who physically killed the Cremers and De Bock," Schutte said in an almost inaudible voice, "but I know whom they acted for. The problem is, no one could believe—"

"I can. I can. They were Germans."

"What makes you think that? What kind of Germans? Some crooked policemen?" Schutte asked.

"No . . . no, of course not! How could I have been so stupid? They were killed officially, Mr. Schutte. They were killed on the highest order. Otherwise, why the publicity, why all the press stories? Those murders were meant to scare only the men who knew what was going on, who knew enough to be scared! Scared not of some mysterious underground but of the German authorities. Am I right?"

Schutte pursed his lips. "But one might ask," he said, "why

Germans would kill people with crowbars, when they seem to have more modern weapons than the rest of the world put together."

"It is quite clear to me now, Mr. Schutte. Again, to instill terror."

Schutte stood up and De Witt stepped backward, but Schutte only walked to the window and pulled the curtain, screening off the sunlight which had reached his chair. He stood there a moment, looking out into the street, then turned and sat down again.

"Yes, Mr. De Witt, a broken skull is more frightening than a bullet. Or I find it so."

His cigar had gone out and he very carefully relit it. "You have given me some comfort," he then said. "I did not think I could talk about this after all. But you deserve—who knows? You may bear witness one day."

De Witt was afraid to make a sound; Schutte's voice sounded as if it would break.

"On January fifteen," Schutte said, "a Sunday, a cold, dark, day"—he was nodding his head up and down and looked a very old man—"seven of us were called in. The seven of us who together held virtually all the stock in the major colonial enterprises of the Dutch East Indies, that is to say, Bandung Tea—"

"Yes, yes," De Witt said in the pause that followed, but almost soundlessly.

"—Sumatra Tobacco, Batavian, Quinine, Independent Rubber, Banka Tin . . . Celebes Oil, one or two more. . . . We were told that all stock was to be handed over at current market price plus a twenty-five percent bonus. It was to be consolidated into one holding company. Under Dutch direction, we were assured. We had fifteen days to comply."

"Assured by whom?" De Witt could not stop himself from interjecting, but Schutte did not seem to have heard the question.

"Afterward, we deliberated. It was immediately clear that a majority would indeed comply. We pretended to believe the stock would remain in Dutch hands, even if the Germans would hold ultimate control. Three of us said they would never sell. Cremer, De Bock, and Wilkens."

Schutte stopped talking and closed his eyes.

"And?" De Witt at last asked.

"And?" He spoke in a clear, almost light voice now. "And they murdered Cremer and called us together and asked again. That time Wilkens went over. Only De Bock held out, but he had more interests than the rest of us put together. And then they killed him. And then we all came and signed and signed that we were not selling under duress. And that is all. I hope you are a happy man now."

"And if you had all refused?" De Witt asked after another long silence.

"Ah, you've hit the nail on the head. If we had all refused, we would all have been safe. They could have killed us all, but that would not have achieved their purpose. It so happened that Cremer's children are minors. De Bock's only heir is his brother and he—but that is not relevant anymore. Yes, if we had all refused, we'd presumably all have been safe. But you see, that was not ever in the cards. In fact, we were furious at Hans Cremer for being so stubborn. We shouted at him. I did, too. Fear is not an ennobling emotion."

"And Evelyn Cremer?"

It seemed to De Witt that Schutte's face shrunk even more. "Evelyn. Yes, there was Evelyn. She came to see us, most of us, she came to see me, and asked us to stick by her husband. And after he—afterward, they had not known, you see, that the Cremer estate was a joint trust fund. I went to talk to her then, I begged her to sign whatever they wanted her to sign. 'What does it matter?' I said. After the war we can undo it again. 'And if they win, they'll take everything, with or without us.' She refused, she said Hans wouldn't have approved. She said they wouldn't touch a woman. But they touched. It is not inspiring, Mr. de Witt."

Another pause. Schutte seemed lost in thought.

"Well," De Witt asked, "Is it true? I mean, that it doesn't really matter?"

Schutte nodded his head almost violently. "Oh yes, it matters all right. These were transfers within the jurisdiction of the board of the exchange. We don't register shares in Holland, you know. They're like money. I would think they will send their new director to the Indies and there, with proof of ownership, no one can dispute his total control. I don't know who he will be, but he will be Dutch and it will be legitimate."

"But how could he get there?"

"Oh, there are channels still open. The German Lufthansa flies a line Zurich-Stuttgart-Lisbon. There are neutral ships. I feel certain those shares are already in Switzerland. They'll let them sit there a while, breathe the neutral air. Like table wine."

"And the hostages?" De Witt suddenly asked. "You did not think about them, did you?"

"Yes, we thought about them. One of us five, Fokkema, got as far as the cabinet of the Reichskommissar. He was informed that it had nothing to do with us, an example had to be set, unrest had to be stopped then and there. Those were Berlin's orders and the reasons given were immaterial. Once more we could convince ourselves that what we did made no real difference."

"Unrest stopped—and they were covering the tracks of their own murders?"

Schutte did not answer.

"I still don't understand one thing," De Witt said. "I mean, now, now that you've had time to think—why don't you raise the alarm, send a secret message to Batavia, somehow, say you were forced, blackmailed—"

"Even if there were a channel of communication outside German control to Batavia—or to London, for that matter— which there isn't, such a message would not change a legal accomplished fact; you'd be surprised how hard it is to shake people's sense of ownership, even in the middle of a war. And, you see, anyway, four of the five of us who are still alive think the Germans have won the war. They think they've saved what there was to be saved. That same Fokkema said the first day, 'Better to sell most than being robbed of all.' Wilkens— once he went over, he was as adamant as the rest of them—'Let the Germans own it.' he told us, 'At least they can protect us against the Japs. It'll give them an interest.'"

"Four out of five. Who was the fifth?"

Now Schutte smiled, a smile that looked ghostly on his chalk-white face. "I was the fifth," he said. "I don't think Hitler has won the war. On the contrary, I think he cannot win it, not anymore. But it will be many years."

"But—?"

"But I was afraid. Very afraid. I have always hated violence. When they showed me a photograph of Cremer, of his broken head, the hair all clotted with brain matter—I was sick then. I have always had a phobia about head wounds. I'm a coward, you see."

"I don't think that's being a coward," De Witt muttered.

"Yes, my friend," Schutte said tonelessly. "The Germans have bought themselves a tropical colony."

43

In his little room above Jopie's bar, De Witt was writing down Jonas Schutte's words as literally as he could. After that fateful sentence, "The Germans have bought themselves a colony," Schutte had not spoken another word, he had sat at his desk with his eyes closed, not responding to questions. Then De Witt had thought, I must get out of here, fast, before someone comes in, before something happens to me. I'll put his statement down and send it—send it where?

He had hurried back to Zeedyk, filled with confusion, fear, and relief. Now everything made perfect sense. He should have seen it before, of course. Why didn't I solve that simple equation? But I was near enough. If I hadn't been, Schutte might not have spoken. Now that I know, what do I do?

When he had finished writing, he put Schutte's confession at the bottom of the sleeping bag with the remaining money.

That done, he lay down on top of the bag, overcome by exhaustion.

The scraping of a chair along the floor woke him up. He saw Titus sitting near the window with a book.

"It's not bad here," Titus told him. "When I was a boy, it was my dream to live on Zeedyk one day."

"Well, it's as chaste as in the YMCA. Jopie doesn't allow lady visitors."

"He has interesting taste in books, your Jopie. You know what I was reading?"

"No, what?"

"Beddoes. *The Second Brother.*"

"Never heard of it," De Witt said wearily.

"I came all the way up here because I got nervous," Titus went on. "You were supposed to let me know what happened with Schutte."

"It was no fun."

"Don't tell me you knocked that old devil's teeth out."

"No, Titus. And he's not an old devil. He's a tortured man."

"And—? But—?"

"I didn't go to see you in Amsteldyk because I've had it. I'm kaput. Dead."

"Let's go out and find some food to put into you. You do look green. Vrede is waiting in that place on the corner, the Sun, with the billiards? We'll try to feed you and you can tell me everything."

"I have something to tell all right."

"Well, come on then."

"I'm really too damn tired to get up off this thing."

"I'll pull you off."

"Oh, what the hell. You win." He scrambled to his feet. "Just let me wash my face. Then I'll come."

This would prove an important decision for De Witt.

He sat with Titus and Vrede. Titus managed better than De Witt in a place like the Sun; he wasn't met with the wariness reserved for outsiders. He had jollied the waiter into bringing a heated-up dish of the midday potatoes and cabbage, although it was four in the afternoon. De Witt was spooning up this stuff while he went through Schutte's story for them.

"Jesus Christ, Jerome," Titus said. "I'm impressed with you. Tenacity killed the cat, or whatever the proverb says."

"Yeah—but now what?"

"That's for us to consider."

"Tomorrow, please," Vrede said. "Don't you see he's about to fall face-first into the cabbage?"

"Yes, tomorrow, Titus. I'll come to you. I have to get about twenty-four hours sleep first."

"Aren't you going to finish that mush?" Titus asked.

"No."

"I'll eat it."

"Good. Tomorrow, folks."

But as De Witt slowly walked back, he saw Jopie coming toward him on the same sidewalk, pointedly looking past him. He stood still, puzzled, and as Jopie passed him he heard him whisper, "Follow me."

Oh God, De Witt thought, now what? Can't they leave me alone for a while? He went after Jopie. On a quiet canal street Jopie waited for a couple to walk by, skipped into a doorway, and came out again with a cigarette in his mouth. When De Witt had come near enough Jopie asked, "Got a light?"

De Witt stared at him, then started to search for matches.

"Cops came to the bar," Jopie said quickly. "Looking for you. I said I'd never seen you. One of them gave me a photograph of you. Here. I'm to call if I see someone like you. 'He lives in this area,' they said. They're working up and down the street, all the bars, the hotels, everything." He lit his cigarette with his own matches. "You're wanted for murder this time."

"What? What?"

"They chatted about it among themselves, as open as you please. Seems you've shot and killed a bloke called Schutte. Thank you, mate." He gave De Witt his own matches and, after a look over his shoulder, took off his cap, planted it on De Witt's head, and walked off.

44

De Witt stood frozen with the photographic print in his hand. He pulled Jopie's cap lower on his forehead. That was a nice thing he did there, giving me his cap.

At least it's a bad picture. I can't place it; it looks cut off from a bigger one. With a sinking feeling, he thought that Lydia must have supplied it.

He started walking, oblivious to his surroundings. When it began getting dark, he found himself standing on a bridge, one of the little high-arched ones of the Walletjes, staring at the water. He was only a few blocks from where Jopie had left him. The wandering men who haunt that district on Saturday nights had appeared, shopping for their weekly fun. He was quite near Geertje's place. I wonder if she'll take me in, he asked himself, now that I can't go back to Jopie. There really isn't any other choice. The situation remained unreal to him; in his tired mind he could not focus on these new developments. He couldn't believe he was being chased, once more outside the law, nor that Schutte was dead. It must be one of the general's weird tricks, to pull me in again.

He was stumbling in the rapidly deepening twilight. Nights get much darker here than in Amsteldyk, he thought, darker faster. The evening was not cold and a haze hung over the water of the canals and began covering the pavements, making them slippery. The men walking by, some alone, some in small, boisterous groups, were visible only as white glimpses of faces. He came to Geertje's window, where she'd sit advertising herself. It was empty, its curtains open. He could just distinguish a shadow moving, farther back in the room, and he decided to knock. She opened the door. "Oh, it's you," she said in a neutral voice. "I haven't gone to work yet. I was making myself a dish of oatmeal."

"May I come in?"

"Sure."

He sat in the easy chair, and she lit a little lamp. He got up to close the curtains and sat down again. He could hear the voices of the passers-by. Someone beat a tattoo on the window and cried, "Hey, Marlene!" He looked at her but she did not react.

"I guess you're mad about last night," she said in a defiant voice. "All I wanted to do was help. That's why I got off the trolley car."

"No, I'm not mad. Nobody was. I couldn't stop though. Schutte would have recognized me."

"Oh. I waited a long time. I near killed myself walking all the way back to a bus stop."

De Witt took a deep breath and tried to smile at her. "No, no one is mad. In fact, Geertje, I'm here because I want to spend the night with you."

"You're a joker. The whole night? And it's a Saturday."

"I'll pay."

"Oh. . . . Business isn't so great, you know."

"That surprises me. You're a very attractive girl."

"You think so?" She got up and peered at herself in the mirror for a moment. "It's that rotten war. The occupation. Men don't get very horny when they're being pushed around."

"Well, what about the Germans?"

"They don't come here. They have their own girls, the gray mice."

"Would you let them?"

"Who cares. But they don't come. Only officers sometimes, in civvies. But they're spooky, they scare me."

"Well, is it a deal then, can I stay?"

She looked hard at him. "Do you really want it that much?"

"Yes. I've resisted it, you must admit."

The words sounded so unnatural to his own ears, he wondered why she seemed to take them seriously. Well, as Jopie says, they like that kind of thing. Every profession has its own weak spots.

"Okay, Jerome," Geertje said. "Just let me eat my dinner."

He had trouble keeping his eyes open as he watched her eat a watery plate of oatmeal; then she took her housecoat off and lay down on her bed, naked except for her stockings and garters.

To his surprise he found this exciting, the light of the little twenty-five watt bulb on her body, the whole scene including the housecoat on the kitchen chair and the empty oatmeal plate with the spoon in the sink. He took off his clothes and went to the bed, but then it was all over in a few seconds and he sank into a deep sleep beside her.

He woke up much later. It was so still outside, he instantly realized, it's past curfew. She can't throw me out now. He felt Geertje stroking him, that was what had woken him up. "Don't bother," he whispered, "I can't. I'm too tired."

"But you're paying for the whole night. You haven't had much."

"It's okay."

She turned on her little lamp and looked suspiciously at him. "You're not cheating, are you?"

"What? How?"

"I mean, you weren't saying all that before to help me?"

"No, no. Please turn off the light. My eyes hurt."

When he woke again, it was day and he could hear the church bells all the way from the New Church on Dam Square. Someone must have saved those from being melted down, he thought.

He lay still, feeling perfectly warm and peaceful, restored. Slowly the horrors of the previous day re-established themselves in his mind, but they did not change his mood. Free choice. I'm a man, I can cope. The murder of Schutte. What could it mean?

Geertje wasn't in bed. She was sitting in the window chair in her housecoat with the bedspread rolled around her, snoring lightly. As if aware of his looking at her, she suddenly opened her eyes.

"What are you doing there?" he asked.

"You were so restless, you were tossing and turning when it got light. I don't mind this chair. I can always sleep." She got up, yawning, and went to turn on the gas under her kettle.

"Well, Jerome, what have you got to say for yourself? You

were bamboozling me last night, weren't you? Jopie threw you out because you're broke. Or you're hiding again."

There was something nervous about her smile that made him say, "Something like that, but I really wanted to stay for you. I swear."

"But you're hiding."

"Yes. Will you let me stay? Just till Monday?"

She rinsed her teapot with warm water and put the kettle back on the gas. "Don't you have any friends?" she asked.

That again. He had brooded about it often enough, but this time it didn't unnerve him. Instead, it gave him a feeling of newness, not of loss. "No, I don't," he said. "There's only Titus, but he's in a little walk-up with his girl, and he's on all their lists."

She kept her back to him, brewing her tea, and he went on, "You know, it is the times, maybe. I mean, before the war a man just sort of carried on with school friends and all sorts of people, even if they were quite different; you could go on having your drinks, going out, all that. Now is when you find out what people are really like."

"Here's a cup of tea, Jerome," she said. "I don't have any milk. And I must say, it sounds sort of sad to me, a grown man, a middle-aged man, who has no one to turn to except a little whore from Friesland."

The way she said this made him laugh.

"Don't laugh," she said. "Isn't it sad?"

"Do you look at me as middle-aged?"

"Aren't you?"

"Well, yes, I guess so. I hadn't thought of it that way."

"I didn't mean to hurt your feelings."

"I guessed you were from Friesland. Not your speech. That name, Geertje. It's a nice name. Wouldn't you want to go back?"

"Are you kidding me? You ever smell a grass pit when they open it?"

"A grass pit? I don't know what that is."

"Fodder grass. We bury it so it won't spoil. Every boy smells of it for six months of the year. And the mud and the cold at four in the morning. And the Sundays. Lord. No, this is better."

"But—"

"But—?"

"Nothing."

She put her cup down and jumped up. "I'll show you something." She went over to the closet and began taking out all the clothes on the hangers, draping them over the kitchen chair. "Look," she said. "Come look."

The back panel of the closet could be lifted out; behind it was an empty space some three feet deep. "My friend fixed that, last summer," Geertje told him. "He was going to go into the black market and use it for storing things. But he figured a person could hide there too, when the police came. It has air. Isn't it nifty?"

"Does that mean you'll let me stay?"

"Yes."

"What happened to the friend?"

"He never came back. I think the Germans got him, at their big roundup in Waterloo Square last December. I've been to ask but they won't say. You know what?"

"What?"

"Bob—that's him—Bob has never gotten out of bed in his life before noon. And that one morning, when the Germans did that, he had gone there at nine. Some fellow he just had to see, he said. That one morning in his whole life. It just goes to show, doesn't it. The only time ever. And I used to tell him, don't be so lazy."

Geertje went to Zeedyk for him to get the money from the sleeping bag, and the Schutte paper, and maybe some clothes if it didn't look too chancy. He went through a rehearsal with her: she was to sit in another café afterward, take her time, make absolutely sure no one was following her. But she was back ten minutes later. Jopie's place was all locked up, with a sign in the door, "Closed. Death in the family."

"I guess he got nervous with those cops and decided to let things cool off," De Witt said. It was a blow all right.

"Now what?"

"Now what. Well, there's still Scheltema. If I make him nervous enough, he'd lend me some money."

"That stuck-up fellow."

"Oh, he's not so bad." Then De Witt recalled their conversation: "Don't you have a coat?" "I live close by now, on Zeedyk." Dammit, of course, Scheltema! Why else would the police have started to comb Zeedyk? William Scheltema and his unchanging human nature. "Yes, let's forget Scheltema," he said.

"Don't look so . . . so lost, Jerome. Let's forget them all, just today. It's Sunday."

No newspapers came out on Sunday and Geertje did not have a radio. They drank herb tea and she toasted bread over the gas. "It's not as grand here as at your place," she announced, "but it's cozy, isn't it? It never really gets cold in here either. I'm having a real vacation day."

"It's very cozy. You're very nice about this. As soon as Jopie shows up, I'll pay you back too."

That had been the wrong thing to say. "Don't worry about it," she answered.

"I just meant. . . ."

By the end of the morning he got so restless that she went to chat with a neighbor, a girl who did have a radio, and to listen to the noon news. She came back to tell him there hadn't been anything about a stockbroker named Jonas Schutte.

It became an endless day for him, a summing up of all the endless, subdued, melancholy Sunday afternoons he had lived through as a child, when the street or the road outside had been as silent as Geertje's street was now, when the sky seemed always to have been low and gray. How different things can be from the words to describe them, he thought. If this scene had been described to me when I was a boy, how exotic and exciting it would have sounded!

Night fell. They looked out for a while with the lights off; fog hung over the water of the canal; no prowling men were about now. The sound of the church bells was carried from the south by the wind. Geertje made potatoes and gravy for dinner and came out with, "Surprise." she said, two bottles of beer. He felt such pity for her then that when she put herself on the bed for him, he made love to her in a most tender way. She fell asleep with the little lamp still on.

46

On Monday morning De Witt, wrapped in a heavy scarf lent by Geertje, and with Jopie's cap on, hurried out of the house to Station Square. It was a somber, hesitant dawn, still misty. He was protected again, by the weather and the people going to work. In a dirty cafeteria he had flower bulb coffee and a mysterious kind of cereal. The fork and spoon on the counter were anchored to chains, like pens in a post office. He had not seen that before. "We have to," the counterman told him. "Last week we lost four forks."

He sat there until after nine, got himself change, and went to stand in line for the telephone booths at the southern end of the square. He waited for the end one, screened from the others by the booth next to it, which was out of order. He called General Buurman.

"General, what is going on? Will you please call off this chase? You know I didn't kill anyone."

"De Witt, Saturday at noon, at the closing of the stock exchange bureaus, Jonas Schutte was found behind his desk, shot to death." The general sounded pleasant, almost conversational. "The only outsider seen in the building that morning was you. We have a sworn statement. You were identified."

"By William Scheltema. He's crazy. Why would I kill my witness?"

"Witness? You did go and see Schutte?"

"Yes."

"And who allowed you access to him?"

"No one. I went."

"The police checked. He had made no appointments. You came in, you threatened him with a pistol, and, when he refused to talk to you, you shot him."

"General, when I left, Schutte was sitting behind his desk, smoking a cigar. That was well before twelve noon. Before eleven."

The general did not answer.

"Is Schutte really dead?" De Witt asked him.

"The funeral is tomorrow at ten, at Zorgvliet. Shot through the head."

Shot through the head. Schutte's phobia about head wounds. De Witt shivered. "He must have killed himself, General. He was a heavily burdened man. If you don't hang up on me, I will explain why. You see, he did not refuse to talk."

"We are not thinking of suicide, De Witt. He abhorred firearms, all violence, we were told."

"But precisely, sir, precisely because of that, he would have— Don't you see? He was a Calvinist, a man who believes in the severest form of self-punishment as the way to eradicate sin. Was the pistol still there?" De Witt guessed, he almost felt, a hesitancy now at the other end of the line.

"De Witt, you admit you went to see Schutte, and that is all I have to hear from you. I warned you. I had your word of honor, your word of honor, that you would not meddle in this affair again. And I in turn gave my word to the SD. I was your guarantor. You broke that word. I cannot save you again."

"Wait, General. Don't hang up."

"I won't hang up."

"General, it is grotesque to invoke honor here. I never, I did not for one moment, take that pledge of mine seriously."

"My mistake then. You are not a gentleman."

"Permit me to say, sir, that you are talking crap. You, just like that German New Order you seem to admire, you are mixing two worlds which have nothing in common. There is

155

no connection between the slightly phoney, all right, but still sort of artistic fantasy about rules of battle and honorable adversaries and all that, and the present, with that same patriotism —a doubtful emotion at best, sir—now carried from The Charge of the Light Brigade to the vileness of war with men, women, and children incinerated with bombs, fooled and swindled by supposed leaders, politicians who believe they're better than anyone else. . . ." He was struggling to catch his breath. "You're using words from a fantasy past to cover the corruption of the present. The Beauftragte, sir, with his iron-fist announcement, knew everything. He not only knew, he handled the whole thing, for your information, sir. Word of honor indeed."

"You interest me, De Witt," the general answered calmly. "You've stopped dissimulating. Prove to me what you're saying."

Holy suffering Jesus, De Witt thought in that same split second, he's listening to all this because he's having the call traced. Fool, amateur! He dropped the receiver and half fell out of the booth. Two girls emerged from the phone booth next to the one out of order and he stepped in between them. "Excuse me, ladies," he asked, trying to keep his voice calm, "do you have change for a guilder?" Out of the corner of his eye he could see a police car enter the square from Damrak and follow the traffic circle. Another one was approaching from the quay. They had no sirens going, no lights flashing.

The girls looked surprised. "No," the first one said crossly, and other added, "We've got to catch our streetcar."

The Damrak police car had stopped and several men were jumping out. People stopped and stared at them. "Let me help you then," De Witt said to one girl, "You have to push these days." He took her by her arm and stepped up into a number 16 streetcar. "Are you crazy? Let go!" she cried.

He pushed past her, entered the car, walked through it and jumped off at the front platform. Screened by it, he ran into Central Station, shouting to people in his way, "Sorry, excuse me, my train!" At the entrance gate to the platforms he saw a ticket collector standing next to a policeman. He ducked into a corridor, ran past a large news and tobacco stand that had been closed for months, turned a corner, and came to people standing in line at the luggage checkroom. He took a place at the end of the line; new arrivals closed up behind him. Breathe slowly, he told himself..

Far off, the sound of police whistles, running steps. The people in the line looked at each other, but no one commented. Then nothing.

When he got to the window, he said to the clerk, "I lost my receipt."

"Can you identify the item?"

"Yes, sure. A brown suitcase. My name's on it. It has two suits, one pair—"

"Wait, wait. Step aside, please. Go through that side door. Someone will come and talk to you."

He spent an hour looking for the non-existant suitcase, refusing to leave, telling every clerk that all his possessions were in it, that they couldn't do this to him. A supervisor showed up who promised they'd look again later in the day when things were less busy. He left a fantasy phone number; they were glad when they finally got rid of him.

Out on the square the police cars were gone. He turned left to the quay, his hands in his pockets, the cap in his eyes, hoping he looked like a seaman, always staying between the canals and the trees, and cutting through at alleyways until he got to Geertje's. She was standing at the window. When she saw him, she closed the curtains and let him in.

47

Shaven, his hair slicked down with brilliantine, his suit pressed by Geertje, and in the raincoat Jopie had got him (fortunately, he had gone out in it that last Saturday afternoon), he felt he looked amazingly different.

He was going to the American consulate. He had written down Schutte's statement again as well as he could and he would take it there; they'd see how crucial it was to transmit it to the outside world and, if they accepted it from him, no arrest could undo that.

Geertje had agreed to come too, as a couple would be so much less noticeable to any alerted policeman. But she was furious, for when she had started to put on the same clothes she had followed Jonas Schutte in, he had said they made her look silly. From that moment on she had refused to talk to him.

They went to Damrak to get a number 2 streetcar; the damp, not very cold weather persisted.

The sky was a pearl gray. A hush seemed to hang over the imprisoned city, and the people at the streetcar stop were very quiet. But one lady, carrying various parcels wrapped in newspaper, engaged him in a conversation about how the post office had refused her parcels although the wrapping paper they had insisted on was not to be found anywhere. Her voice sounded unnaturally loud amidst the silence. She kept addressing herself to Geertje, who did not answer, and De Witt gave the woman an apologetic married-man smile. When the streetcar finally came, he and Geertje had to stand and at each turn they were thrown against each other. Even then she refused to meet his eyes. We look a genuine couple all right, De Witt thought.

They got off at Keizersgracht. "Let's walk along the even side first," he asked, "and see how it looks. I know you're mad at me, but please take my arm."

The consulate was on the odd side, number 473. He noticed the American flag from a distance and as they came abreast of it, he saw from across the canal the Dutch policeman who guarded the entrance, looking bored and biting his nails.

They walked on. "You must distract him for me," he said. "Can you ask him directions or something? Or perhaps—"

"Don't worry. I can handle policemen."

They crossed the next bridge, turned right onto the odd side of Keizersgracht, and went back; De Witt now following her at some distance, trying not to walk but to *stroll*. A citizen taking the air. Geertje approached the policeman; De Witt could see the man's face brighten and then he heard him laugh. The policeman pulled out a street guide, and De Witt skipped into the doorway of the consulate and pushed the glass door. For one moment he thought it was locked, but it swung inward and he stood in a dimly lit hallway.

A receptionist was sitting behind a low table at the foot of a staircase. "What can I do for you?" he asked in an English that showed a Dutch accent.

"I've come to see Mr. George Canty." De Witt had felt that knowing the name of the man was one of his trump cards.

Nevertheless, the receptionist spoke the sobering words, "Do you have an appointment?"

"No, but it is a very important economic matter. I am the mayor of a community here."

"In general, under the special circumstances, the consul is accessible only to American citizens. You're not an American citizen?"

"No, I just told you. I am the mayor of a Dutch town. How could the mayor of—"

"I'll see what I can do." The man vanished through a door under the staircase.

It became still in the dark hallway. Through the glass door, he could see a rectangle of the greenish water of the canal. Geertje and the policeman were not visible. He heard a clock strike somewhere upstairs. Suppose I run up there, ask for asylum? Is that possible? I'd be a genuine political refugee, with important information. Maybe they'd even get me out, with diplomatic immunity. Imagine driving through these streets, untouchable, off to Lisbon—Geertje could have all the sleeping-bag money.

"This way." The receptionist had reappeared and led him to an office where a very young man was seated behind a desk.

"Mr. Canty?" De Witt asked.

"No, I'm not Canty. The consul is not accessible under the special circumstances. But you may talk to me. I'm Eliot. Your name is?"

"Mr. de Witt. I've come on a very important economic matter."

"When you say, 'important,' you mean important to the United States?"

"You may judge for yourself. I have information that the major producers of raw material in the Dutch East Indies have lost control—that is to say, the shareholders have sold control into German hands. I have here written down, a—"

"Just a moment, Mr. de Witt. I am afraid I cannot listen to this. We're a neutral country. The consulate is here under the express understanding that we are to take care of our own nationals only."

"Do you understand the importance of what I'm trying to tell you? You must transmit this information. You must—"

"We must do nothing of the kind. We would make ourselves guilty of espionage. I don't know who you are or who sent you."

"No one sent me. Surely your embassy would transmit essential economic news to Washington?"

"Our embassy, or better, our legation, for your country and mine are mutually represented by ministers only, was closed on July 15 of last year at the request of Germany. Our minister Gordon left The Hague on July 16, 1940."

"Even so, surely your consulates still function as listening posts?"

"Why don't you take this information elsewhere?" Eliot asked in response.

"Like where?"

"I can't decide for you, sir. The board of the Amsterdam Stock Exchange?"

"The board—you must be kidding. Don't you realize you are the last free listening post in an occupied country?"

"I'm sorry, sir. Now you must excuse me."

"But I've risked my neck to get this! And I've come here, in the middle of the day, and Geertje—"

Eliot stared at him, and De Witt checked himself. He thinks I've gone crazy. But this fucking wall which people build around themselves, this fucking smugness. . . . "I demand asylum then," he said.

Eliot stood up and pressed a button on his desk. "Really, sir. The United States has never acknowledged that concept. We think of it as rather medieval. Imagine if all kinds of people walked in here."

De Witt stood up, too. He had decided to give up on the whole thing and his face must have shown it, for Eliot said, more friendly now, "Perhaps your motives are of the best, sir. You must appreciate our position. Even in times of war, one has to heed basic rules and conventions."

"Of civilized nations."

"Precisely."

The receptionist had entered the room.

"You must understand," De Witt now told Eliot, "that I don't hold with the idea of colonialism. I'm with you people there. However, if it is a matter of allied against German control of oil and rubber in the middle of a war. . . ." His voice petered out.

"This gentleman is leaving," Eliot said. "Perhaps the garden gate would be better."

He held his hand out but De Witt, ignoring the gesture, left the room.

"You shouldn't have refused his hand," the receptionist said, once they were outside.

De Witt shrugged.

"No, this way, sir. You see, he's letting you out the back way. We're never supposed to do that. Now that policeman at the front door can't see you or stop you."

The sky had cleared, the day seemed unnaturally bright now. He had come out into a side street, he looked around the corner and saw the policeman pacing up and down on Keizersgracht. Geertje had gone, of course; he'd have to get back to her place alone. What would be safer, walking or the streetcar?

He walked. He felt desperately vulnerable, as never before, he thought, worse even than with that SD officer. It was terrible to be afraid, afraid not in a room but outside; that glaring blue sky seemed like a magnifying glass with him under it—people's sense of ownership—rules and conventions of civilized nations. I am hysterical, he said to himself. Cut it out.

It took him twenty minutes to get home but it felt like a long time. He was drenched with cold sweat.

48

That evening the newspapers had De Witt's photograph on page four, upper right-hand corner. "Former mayor wanted on homicide charge," its caption said. No more anonymity. "Jerome de Witt, age 39, tall, slight figure, hair dark brown or black, eyes light brown, oval face, when last seen wearing a gray suit, dark tie, no overcoat or hat, is wanted in the death of stock exchange board member Jonas D. Schutte. A police spokesman would not confirm or deny previous reports that De Witt was involved in the other violent deaths among members of the stock exchange, but we were informed that there is concern for the public safety as long as this man has not been apprehended.

"The public is reminded of the ten-thousand-guilder reward, made available by the Board of the Stock Exchange and the German authorities with the Netherlands State Bank, for information leading to the arrest and conviction of the perpetrator or perpetrators of the so-called Stock Exchange Murders.

"The funeral of Mr. Jonas D. Schutte will take place tomorrow morning at 10 A.M. at Zorgvliet cematery in the presence of high officials of the Dutch and German financial community."

De Witt folded the paper over and looked where he could put it out of sight.

"I saw it, Jerome," Geertje said. "What are we going to do? You said you wanted to stay till Monday only. If I don't go back to work—Frieda already knows there's someone here. She's the girl with the radio. And now they have your portrait in the paper."

"Portrait? It's a terrible likeness. But, eh, yes, you're right."

"I've gone by Jopie's place again. It's still all dark and closed up."

As he sat there, staring at the folded-up paper, he noticed an item in a column called "Personalities." "Indies heir Jonkheer André de Bock," it read, "has returned from our colonies. After an odyssey of travel by boat and airplane, Jonkheer de Bock expressed gratification at being back in the Motherland."

"What is it?" Geertje asked, seeing his face change.

"Geertje, Marlene, see! Never say die. There's always at the last moment—here's the answer to a working man's prayers. Saved. He'll help. I'm sure of it. Don't worry another second. I'll be out of your hair first thing in the morning. All's going to be well after all."

To his surprise she seemed to get tears in her eyes, which she wiped away with the sleeve of her housecoat, and then she gave him a warm, motherly smile, sitting oddly on her sharp little country-girl face in the big city. She came over to him and stroked his hair. "Poor bloke," she said. "And this afternoon it was the American consul who was going to save you. You expect too much of people. But it's sweet." She kissed him. "It's okay then, you sleep here."

"Never. You can't. Expect too much. People rise to the occasion."

He was out of the house before it got light. Geertje had offered to give his hair a peroxide rinse this time, but he now felt such tactics were amateur stuff, useless. People were spotted through their behavior, their movements and hesitations. Lying awake in the night, he had decided that, if he moved and acted like everyone else, no cop could pick him out of a crowd on the strength of a bad little picture and a description fitting thousands. And if he stayed away from places like that Damrak café. It would be extraordinarily bad luck to run into another routine police check so soon. Acting natural counted, not hair color.

But when he entered the vast lobby of Central Station, he sensed danger; there was an uneasy mood among the people streaming past him, and he overheard fragments of conversations about arrests and road blocks. "Baarn, Amersfoort, platform 6, " he read on the board. The ticket collectors at the gates to the platforms each had a policeman at their side. Was that standard practice now? He joined a group at a refreshment stand, a ragged line broken by pushing and shoving. A sign above the counter said, "Coffee and pastry, one guilder. No ration coupons needed." He let himself be carried forward while watching the platform gates: No one was being stopped by the police.

At the counter they poured him a chipped mug of coffee—a strange taste, not bad, who knew what was in it—and gave him a spongy, pink chunk of something or other, which was the pastry. He sipped the coffee and saw one of the policemen take a passenger by the arm and pull him aside. The man produced a card and the officer, joined by a colleague who had come over, studied it. Then they gave the passenger his card back and waved him on. He was a thin, dark man in a raincoat, looking rather like him, De Witt realized.

He put the mug back. He couldn't get through here at the station. He had to get back to Geertje before it was full daylight. At the main entrance he looked around one more time (useless, and thus a terrible mistake, he told himself later), straight into the eyes of two other policemen who had posted themselves with their backs against one of the large pillars in that area. Their eyes did not rest on him but then, as he made an involuntary movement, a movement with his whole body although nothing more than a kind of shudder, their eyes returned to him; they stared at each other, he and they, and he lost his nerve and ran out, knowing that they had already started running toward him. He heard the police whistles behind him and dodged in front of a streetcar with an inch to spare—he could hear the motorman curse—before jumping onto the rear platform of another streetcar in motion. Goddammit, here we go again. This car crossed the water and entered Damrak; he was aware of his fellow passengers' staring but did not look back; he jumped off. He ran into the alley alongside the C&A department store. A man carrying two garbage cans was disappearing into a side door. De Witt slipped in after him; "I've come for the job," he said. "I'm all out of breath—am I the first?"

The man began to laugh. "You're sure an eager beaver. I don't know of any job. Did you see an ad?"

"Yeah. Elevator man. In the morning paper."

"You'd better wait then. No one's here till eight, eight-thirty."

"Thanks. It's nice and warm here."

"You wouldn't have a cigarette to spare, would you?"

"Well, no, but I can give you a sheet of cigarette paper."

When he slipped out of that same door an hour later, bright sunlight filled the streets. He turned west, hastily crossed Nieuwendyk and the Westside Voorburgwal, and turned north on Spui. I'll get past the station in the docks area, he thought, and then cut back to Geertje. She won't be very pleased to see me again. She has to find Jopie for me as a very last favor. I'm lost without money and a good ID card. Stop. Why is it so quiet here?

Ahead of him the road lay virtually empty. Did I walk too far west? he wondered. He stood still to orient himself and heard the screeching of car brakes beside him. He started to turn his head; a hand closed around his neck while a heavy voice shouted, "Got you. Got you! Try and get away this time!"

For a brief moment the world turned black in front of his eyes. Then he tried to wrench himself free and saw the face of his attacker. "Goddammit it to hell!" he cried. "It's you! Are you crazy!"

It was Adriaan who now let go of his neck and laughed. "Scared you, didn't I?"

"You stupid bastard, what's the matter with you?" De Witt

165

looked around to see if anyone was watching them.

"I want my raincoat back, that's what's the matter," Adriaan said complacently.

"Oh, for God's sake. For God's sake." De Witt's legs began to tremble. He had to sit down on the bottom step of a house stoop.

49

Adriaan seemed sorry now. "Come on, man, can't you take a joke?" he said.

De Witt produced a weak smile. Staring down at him, Adriaan asked, "You're not in trouble are you? I mean, with the Germans?" He took a handkerchief out of his pocket, spread it on the step next to De Witt, and sat down on it. "I know I wasn't much help that evening. I figured you were just in girlfriend trouble. No, that's not true. I didn't figure anything. I was busy with my own affairs. I couldn't be bothered." He patted De Witt on his shoulder.

"Okay, Adriaan. It's okay."

"You look down and out, that's for sure. How come?"

"Nothing really. Trouble with my ID card. I was fired. I'm no longer a mayor. And you?"

Adriaan pointed at the car that was pulled up at the curb, its rear sticking out into the road. "All mine. Pontiac 1938. Look." And he pulled out his wallet and showed De Witt a sheaf of documents.

"I'm impressed," De Witt said.

"No, read them."

Licenses and *Ausweise* in German and Dutch: permission to drive, permission to buy fifty liters of gasoline a week, ration cards for gas and oil, a paper with seals and picture stating that Adriaan Veen was engaged in work important for the supply of food and raw materials to the German garrisons "in Amsterdam and surroundings."

"That's the big one," Adriaan said, tapping his finger on it, and then carefully returning them all to the wallet.

"You don't want that raincoat back," De Witt remarked, touching the fur collar on Adriaan's Chesterfield overcoat.

Adriaan grinned. "Pretty snazzy, eh? No, I was joking. Keep it, with my compliments."

"Well, actually, it's hanging in the Marnix Street police station," De Witt said, standing up.

"No kidding. Let's go get it."

"Hmm. Perhaps better not. I must get a move on."

"Nonsense. I want to know what happened to you. Come, I'll buy you a coffee. And I mean, coffee. I know a place."

De Witt shook his head. "I don't want to go anywhere. And I really must get to where I was heading for."

"I'll give you a lift."

"Okay then. You can drop me on the corner of Gelder Quay and the Walletjes."

"So you've hit the jackpot," De Witt said as they drove north on Spui, De Witt with his legs stretched out in front of him, keeping low in his seat.

"You could say that. Remember the *Imitatio Christi* I showed you? And you weren't very interested? You could say it all started with that. I sold it to a quartermaster major from Erfurt. And the rest, as they say, is history." He laughed, sounding so pleased that De Witt, while telling himself he should be disgusted, couldn't help laughing too.

"It all started with that," Adriaan repeated. "The imitation of Christ. The miracle of the loaves and the fishes, the water turned into wine, staged in a new version specially performed for the Germans—"

"Yes, Adriaan, that will do," De Witt interrupted, falling into the tone with which he used to berate Adriaan in the days he considered him a friend.

Adriaan gave him a long look. "You *are* in trouble, aren't you?"

"You could say that."

"First and foremost, always, comes money. Do you have any?"

"Yes, I do. But the damn thing is, I can't get to it."

He let Adriaan drive him past Geertje's place—all quiet and normal there—and then he got off at the corner and walked back. She was indeed upset to see him again. "So you weren't saved by that man after all." "I never got there, I never got farther than the station."

"Don't worry," he told her. "Someone's coming to pick me up here after dark. A friend I met. He says he'll put me up. Guess what, he has a car."

"A car, with gas and everything?"

"Yes! He's also promised to *drive* me to Baarn. Isn't that a break? The train station is just too tricky."

"Oh—can you trust him?"

"Yes. He's a bastard, but in a different way. He's become a black-market big shot with the Germans. You know what he's going to do before picking me up? He's going to break into Jopie's bar, well, break in, he says he has special keys. And he's going to bring me my sleeping-bag money."

"Gee. That's marvelous."

"He's running a risk, of course. I'm giving him half the money."

"Half?"

"What's wrong with that? There's a lot, several thousand guilders, I never counted it properly. And I'll pay you, of course."

"That's all right. I don't need it."

"Fair is fair."

"Fair is fair," she repeated tonelessly.

Adriaan showed up on foot. "Left my car on Warmoes Street," he explained. "More discreet. Phew—I'm not used to walking anymore." He looked around. "Not bad. What's your name, honey?" This to Geertje, who had stayed at the sink, hardly looking up when he came in.

"Her name is Geertje Zondervan," De Witt said. "Did you get into the bar?"

"Sure. Nothing to it. Walked in and out. Here's that paper you asked for, and your half." He handed De Witt a little pile of bank notes. "Don't you want to count it?"

De Witt was folding up the Schutte statement. "No, why?"

"It's not as much as you thought. There was only seven hundred guilders there. That's three fifty."

De Witt looked at Adriaan, started to pull the money back out of his pocket, then shrugged and let it stay where it was.

"Jerome!" Geertje cried, turning around.

"What?"

"Oh, nothing."

"Okay then," Adriaan said. "Are you packed?"

"There's nothing to pack."

Adriaan did not like that. "You mean you don't have another pair of underpants, another anything, to your name?"

De Witt smiled at Geertje, who was now leaning against the counter with her back, and shook his head.

"Okay then," Adriaan said again.

"Why don't you stay here, Jerome?" Geertje asked at that point. "Isn't it safer? The more you fidget around, the more risk you run."

"But you said—"

"Nothing. You're fine here."

"I must admit," Adriaan announced, "There's an offer I can't compete with."

An uneasy silence.

"Okay then," Adriaan said. "You lie low, Jerome, you stay put. Tomorrow morning, without fail, to Baarn. Wait on that corner where you got out before, between the trees and the water. You'll be all right there, it'll be dark. Half past seven on the dot."

"You're sure now?" De Witt asked Geertje.

"Yes, she's sure," Adriaan answered for her, getting up. "See you, Geertje."

At the door De Witt asked him, "You're going to be there? I don't want to hang around on a street corner for nothing."

"Jerome, old friend, I'll be there. A deal is a deal." And then in an undertone, "But I must say, you sure seem to have gotten yourself up some kind of shit's creek. You should have stayed mayor of Amsteldyk, my friend. You had a good berth there."

50

At seven twenty-six De Witt softly closed the door behind him and made his way to the corner of Doelen Street. Geertje was still asleep. He had left two hundred guilders in her money jam jar; he himself now carried almost two hundred too, and the Schutte paper. He went slowly in order not to trip over the bolts along the water's edge, once used to moor boats, and which he remembered rather than saw. I wonder why the Germans aren't collecting them for old iron, he thought. Too hard to get out. I hope Adriaan shows up. Maybe he'll show up with a vengeance, with a bunch of Germans, to collect the reward.

Did I make another whopper of a mistake? Could he have been just pretending he didn't know about Schutte and the reward and everything?

No, he can't play-act that perfectly. Besides, they would have come for me last night. He doesn't need it, either; think what that coat he's wearing must cost these days. True, he stole most of the sleeping-bag money, but that was already in his hands, he knows I know, it's his fee. "I'm a businessman," he'd say. That's not like giving me away to the Germans.

When De Witt had reached the corner, he saw on his new watch that it was half past seven. In the total silence and darkness a little blue light became visible, swaying, at a distance. He stood behind a tree and realized it came from a lantern hanging from a cart, pushed by one man, pulled with a rope by another. It passed close by but remained a shadow; what gave it reality was the unpleasant smell it spread. He heard it creaking up the bridge and thought of a Selma Lagerlof story he had read in high school. Death arriving in a cart whose creaking is heard only by those about to die.

A hint of light in the sky. Ten minutes to eight. Well, he has not given me away, Germans come on time. He leaned against the tree, suddenly feeling miserably weary.

Then he heard a little beep from a claxon and saw the blue headlights of a military truck going up the bridge at great speed, silhouetting Adriaan's car. He ran toward it, fell into the right-hand seat, and closed the door. "Sorry to be late," Adriaan said, accelerating sharply up Doelen Street toward Dam Square.

"I thought—that's one-way," De Witt muttered.

"Please, Jerome, no backseat driving. It's bad enough to be up at this hour. I wouldn't do this for everybody."

Well, you could at least acknowledge you got well paid, dammit, De Witt thought, but he kept silent. This dark world. Think how blacked-out Europe must look from the sky.

They had crossed the Amstel River—he could tell from the different sound of the pavement when they drove across the Berlage Bridge—when morning began to break in earnest. As the darkness lifted, he saw there were no longer houses on each side of the road but fields and copses and single lightless villas whose outlines were drawn against the eastern sky. He climbed over the seat and sat on the floor behind it.

"What's that you are wearing?" Adriaan, who had watched him do this, asked.

"Nothing special. Stuff Geertje borrowed for me." Geertje, in a burst of goodwill after Adriaan's departure the evening before, had gone out and returned with a borrowed sailor's turtleneck, a blue woolen hat, and an oilskin coat for him.

"That's a sad dame, isn't she?"

"Oh, I like her," De Witt said.

"Hmm. No accounting for taste. There's a road check coming up. Just keep quiet, pull that plaid over you."

Adriaan slowed down, then speeded up again. "They waved me through, they're getting to know me," he announced.

"It must feel pretty strange to dash around like this."

"You get used to it." Then he chuckled. "It sure is a change from peddling books from a cart, no? Isn't it something? Imitatio Christi."

When they got to Hilversum, it was fully light and Adriaan

started to blow his horn almost without pause. "Fucking cyclists," he told De Witt.

"Pipe down, you Nazi," De Witt heard an old man's voice shout after them.

"Up yours, pop," Adriaan said to the rearview mirror. "Oh, shit."

"What is it?" De Witt asked, pressing himself against the floor.

"I don't know. Oh. Nothing. A convoy."

They had come to a stop; De Witt peered over the seat. A German on a motorcycle was standing at the crossroads, holding up a red disk on a stick of the type station masters used to carry. A row of German army trucks was rolling by, closed trucks, trucks pulling flatbeds with light cannon on them, and trucks with the back tarpaulin open, showing soldiers sitting on two benches facing each other. Shreds of singing drifted toward them; he even recognized the "Tomorrow the whole world" song. It didn't sound hearty. "Anti-aircraft guns," Adriaan said. "Bad news for the RAF, poor devils."

They were waved on, and a mile out of town Adriaan turned sharply right onto a secondary road. De Witt popped up.

"I have to run an errand," Adriaan told him. "Don't worry."

"Well, dammit, I do worry. They're looking for me, we're not on a sightseeing trip."

"You can't be safer anywhere than with me," Adriaan answered. "I have to combine things, you know. That's efficiency."

"You learned that from your German friends, no doubt."

"No doubt."

Adriaan stopped at a cluster of buildings and, reaching over De Witt, grabbed a briefcase. "Ten minutes. Don't worry."

De Witt lay down again and closed his eyes. You bastard, it's no fun being at your mercy.

Adriaan did come back very quickly. "You know," he said as he swung the car around, "it's true. We can learn something from the Germans. We're too damn lackadaisical. That's why we lost the war in five days. Liberals."

"Oh, bull. We lost because you can't defend a little country as flat as a football field in a modern war with tanks."

"You think everything was so great here before?" Adriaan asked with an edge to his voice.

"Certainly not. What's that got to do with it?"

"Let me tell you it wasn't. You know, when a man was on the dole here, they gave you a free license tag for your bicycle, but it had a hole in it, and that meant you weren't al owed to use it on Sundays, you could only use it to go and look for work? Did you know that? They wouldn't fucking let you bicycle on Sundays in your own country. It was a rich man's game. Democracy my ass."

"While Germany?"

"Oh, the same deal. Kill and rob to glory. The only difference is, they've cut the cackle."

"And that's why you want them to win?" De Witt asked.

"No, I don't. It makes no fucking difference what I want. They'll win or they'll lose. I'm not going to be a hero for a country that wouldn't let me use my bicycle on Sunday. Where to now?"

"Baarn-Amersfoort road. Eight, maybe ten miles."

When they pulled up at the De Bock castle, Adriaan rolled down his window, stuck out his head, and had a long look. He nodded with satisfaction. "A rich man's country. Okay, let's go see."

De Witt had crawled back into his seat; "I don't want you to come with me," he said, and got out of the car.

"How do you know he's there? How do you know he's going to receive you? You may still need me, you know. Don't worry, I won't spoil your scene. I'd just like to have a peep at a fellow who lives like that. *Look* at that!"

Close to the entrance door a car was parked, a low-slung beige convertible, which was in the process of being polished by a chauffeur.

"That's a Bugatti," Adriaan said in an awed voice.

51

The same valet of his first visit opened the door for De Witt. The man recognized him but showed no particular surprise that this mayor was now appearing in a sailor's outfit. "Yes, Mr. André is home," he said, "but he is still dressing. I will announce you. Mr.—?"

"De Witt. And friend."

He came back a few minutes later and took their coats and hats. "This way, gentlemen. Mr. André will be with you soon." He showed them into a sitting room but remained standing in the doorway. He smiled at De Witt. "You are the mayor who came to talk about the Jonkheer, didn't you, sir?"

"Yes, indeed. And you are—"

"Teun."

"Teun, isn't André de Bock a jonkheer too? You kept saying, 'Mr. André.'"

"To be sure. But to me 'jonkheer' signifies Jonkheer Johan only. If you get my meaning."

"Eh . . . well—yes, I see."

"How's that?" Adriaan asked.

"It's not like an English title, going to the eldest son," De Witt said, "All men in a family have a right to it."

"But, of course, Mr. André is the heir anyway," Teun added.

André de Bock came in, dressed in a city suit, a cup of coffee in his hand, and Teun vanished. De Witt introduced himself and Adriaan. This De Bock looked no older than twenty-five or so. He was a handsome young man—though with the slightly yellowish face often seen on people who grew up in the Indies—with curly hair, and already getting a bit heavy. He eyed his callers, De Witt thought, with not more than mild curiosity.

"Mr. de Witt," he said. "My brother often mentioned you in his letters."

"He did?"

"And you, Mr. Veen? Did you know Johan?"

"Mr. Veen was kind enough to drive me here," De Witt answered hastily. "He is not involved in the purpose of my visit."

"And I might add," Adriaan said with a smile at De Bock, "that that makes it one of the very few things I'm not involved in these days. Let me give you my card." Pulling out his wallet, he looked at several calling cards and then handed one to De Bock.

"Mr. Adriaan Veen, National and International Transactions," De Bock read out.

"You must excuse me, I have business in the area," Adriaan now announced. "I can come back for you around noon, Jerome, and take you to a very nice little place in Baarn, where they—"

"Adriaan, I'm not going to any little places, cut it out," De Witt interrupted in an angry, low voice.

"No, no, Mr. Veen," De Bock said. "Why don't you come back here and have lunch with us. We'll find something edible for you."

De Witt was shaking his head, but Adrian ignored him. "That would be nice," he answered. "I will see you later then."

"National and international transactions," De Bock repeated after Adriaan had left. "Is your friend a crook?"

De Witt shrugged. "Soon he'll be called a financier."

De Bock sat down across from him, took a sip of his coffee, and looked expectantly at De Witt.

"That was a trivial beginning," De Witt said, "but this visit of mine is not trivial. It's very serious indeed; Adriaan, Mr. Veen, that is, doesn't know why I am here. I should—" He had thought out in the car how to approach this, but Adriaan's chitchat about lunch had confused him. How was he to deal with this man? Was he as committed as his brother had been, or was he the younger son playboy? He looked that way a bit. De Witt hesitated, and the smell of De Bock's coffee made him dizzy. "I wonder if I could have some coffee?" he asked. "I had no time for breakfast this morning."

"But, of course. I should have thought of it." De Bock rang and asked Teun to bring a pot of coffee and some rolls.

They waited in silence. Teun came back quickly and poured De Witt's coffee. He put it beside him on a little table, with the tray.

"You see," De Bock said when the door had closed, "Teun smiles at you. That's rare with him. He knows you were a friend of my poor brother. And that is enough for me, too. Trust me, Mr. de Witt."

These words released De Witt from his uneasiness. Things seemed simple suddenly. "The basic question, Mr. de Bock, is always this: Are we peasants plowing our fields with our backs turned to the Battle of Borodino? Or, even worse, do we search the corpses afterward for valuables and pull out their gold teeth? Or do we join the fight?"

It was obviously not what André de Bock had expected, but he nodded his head.

"What do you know about me, Mr. de Bock?"

André de Bock smiled. "Enough not to be tempted by any ten-thousand-guilder reward."

This startled De Witt. "You know?"

"Yes, of course. Didn't you think I would?"

"Well, yes. I had not thought it through."

"Mr. de Witt, relax. Your wanderings are over, you are as safe here as humanly possible under the present rotten circumstances. Tell me everything you know."

52

De Witt told his story, from the murder of Hans Cremer to his visit with the Beauftragte, ending with the statement and then the suicide of Jonas Schutte.

"Much of this I knew, obviously," André de Bock finally said. "If you wondered how I got back so quickly—quickly for this Year of Grace, 1941, that is—I left Batavia before my brother was killed; I left when he wrote to me that he was being threatened. I knew it must be very serious, for him to mention it at all."

"Why did you say he had mentioned me in his letters?" De Witt suddenly interjected. "He couldn't have."

"Oh. I don't know if he did or not, I always say that to make people feel good. Johan had so many friends. Well—threats. Some of my friends on Java implied Johan was being threatened because he was a collaborator with the Germans. I knew that could not be so. Our great-great grandfather, after all, fought in the Battle of Waterloo, at the side of the Prince of Orange. To the contrary, the threats had to come from a German source. As you, or rather Schutte, confirm. On the other hand, I am inclined to think that we have to deal with a criminal conspiracy in some little corner of that vast network spread by Berlin. I have difficulty with this 'they bought a tropical colony' idea. It sounds too simple."

"Schutte was very clear about it. Its simplicity is presumably its great merit in German eyes."

"Yes, but what you don't know, is what we knew and what Johan commented on, is that Schutte had a genuine persecution complex. Paranoia, if that's not too strong a word. Had no one informed you of that?"

"I haven't discussed this with anyone but you. There's no one to discuss it with. Obviously. It's a ticket to the concentration camp. The only other copy of Schutte's statement. . . ." De Witt had been about to say, ". . . is in a certain Geertje's closet." But that seemed in terrible taste. Without really knowing why, he finished his sentence with ". . . is with Mr. George Canty, the American consul in Amsterdam."

"That was a very wise precaution. I didn't realize there was still an American consulate here."

"Yes, there is. At that time I didn't know you were already back. If I had got caught, Schutte's statement would have vanished into thin air."

"Still, there is something wrong with that statement, as I will presently prove to you. But I had not realized you actually have it in black and white. Read it to me, will you?"

De Witt pulled out his notes, written that Saturday in Jopie's room, and started reading, from "sit down, De Witt" on. "I wrote it down like a court stenographer," he explained to De Bock.

"Quite so."

De Witt came to the sentence, "It so happened that Cremer's children are minors," and, reading ahead, he saw, *"De Bock's only heir is his brother and he—but that is not relevant anymore."* He decided to skip that sentence; there was something about it that disquieted him. He swallowed nervously.

"Yes, Mr. de Witt?"

"I'm sorry. When I said, 'like a court stenographer,' I meant of course that I tried to reconstruct it afterward. It's not letter perfect, it doesn't all run smoothly. To continue. 'If we had all refused, we would be . . . we would have been safe.'"

He read to the end.

"Right," André de Bock said. "Now it is my turn to show you why we have to look beyond Schutte. Come to my study with me."

De Witt followed him through a series of corridors with parquet floors and bright windows, past portraits, statues, and large potted plants. The study was a small but beautifully furnished room, with French windows looking out on lawns. De Bock opened a desk with a key on his key ring and handed De Witt a large engraved document.

It was a stock certificate issued by the Batavian Petroleum Company, an elaborately decorated paper with, on the left, a picture of a palm tree and, on the right, the likeness of a bewhiskered gentleman in a topee. "Ten Thousand Preferred Stock Shares," it said, and it was dated, Batavia, July 1, 1892.

"Ten thousand," De Witt said.

"Yes, think of it! I don't believe they issue such very large denominations anymore. But, of course, those have been in our family for half a century."

"You mean this is from your brother's portfolio?"

"Indeed, that's just it. Johan was an old-fashioned man, he

liked to keep things at home. It's all here."

De Witt handed the paper back to De Bock, who locked it away. "You see why I want to poke holes in Schutte's story," De Bock said. "We have to separate the truth from what the poor man must have imagined, those last terrible hours before he killed himself."

"I can't understand it."

De Bock sighed. "We must get ready for your friend now. We will have lunch with him first."

"I would rather we didn't, in all honesty."

"I don't blame you, De Witt. My thoughts are elsewhere too. Nevertheless, no point in alienating Mr. Veen. He knows you are here, and he's friendly with the Germans."

"Yes, true," De Witt muttered. "Not friendly, really— screws them rather, I think."

De Bock clearly chose to ignore this remark. "I'll give some instructions for lunch," he said. "You just sit somewhere and pull yourself together, wherever you're comfortable."

"I'd like to use the bathroom if I may."

"I will show you the way."

53

The second he stood in that absolutely Roman bathroom, he knew what he was going to do.

Jerome de Witt, the toilet escape artist. I'm going to develop this to perfection. It will become famous. All over Holland people with the runs are going to be arrested.

The bathroom had a window that looked out on a courtyard. He opened it and easily climbed through, stood still to work out where he was, and started walking. Smoothly now, you're not to arouse surprise. You're a guest taking his constitutional. He passed a pantry where he saw Teun, reading a paper with his feet up. Their eyes met and De Witt smiled at him. He rounded another corner and found himself in front of the castle. Looking toward the road, he saw Adriaan's Pontiac approach. He started to run toward it, waving his arms.

Adriaan stopped the car and De Witt opened the door and jumped in. "Quick, quick, keep going."

Adriaan turned off the engine. "What's the matter with you? That fellow is your best bet!"

De Witt got tears in his eyes from frustration. "Start the car, Adriaan. He's sending for the Germans. Do it."

Adriaan sighed, turned the key, and drove off slowly.

"Adriaan, they'll shoot. They'll damage your car."

"Okay, okay. You're one crazy guy, Jerome. I'm washing my hands of you after this."

"Wash as much as you want. Just get off this road. Here, here, take this side road."

They were going fast now. "Don't worry," Adriaan said, "I know these roads better than any German cops. Now may I know what's going on?"

"Listen to this. 'De Bock's only heir'—that means, Johan de Bock's only heir—'is his brother, and he—' how would you finish that sentence?"

"I don't know what the hell you're talking about."

"And he's away? No, because at the stock exchange they know everything about each other. Everyone knew André was on his way home. 'And he. . . .' Something about him to show he'd play ball. Don't you see? 'And he's a Dutch Nazi.' What else could it be?"

Adriaan stopped the car. "Is that what we are bumping down this road for? How about, 'And he's only interested in screwing native girls'? No wonder you're in such a fix, Jerome. You get carried away with yourself."

De Witt smiled. He felt good now. "No, my friend. No, Christ imitator. I know I'm right. Either that, or Schutte was going crazy. And he was not. He was a stern Calvinist Protestant about to face his Maker, he already felt himself standing in the icy light of Truth."

Adriaan gave De Witt an odd look and started his car again. "Jerome, maybe you do know what you're talking about. I must say, I had looked forward to a posh lunch, not to mention some nice business deal or other with the jonkheer."

"He showed me a certificate for ten thousand preferred stock shares in Batavian Petroleum. That was a piece of paper worth perhaps three million guilders. I think there were several of them."

"Holy Moses. See what I mean? Think of it."

"He wanted to prove to me that Schutte was wrong. That's why he showed it to me."

"And why would he bother then, if he was going to have you taken away?"

"I can guess. I've been pretty much up on things this morning, Adriaan. I'm learning. I told him I knew the American consul and that I'd given him a statement by Schutte. It would still be worth his while, De Bock's, I mean, to turn me around on that. Just in case."

"But you didn't? Know the consul and the rest of it?"

"Well, I did go there. Otherwise I'd never have thought of saying that. But I only got as far as his fifth assistant."

"Okay. Maybe you do know what you're talking about," Adriaan said again. "I sure hope so. That jonkheer would have been a very nice connection."

"After you'd left, he asked me if you were a crook."

"So what? How do you think that castle got built? You think he was drinking acorn coffee there?"

"No. . . . Shit!" De Witt cried.

"Now what?"

"My oilskin. I left my oilskin. Geertje had borrowed it for me. I hope there's nothing in the pockets. I never looked."

"You seem to leave a trail of coats across the landscape."

De Witt started to climb over the seat to hide on the floor once more, but he stopped as he was perched on top of it. "Holy heaven," he muttered. He slid back into the seat beside Adriaan and put his hand on Adriaan's arm. "Stop. We have to go back."

Adriaan braked so strongly that the engine stalled. "Now what? Now what?"

"I just realized something. I have to go back, there won't be another chance, not easily. Not all the way back, just to where you turned off. I can walk the rest. Please. I'll explain."

"Jerome, you are crazy. I don't want to hear more. You tell me the Germans are after us and now we're going back? I'm not going back."

"I don't blame you. I'll walk." He opened the door and jumped out.

"Mr. Mayor, are you sure you know what you're doing?"

"No."

"But we're quits now, right?"

"We've never not been quits, Adriaan."

"Okay then, if that's understood. Close the door." And the Pontiac drove off in a spray of dirt mixed with very old snow, while De Witt was left standing at the edge of a country road in a silent landscape.

54

De Witt stared after the car until it had vanished around a curve, and then he started walking back towards the castle. He was very cold, but he was glad now to be without the oilskin and the woolen hat, which would have made a very strange outfit to be seen in on a country lane. He picked up a straight branch for a walking stick.

The only sound was a trickling of dripping water in the trees. Patches of snow were still ensconced in hollows and forks of tree trunks. Every now and again a bird struck up a few notes but stopped again as if realizing it was too cold. A white haze covered the sky, the sun was invisible. Someone approached from the opposite direction. De Witt thought that perhaps they were both equally apprehensive, equally struggling to resist the idea of running off into the woods along the road.

It was a man, a farmer in old boots and a felt cap, with a

mongrel dog on a piece of rope. They nodded at each other in passing, and after a few steps they both looked back at the same time.

He now found that Adriaan and he had driven much farther than he had imagined. It took him more than two hours to reach the crossroads where he had made Adriaan turn off. Here was the Baarn-Amersfoort road again, and the castle was not more than a mile or so to the west, although it was not yet visible. He decided to pass it, on his side of the road, and if he were lucky, he'd be able to see if De Bock's car was still there. If it was, he'd wait to see it leave. If De Bock stayed home, he'd have to play it by ear, wait till after dark. De Bock had certainly been dressed as if he meant to go to Amsterdam. But who knows, maybe he dresses like that for a sandwich at home. He sat down on a tree stump and felt tired and troubled; his sense of euphoria had worn off.

He got out of his shoes, one at a time, and rubbed some life into his feet, then he continued west, not walking on the road now but through the trees. The going was easier than he had thought; the soft moss was almost dry. Now he could see the castle, the entrance road across the moat, then the high oak door. The Bugatti was gone.

He crossed the road and started to make a wide arch around the house toward the kitchens, where he had seen Teun reading his paper. There were stone guide marks here, a wired-in vegetable garden, but the estate was not fenced off. Unless, of course, all this side of the road is his, he thought. There may be a wall much farther east.

There was nothing in his way as he turned and made for the pantry door. He was about to open it when Teun came walking along, smoking a cigar. De Witt jumped. Teun took the cigar out of his mouth and said, "Good afternoon, sir."

"I was looking for you, Teun."

Bless this Teun who didn't ask questions but steered him away from the house, between two outbuildings and around a kennel. They sat down on a bench. "You can still smell the dogs," Teun said, "and it's more than a year now. The Jonkheer sent them away to some farm when the war began, in 1939."

"Teun—"

"Sir?"

"Don't call me 'sir,' I'm here to ask your help. Did the German police come for me?"

"Two men came. I don't know who they were. I didn't hear them talk. Mr. André had sent Ralph out on his bicycle, for we still don't have a phone. Mr. André came out to meet them. They looked for you."

"Was Mr. André angry or surprised that I'd gone?"

"He'd never show it."

"Teun, you know that Johan de Bock was an exceptional man?"

"Yes. I know."

"And that your Mr. André is a bum?"

"I know that too."

"I thought you did, I thought you did! From when you said —I'd never have dared come back here otherwise. Will you help me?"

"With what?"

"Is Mr. André coming back soon?"

"Yes."

"Okay, I'd better be fast. Jonkheer Johan de Bock refused to join a German scheme, a big thing. They needed his Indies shares, they were supposed to have grabbed them before or after his death. André showed me one to prove they hadn't, to prove that I was all wrong. But that's not what it proves, of course! I just figured that out. It proves that André is not only on their side but that he is the very man who is the new director of the combination they cooked up; they didn't leave him with only his brother's shares; he has the lot, and he's going back to Java to take control. Who else? You see? It would be a very good thing to stop him, Teun, and with inside help—"

"I'm not sure I follow all that," Teun said, "but I do know this: Mr. André would not be part of anything to do with his brother's death. That couldn't be. These people are very fami-ly-y. You wouldn't understand, sir. Family is everything for them, it's their religion."

"But Mr. André has made plans to go back to the Indies, hasn't he?"

"No, he hasn't."

"He hasn't? Oh—but then, of course, you see, he'd keep them secret. He must have *some* travel plans, to go to Switzerland, or to Portugal?"

"Can anyone, nowadays?" Teun asked.

"Sure, if the Germans want you to. He came back here that way, didn't he?"

Teun picked up a stick and started to scratch circles and crosses in the dirt. "If it's sides, I'd be on your side, Mr. de Witt. But he's not going anywhere. He says how good it is to be home. He said he's so sick of traveling, he doesn't even like going to Amsterdam. He's talked about spring cleaning, and setting the trees aright, and laying in a supply of wood from them to get through the next winter if there's no more coal, all sorts of things like that. You'd better go now. I think I hear Ralph, and Mr. André is due any minute. I will not say a word about this."

"Teun, if he suddenly decides to leave the country again, will you believe me then?"

Teun thought about this. "Maybe."

"Would you know, in advance?"

"Chances are. If it's telegrams, he sends me to Baarn to the post office. He'd never go himself, not with the waiting lines they have there now."

"Would you let me know if that happens? Would you, please? Even if he says it's just for a week, a trip to Geneva, say?"

"Hey, Ralph," Teun suddenly shouted. "I'm coming, I need you with the stove."

"Would you?" De Witt repeated.

"How? How could I?"

How. "You call from Baarn. You call the Sun Café, Zeedyk,

Amsterdam, or maybe it's now called 'Zon,' in Dutch. The number will be in the book. Someone will be at that phone, every morning, at eleven. Okay?"

"You'd better run, Mr. de Witt. Go that way, toward those trees."

"Will you, Teun? Will you? The Sun, Zeedyk, every morning at eleven."

"The Sun, Zeedyk. Okay, Mr. de Witt, I'll do that."

De Witt pressed his hand and hurried around a shed and toward the trees.

55

He walked all the way north until he could smell that cold, slightly muddy odor in the air that spells the nearness of the former Zuyderzee, now a lake. Then, without getting out onto the road, he turned left, as precisely west as he could guess under the sunless sky. He sat down in the lee of a little hill and waited for it to get dark.

He was very tired, for he had walked miles, and his rations so far for that day had been two cups of prewar coffee and two rolls, unfortunately very elegantly tiny ones. He was afraid to fall asleep and kept flapping his arms about to stay warm and awake. It's been some day, he thought. De Bock in Java, shipping oil and rubber, to third parties maybe if it can't reach the Germans, or maybe he's just supposed to keep the output low, hold it in escrow, so to speak—maybe the Germans figure on flying there from Egypt. Could they? Men in topees with little swastikas on them, the Beauftragte with two naked Balinese girls on his knees; they have such beautiful breasts, those girls —damn, stop, I was dozing off.

He got up and rubbed his face with wet grass. Let's move on, it's getting dark.

He came to a footpath going in the right direction and started following it. His feet hurt badly. He passed a farm where a dog began to bark hysterically, but nobody stirred.

People seemed as serious about the blackout here as in the city; the farmhouse lay without a glimmer of light. On he plodded, through a pasture where he heard the heavy breathing of cows or horses without seeing any, through a cattle gate, and out onto the road again. The road became paved and he saw shadowy houses. Cyclists passed him. "Is this Muiden?" he called after one of the shadows going by. He heard a woman's laugh. "Muiden? It's Naarden," a voice answered.

Hell, Naarden only. He tried to visualize the map. Three hours more, perhaps four. I have to get in before curfew, I just have to. Let's march. He started to whistle, "Und heute gehoert uns Deutschland."

He stayed on the road now. A vague outline of a half-moon had crept over the horizon and helped him find his way; there were more bicycles on the road, and once an army truck rolled by. Walking on the asphalt might actually be less suspicious than stumbling through woods. Besides, from here on, the land was all cut up with fences, houses, walls, gardens.

"Out for a stroll?" a figure in a dark doorway asked.

He couldn't see the man too well, but he seemed to be wearing some kind of belt; there was the glimmer of a buckle. Maybe a rural policeman.

"No, I live in Muiden," De Witt answered. "First one flat tire, then the other."

"Bad luck."

"Yeah."

Onward. He walked in a trance now, stopping would finish him, he had to keep going. He stayed on the narrow road, to the right of the main road where the Germans had that checkpoint. It was ten o'clock when he recognized the stone gate of the Eastern Cemetery on his right, a whitish arch in the moonlight. Ten minutes later he crossed the Berlage Bridge. No one stopped him or hailed him. He felt he couldn't take another step with his shoes on; he took them off, put them in his pockets, and started to walk as fast as he could. In his socks, he continued up along the Amstel, past the Free Hospital, and right on Voorburgwal. It was ten past eleven on his watch when he tapped on Geertje's window. And by some good and great dispensation from the heavens, he thought, she opened the door instantly and without a word. He stepped inside and stumbled into her big chair. He closed his eyes and was asleep.

56

Geertje made warm water with borax for him to bathe his bleeding feet, and she cut the backs off a pair of old slippers of hers for him to wear. He woke up in a panic later that night; the next day she got him a bottle of his sleeping pills, under her own name, from the municipal doctor whom the Walletjes girls had to see once a week for a venereal inspection.

"What I have to do now is get to Titus," he told her. "He must put me in contact with the underground, he must. This is worth their while all right, and I cannot handle it on my own." After the fatal Saturday of Schutte's death, he and Titus had agreed it would be too dangerous for them to see each other again.

She did not answer him.

"If I go to Amsteldyk myself, I may as well jump in the canal right here. Geertje, will you try and speak to him on the phone, just this once more?"

"And you'll be saved, for sure this time?"

He made a face.

"Dear Lord. Jerome de Witt, what *are* you after? Do you aim to hide in my room till this war is over? What do you have to do with the oil and the rubber in the East Indies?"

"Yeah, I guess you're right."

"If I must," she said then. "How?"

"He's hard to reach him, he's a gas fitter, he works all over the place. His girl, Vrede, works at the gas factory, but they don't accept private calls. If you say it's an emergency."

"What about Eddie's café then?"

"Oh, of course. Much better. If he still goes to the place."

"I know a girl," she said. "She works on Weteringschans, very fancy. Let's tell Titus to go there, customerlike. It's in a busy block, so you can go there too. I'll warn her, she's good. Then you and he can talk in her kitchen."

"I don't know how I can make up to you for all this, Geertje."

"No, I don't either. I'll tell Titus to put a suit on. Does he have one? My friend doesn't have gas-fitter customers."

"What's her name?"

"Sheherazade."

"No kidding. I can see she wouldn't. Have gas fitters, I mean."

Geertje wanted to come with him—the couple dodge, which made it less risky for him to be in the streets. She's really with me in this, he thought. She must like me a lot. I'm not much of a catch right now, to say the least. That evening when she was scared, or lonely, and I sent her home—I won't forgive myself for not treating her better when I could have, when I was Your Honor.

Titus was half amused and half furious that he had been summoned to Weteringschans. "Glad to see you, Jerome, but I hope it's important. This sure is a place, though. A whore with an American refrigerator, my father wouldn't have believed it."

De Witt told him about André de Bock. "Their plan can be wrecked," he said. "But I can't do it. Not alone, that's certain."

"Can I look in that refrigerator?"

"For Chrissakes, Titus."

"Empty. Poor girl. Okay, Jerome. I admit, it would be more important than putting sugar in German army trucks, which is what some fellows are doing. If it's all as you say. You've done a lot of surmising out there in Baarn."

"I have all the pieces in my mind. From the tire iron on the rug in Cremer's living room to . . . to Schutte smoking his final cigar. It's complete."

"Let's say you've convinced me, for argument's sake. How are we going to convince those men and women you're asking for help? How do you see this? Breaking in? Shooting De Bock? Both? Didn't Schutte tell you most of those shares would already be stashed away in Switzerland? Wouldn't the Germans simply send someone else?"

"Yes, but, on the other hand, there aren't many Andrés around, men who belong in the Indies, who are credible when they show up and say they're in control. Are there *any* other men or women who, even theoretically, have the wealth to buy themselves legally into that position?"

"And you, are you volunteering to shoot this André dead, if that's part of it?"

"He's an accomplice in the death of his own brother. Think of Evelyn Cremer, and of Waldemar, and of Dr. Felleman's wife."

"You haven't answered. Have you ever killed a man?"

"No. Have you?"

"I'm asking. A kitten?"

"No."

"A chicken?"

"Go to hell, Titus."

Titus sighed. "I'll see what they have to say. I will do my best. Don't overestimate them; their resources are very skimpy."

"Can we meet, say, this same place tomorrow?"

"Tomorrow? We, they, they can't just assemble at the Rozenboom bar, you know. On Wednesday I may have something. You lie low, let Geertje call me, at Eddie's. She's doing okay now."

57

The following days were mysteriously peaceful. During the day, with the curtains closed, De Witt helped Geertje clean and cook. He peeled potatoes and scraped turnips. He even read to her. But evenings, when a customer knocked on the window, he went into hiding behind the panel in the closet while Geertje was doing her job. She had insisted on that arrangement, it was the only way she had agreed to let him stay. She didn't mention "her future" as she had once; "If I don't," she had told him, "the cops will be here as sure as Christmas. They smell a rat from a mile. Business is bad. It won't be that often."

De Witt wondered at himself as he sat on his crate behind the panel. With the clothes hanging in front of it and the closet door closed, he couldn't make out any words, just the mutter of voices, setting the price presumably, then silence. Thank God the bed didn't creak. Sometimes he heard Geertje's moaning—only for Johns who paid ten guilders or more, she said —or the man cursing for some reason or other. De Witt had gone through various stages: humiliation first, then a mixture of disgust and anger combined with a secret hope of a loud argument out there, with him bursting on the scene to help her. Then, excitement. It embarrassed him, but the knowledge of what was going on beyond his closet suddenly seemed breathtaking. He would have liked to look, and afterward he had to make a painful effort to hide his mood. Geertje would have accommodated him, no doubt, but the idea of entering her, touching another man's seed—he took his sleeping pill and turned away from her at night. He knew she was offended by it but she didn't say anything.

She had agreed to take up the telephone watch for him at the café the Sun; that was a big thing. She timed her shopping accordingly, standing in line for whatever was to be had, with an occasional foray into the dock area, where a fisherman might show up selling mussels at ten times the prewar price but without demanding ration coupons. She'd walk all the way to the Mint Tower to buy a miserable sprig of flowers for two or three guilders; by eleven she was in the Sun with her shopping net, seated in the chair nearest the telephone booth. When the booth was occupied, she'd look daggers at whoever was in it; then she had to pretend afterward she was making a call. Once the phone had rung at eleven sharp, but it had been for the café owner, who had no phone of his own.

On Sunday she went to the movies with Frieda and came home pale and frightened: after the ads, De Witt's picture had been shown on the screen, his and those of two other men, one

191

after the other, with the caption, "Bandits, these men are dangerous. Reward for all information leading to their arrests."

"It was dead silent in the movie house when they showed it, Jerome. One fellow started to clap but he was shushed. I don't know why he did." She burst into tears.

De Witt put his arms around her. "Please, Geertje. Please don't cry. That fellow who clapped—he knew we're no bandits, everyone knew. The Germans aren't interested in *bandits*. We're, we're resisters."

"But they have won."

"No. They haven't. And even if they had. Didn't you tell me once, we're all going to get it, sooner or later? Isn't it better then to act decent, not to cave in? Wouldn't you? You know, most people feel that way, they're just afraid to show it."

"I don't think so, Jerome. Most people don't give a shit. All they think of is their coffee and butter and sugar. All they think of is their own selves."

"Oh, Geertje—we're all sad sacks. I just got into this, I don't know myself how. Others will, give 'em time. It's just begun, you know."

There was a silence.

"Did it say anything else?" De Witt then asked.

She shook her head.

"For sure?"

"It said whoever gives them shelter will be punished as severely."

"Oh God. God help us. Was it a good likeness?"

She studied his face. "I knew it was you all right. Your hair has grown again you know, a lot."

"Okay, let's shave it off. Can you do that for me?"

"All of it? You'll look spooky."

"Let's shave it off and then I'll put that Sportsman's Tonic stuff on my skull. You still have it? Maybe that'll do it, make me really look like an old sailor. And how was the movie?"

That made her laugh, and they were laughing and splashing while his hair was shaved off. When he looked in her mirror at the end, he screamed, "This is terrible! That's not an old sailor, it's a dirty old man."

"No, it's sort of handsome. Manly, you know."

"No kidding?"

"No kidding."

She kissed him on his head and, for the first time since his return from Baarn, they made love. He didn't think about her customers and his waits in the closet.

58

Geertje's call to Titus turned out differently from what he had expected. The word was that Titus' friends had no means to tackle this.

"And was that the end of it?" De Witt asked her. "Was that all?"

"No, they didn't kill it. One of them is going to see if that place in Baarn is guarded now. And, Titus said, they might be able to help you get away somewhere."

"I've an uncle up north. I guess he'd let me sleep with the cows for the next ten years."

Should I give up? The original purpose is surely lost, anyway. There's no one in Amsteldyk I can protect. What do I want then? To be a patriot? Get even with Buurman and his Beauftragte? Someone should spoil their little plan.

But the following morning, only a few minutes after eleven, he saw, through the crack in the curtains where he used to stand and watch the street, Geertje come running. She came in, locked the door, and looked at him with shining eyes. "Your call came!" she cried.

"Jesus." He sat down. "Where's your shopping bag?"

"What? I left it in the Sun. Aren't you curious?"

"Yes. Scared, I guess."

"I wrote it all down. The man spelled it out twice. Here you are." She gave him the piece of paper on which she had written the message in pencil:

Maybe your right. Sleeper to Zurich March 24. Hotel Boor

Lac March 25 to March 27. Sleeper to Amsterdam March 27.

No maybe about it, he thought, I was right. I am no longer an amateur.

"What does it mean exactly?" she asked.

"It means André de Bock is going to take the shares to Zurich in Switzerland. Or, more likely, they're mostly there already. He's going on to Java with them. He's not taking any sleeper back to Amsterdam; that's make-believe to cover his moves. For sure."

"Did I do all right? I'm getting to be a good telephone messenger, no? The fellow at the other end sounded funny. And he didn't say B-o-o-r but B-a-u-r, twice, but that didn't make sense."

"It doesn't matter. I know the name of the place. You did beautifully."

"I'd better go get my stuff from the café before someone pinches it. I was so excited, I had to come tell you first."

"Don't think I'm not excited. Sort of scared too, I guess. It was cozy here."

"Scared? You mean you want to go after him?"

"I guess so."

"To Switzerland? But you couldn't even get to Baarn that day." She gave him a smile. "Poor Jerome. At least your feet are no longer sore."

"True."

When she had left, he looked at himself in the mirror. Look at that head, he thought, that skull with the bumps and the Outdoor Effect on it. This middle-aged, skinny, tired person. Is he going to make a dent, influence a whole big war? The odds would seem against it. The only action I've seen is Geertje's moaning and groaning, for the ten-guilder customers. About that, I've learned a lot.

59

Titus's underground contact, a young woman, reported on De Witt and the Baarn phone call to her group. They were sitting around in an Amsterdam kitchen, which looked like any other kitchen except for a very old-fashioned mimeograph machine which had been put on the table.

"It still sounds very ephemeral to me," a high-school teacher said.

"It's hard to get very excited about stocks and bonds being stolen," a young man announced.

"They stand for oil and rubber, that's clear enough. Oil and rubber kill people."

"The economics of war—" someone else began.

"Come on, folks," the leader of the group said. "Look, it's very simple. That castle in Baarn is guarded. We're not going to risk our little group and our two pistols on a shoot-out. All we can do for this fellow De Witt is give him our escape route addresses, or we don't. In favor: Titus says he's one hundred percent sure the man's on the level. With the reward, and that picture of his on show in the cinemas, they'll catch him soon enough if he doesn't get out. If we help him hide in the country, we risk more people. Against: he's not really one of us. If they catch him on the way, they'll probably beat those names out of him."

"He must be a pretty committed guy," the woman said. "He gave up his job as a mayor and all that."

"The SD is pretty committed, too," the teacher said. "How do we know that jonkheer is taking that stuff to the Indies?"

"It makes sense," the leader said.

"Well, what is this De Witt going to do, supposing he does get to Geneva, or wherever it is?"

"That's his concern."

"There are Dutch consulates there, you know, representatives of the London government."

"Are you kidding? Those guys have been there since the year zero, collecting dust. You know about Patrice? The consul in Geneva said, 'Do you mean to say, sir, that you came into Switzerland illegally?' And Pat—"

"Let's please vote," the leader said.

The vote came out in favor of giving De Witt the escape addresses, four against two.

60

De Witt had gone with Geertje to the new Weteringschans rendezvous. It wasn't fair to leave it to her, and if Titus was going to arrive with another refusal, he wanted to be there and face him. However, Titus now brought a yes.

"Yes," he said. "My friends think it is very important that you try and stop this scheme. They accept the fact that a lot of it is guesswork, but they trust you. They're behind it."

"Well!" De Witt felt a surge of relief go through him. To be part of a team—

"There isn't *very* much they can do to help," Titus added hastily. "For instance, I tried to get a pistol for you, but no soap."

"I don't want to travel with a pistol. They hang you for that."

"Yes. True." Clearly Titus felt they'd hang him anyway if they caught him. "Do you have any idea how you're going to tackle that jonkheer of yours?"

"I'm working on it. Don't worry about my part. You try walking from Baarn to Amsterdam in your socks and without an ID. But what—?"

"They're trusting you with two contacts," Titus answered. "These are very precious. You are lucky, I tell you."

"I know, Titus, I'm very grateful to you."

"Then they found you a bicycle," Titus went on, "a shabby one, but a bicycle with real tires. It's in the hallway downstairs, and I'll explain to you where it comes in."

"A bicycle," De Witt repeated. It wasn't the kind of thing he had expected.

"I'll explain," Titus repeated. "Then there's some Belgian money, a hundred francs, which is less than it sounds. I also brought you a raincoat of mine."

"A shabby one," De Witt said with a little smile.

"A shabby one, but a raincoat." Titus didn't add that the bicycle and the Belgian money had also come from him. "You're lucky, I tell you," he said once more. "The first address is a smuggler in Breda. He'll take you across the Belgian border. You need a bicycle for that and you leave it with him, by way of fee. In Belgium there's an old steam trolley that runs from near the border to Antwerp; he'll show you. Then you'll go from Antwerp to Brussels on the train. In Brussels you'll go to the second contact and they'll take it from there. It's *our* Belgian border that is the hard part. Belgium and northern France are one military administrative district for the Germans, you know. Workmen go back and forth. It's the getting out of Holland, since we're earmarked to become part of the Reich, that's the real hurdle. Now here are the two addresses you must memorize."

"Can I see them too?" Geertje asked.

They hadn't been aware of her listening; she had posted herself at the window in the large kitchen of that establishment, smoking a cigarette she held between thumb and forefinger.

De Witt looked at Titus.

"Yes," Titus said, "help him remember them."

On the way to their meeting with Titus, De Witt had had a strange encounter. As he and Geertje were walking up the street from Utrecht Square, arm in arm, trying to be a married couple from a fishing village visiting, they met the Geelkerkens. He had seen them approach, on the same sidewalk, too late to dodge them. Max Geelkerken had seen De Witt too. He had recognized him all right; he hadn't spoken, he hadn't drawn his wife's attention to him, he had not slowed down. He had, however, blushed scarlet.

De Witt had puzzled over this. Here De Witt was, outlawed,

recognized, and therefore in principle caught. Yet it was Max Geelkerken, not he, who had acted caught. Red-handed. Red-faced. It was strange and yet it made sense. He felt the incident meant the real and final good-bye to his old life. Geelkerken, even Geelkerken, had shown him he was doing the right thing, hadn't been able to help himself from showing that, from showing that he was ashamed not to be on his side. People are turning.

"Here's something else," Titus was saying to him. "Something to interest you. I knew last week, I was saving it for you. Some of ours are keeping an eye on some of theirs, on the worst of them. Well now, it appears there's a policeman loose in this town, a Scharfuehrer or whatever it is, and they call him Heinz Reifeneisen."

Geertje started to laugh and then stopped abruptly.

"Reifeneisen, which means 'tire iron.' That's his nickname. His name is Heinz Oberwalt of the criminal police, Kriminal-polizei. They're in the RAI building. They're not SD but a competing outfit; apparently those two hate each other about as much as they hate the rest of the world."

"And he is called Heinz Tire Iron because—"

"Because he always carries one. Like, what do you call those things, in that movie 'Bengal Lancers'? Swagger sticks. Reifeneisen has a tire iron for swagger stick. He uses it on his arrestees, it seems. The sharp end in their—"

"Stop it," De Witt said.

"Heinz Reifeneisen *né* Oberwalt."

"Is someone going to get him?"

"No. We'll get them all if they don't win this war."

They hugged each other. "Take care, Jerome. You may think you're unrecognizable but you just look weird." He shook his head. "Masquerades. I guess I should be glad you didn't show up in drag."

He kissed Geertje. "You two leave here first," he said, but when De Witt and the girl were at the door he cried, "Wait! Aren't you going to ask me how you're to get on that train to Breda? You weren't going to cycle all the way, were you?

Here, a Dutch ID card. It's not great, but it should get you through the station."

De Witt looked at it. He stared at Titus and then he turned to Geertje. "Jesus," he said. "It's his. His own."

Titus laughed. "It's okay. I've lost it. In Brussels you can tear it up. We look a bit alike, you know."

"You do, Jerome, you do," Geertje said.

When they were outside, De Witt pushing Titus's bicycle, she said, "I'm going with you."

"Oh no."

"As Titus says, you look too weird. You need me. That way people will stare at me instead of at you and think, what does she see in him. Also, I've got a hundred guilders or so to spare."

"You don't have a bicycle."

"I do. It's in the cellar, I never use it."

61

That night De Witt slept so deeply without taking any pills that Geertje had to shake him after her alarm had gone off. Things are in motion anyway, he had thought. No more either-or.

When they went outside, they were met by that same perpetual hard wind blowing in from the harbor. She was carrying a basket with food and underwear in it; De Witt had their toiletries in the pockets of the shabby raincoat. You couldn't set out for secret border crossings with suitcases. He had hidden the hundred Belgian francs in a shoe, for they could be a giveaway. And then they got on the morning train to Breda as easily as if it were peacetime, after having checked their bicycles in the luggage car. The platform gate policeman, unshaven and yawning, didn't look at them.

Geetje hung on De Witt's arm, whispered in his ear, and sat even closer to him than the full train compartment made necessary. She was acting a lovers' outing. "Aren't I good?" she whispered. "Terrific, you should be an actress." "I've always wanted to be one. Our work isn't so different, you know?" He didn't smile at that, she was serious.

Indeed, maybe she did prevent people from looking at him as a person by himself, someone whom they might recognize from those alerts projected in the movie houses.

In Breda nature was friendlier, a bit of blue in the sky, the air almost still; you could tell you were inland, and some three hours south of Amsterdam. They bicycled down the quiet streets to their smuggler's address. "It's nice to be in the country," Geertje said.

A girl of about sixteen opened the door for them and said, "Dad is away."

"Away?"

"Yes. For a couple of days. Could you come back?"

"Come back!" De Witt cried. "What are you thinking of!" Geertje plucked at his sleeve. "We could go to a hotel."

"Oh, shut up, Geertje," he whispered, "A hotel, without papers?" "Sorry, miss," he told the girl, "I didn't mean to holler at you. But it's very urgent, you see. We have no time. It's my wife's mother, in Brussels. She is dying."

"Oh, dear." The girl thought about that. "I could take you across myself," she said.

"Can you? Will you? We'd leave you our bicycles of course. You know the way, do you?"

"I've gone with my dad, often. You two just sit here. We can't leave before two o'clock. The Turnhout trolley, the Belgian trolley runs at four. You don't want to hang about out there in the fields."

She left them in what was obviously in Dutch farmers' style the "Sunday room," smelling of furniture polish and caustic, the table covered with sailcloth and on top of that a white lacy tablecloth, the chairs in geometrically precise positions, everything gleaming and unused. A glass breakfront with seashells and souvenirs. A Virgin with a little oil light burning.

"A respectable smuggler," De Witt muttered. He was inspecting the seashells, putting them to his ear. The room depressed him and made him nervous again.

"Don't break anything, Jerome. Do you think she knows the way?"

"Since she offered . . . since they seem to let her—I have to pee."

"Me too."

"You ask."

"No, you."

In the toilet he saw on a birthday calendar that a girl called Katryn was fourteen that month. It was the only girl's name on the calendar.

They ate everything edible in the basket. Then they just sat there without saying anything, staring at the pictures and the Virgin.

"Is your name Katryn?" he asked the smuggler's daughter when she came to get them.

"Yes. How did you know?"

"From the calendar in the—you know. God, she's only just fourteen," he whispered to Geertje.

He saw the girl cross herself as they set off, she in front, he and Geertje cycling behind her. The road signs, removed at the start of the war, had never been put back, and De Witt had no idea where they were going; the sun had disappeared behind dark clouds.

An hour later they turned off the asphalted road and entered a small village. "Zundert," Katryn said. "We leave our bicycles here, behind this hedge. We have to walk now."

She looked around and listened. It was very quiet and there wasn't a soul in sight.

They walked down a narrow dirt road and then on a little dike between pastures.

"Are we near the border?" De Witt asked after a long while. Katryn nodded.

"Aren't we sort of conspicuous up here, I mean visible?"

The girl laughed nervously. "I'm a bit mixed up," she said.

"That way, I think." She started crossing a pasture in which a solitary cow stared at her.

"Oh, fuck it," De Witt muttered.

"Jerome, let's go back," Geertje whispered.

"We can't, not now."

"Come," the girl said, turning around at them, "or you'll miss the tram. There's only one." She started to run and they ran after her.

"Wait. My shoe," Geertje asked. He took her hand. "Come on, girl."

They came to a line of poplars and Geertje suddenly uttered a plaintive little sound, like a cat that's been stepped on, and fell. Her fall came so unexpectedly that he fell too. "What—?" he began, but she dug her elbow hard into his ribs.

Fifty feet away from them a German soldier approached, a bicycle at his hand. De Witt, lying with his chin on reed stubbles as pointed as knives, stared hypnotized. He had never seen another human being as sharply: soft black boots of leather or maybe some kind of imitation leather; a stick hand grenade on his wide-buckled belt; a dagger; a rifle on a brown strap hanging from his shoulder. Short hair, the ugly green cap. The face came last: a red, nondescript face, a farmer's face, the eyes staring ahead. A man absorbed in who-knows-what thoughts, who would shoot them if he saw them. He could feel the beating of Geertje's heart against the hard ground.

The soldier walked by. Silence. Nothing stirred. All De Witt saw was reeds, winter grass, the bare trees.

They heard a low whistle. The smuggler's daughter was standing beside a tree twenty feet in front of them, beckoning them. "Quick, the trolley."

They ran past another line of poplars, across a dirt road, past more trees, before coming upon a wooden railroad shanty with a little steam tram just starting up.

"Quick, jump," Katryn said, and De Witt and Geertje jumped on the rear platform and stared at the girl who waved, gaily it seemed, and then turned around.

"Now there's a tough fourteen-year-old," De Witt said. He

202

pulled out his handkerchief and wiped the dirt off Geertje's face. She took it and wiped his.

"Were you scared?" she whispered.

"Jesus, yes. I don't know. It all went so fast. So different from how you imagine it. You saved the day, Geertje, that's for sure."

She shivered.

The steam train was full of Flemish women toting bags full of food they must have bought on farms to take to Antwerp. There was a lot of chatting, a different mood from that of the trains and streetcars north of the border. He wondered why; did they care less? Know better how to cope? The conductor entered their car and De Witt went back out on the platform to get his Belgian money out; when he started to take his shoe off, the note fluttered away and he only just caught it.

The station in Antwerp was full of German soldiers, but there were no police in evidence, neither Belgian nor German. They caught a Brussels train (one left every hour) and even got a seat. It was almost dark now and oilcloth blackout curtains had been lowered over the train windows.

It was not a very long ride. When the train began to slow down, he peered around the little curtain and could just make out the towers and cupolas of the approaching city rising in the gray sky.

62

The contact address in Brussels was an easily found house on a wide, rich-looking avenue. The man who opened the door for them didn't ask anything and took them up three flights of stairs to an attic that held several cots with blankets. "There'll be no one here but you," he told them in Dutch with a French cadence. "Come down in an hour and we'll have something for you to eat."

"Will we—?" De Witt began.

"It'll be a day or two. We need time to get your ID cards."

"I don't—" from Geertje.

"Later," he said with a smile, and vanished.

De Witt fell down on a cot. "What were you going to say, Geertje?"

She moved another cot against his and lay down too. "I wanted to tell him that I don't need a card. I'm going back, tomorrow."

"What? What are you saying? Because of that girl getting lost?"

"No. No. I'm not scared anymore. But I always meant to go back. I'm going back tomorrow because you'll be okay now. I can't go to no Switzerland, what would I do there?"

"Oh, cut it out, Geertje. You'll be with me."

"You don't know what's going to happen to you there."

"No . . . but you'll be better off anyway than in Holland. It's a big break. Those friends of Titus don't do this all the time, you know. They'll help you in Switzerland; there's a Dutch consul there. A man from the London government. It's a neutral country, for God's sake! No war!"

"No."

"You know I'm fond of you."

"Don't confuse me, Jerome. I have a nice place in Amsterdam and a job."

He swallowed the snide remark he was about to make. "Geertje," he said, "I love you, sort of."

"Don't confuse me," she said again. She turned and hid her head in the pillow.

"Are you crying?"

"Leave me alone."

He was lying on his cot in the pitch-dark attic. Not a sound penetrated from the avenue. Geertje was breathing so lightly, at times he couldn't hear it at all. Like a child, he thought. I mustn't get carried away with myself. I can't mess up my life again, and hers maybe, because I'm feeling friendless and lost. No more Lydias.

But she's the opposite of Lydia. She hasn't got a mean bone in her body. Perhaps I do love the girl, whatever that word may mean. She's very skinny and she's a bit stupid, no, not stupid, she just hasn't ever learned much. She's a whore. If she's been at it since the war, she must have had five hundred men in her.

He swung his legs over the side of his cot and shook her. Immediately she sat upright. "Something wrong?" she whispered.

"No. I had to wake you. I don't love you 'sort of.' I love you, and I like you. We'll stick together. Get married, the whole bit."

"Oh, Jerome, you're just chatting. Please go back to sleep."
"Is it a deal?"

"No." And she pulled the blankets over her head.

Just as she did that morning in her own place in Amsterdam, when I offered her the syphilis ward.

He woke up, it was day, and he saw Geertje sitting on her cot, fully dressed, looking at him.

"Hi," she said. "I'm off now."

He could feel his heart starting to pound. "Don't. How would you get back, anyway?"

"Just the way we came. I'll say I was visiting my boyfriend. They won't worry about someone like me. I've already been downstairs. He's a nice man, he gave me fifty Belgian francs for guilders. That's all I need. Here, I want you to have these," and she put two fifty-guilder notes on his blanket.

"I don't want it."

"You can pay me back after the war. And you know, Jerome, that Sunday, when we toasted the bread, that was maybe the best day I've ever had." She bent over to kiss him on his mouth, and was gone.

He thought, I must run after her, stop her, but he did not move.

63

Two days later De Witt was on the train to Reims, in his pocket a Belgian identity card showing him to be a miner from the town of Huy on the Meuse River. In a window seat of his compartment a young blond man was leafing through the French-language edition of the German magazine *Signal*, which identified him as the person De Witt had to follow when he got off the train at Couvin, just before the French border.

The Brussels contact man had explained it to him painstakingly, and clearly with some doubt about De Witt's acumen. But he had been as calm and matter-of-fact about it as if he were sending a not very bright child on a school outing, and De Witt had found it impossible to get nervous. The man hadn't commented on Geertje.

At Charleroi Station, two German military policemen boarded the train, and his *Signal* friend threw him a brief but reassuring glance. The train had started again when one of these men came into their compartment and demanded all papers. He was a heavy fellow, and he wore a metal plate on his chest, which hung from a chain around his neck—like the wine waiter in the Victoria Hotel before the war, De Witt thought. The idea helped. He quietly handed over his miner's card. The man read it, looked at him, and handed it back without a word.

At Couvin he followed his guide, off the train and down a road that led away from the little station toward a cluster of farms in the distance. After a while his guide stopped and let him catch up. "Vous parlez français?" he asked, carefully enunciating the words.

"Oui. Not too well. School French."

"That is good."

They walked on in silence. A nice day. Spring comes earlier here, De Witt thought. How different the landscape looks from Holland. And yet it's hard to say why precisely. More stone, more walls. No water.

They passed the farms and then found themselves in a little village square. His guide turned toward him and smiled. "Well, my friend, you're in France."

"Really?" God.

A man in a black suit suddenly appeared, went up to De Witt and shook his hand. "Bienvenu," he said. "Welcome to Monthermé." and then something about bravery, which escaped De Witt.

"Who was that?" De Witt asked when they were left to themselves.

"He's the mayor of Monthermé. He thinks you're a French prisoner of war, escaped back from Germany. We have quite a flow through here."

"You are well organized. Wow."

They entered a little house; a bell sounded when they opened and closed the door, but no one came. De Witt found to his surprise that it was a photography shop. "They can't have too much business with nothing but farms around," he said, but his guide either didn't understand his French or paid no attention.

"We wait in the kitchen," he said. He held a curtain aside for De Witt to go first.

When the little bell sounded again, he went to look; De Witt could hear his voice and another's. It was nice to be guided and follow orders and directions; it was all so much simpler than he had thought. If only Geertje had stayed put. Two days only. Think of all those nights beside her when I didn't want to touch her.

The guide came back with another man. "This is Charles," he said. "You will sleep here tonight. Tomorrow morning Charles will put you on the train to Belfort. You will travel alone."

"Very early," Charles said in English. "You are a good early riser?"

"One must not chat on the train," De Witt's guide went on.

"The best thing always is to sleep. It is a long ride. The service is bad now. Ten hours, twelve perhaps."

"We will give you some provisions," from Charles.

"In Belfort you will stay on the platform of arrival. You cross it to the other side. There will be a little train there. It goes to Montbéliard. Fear nothing, it waits for the connection. In Montbéliard you will be met."

"How will they know?"

"He, the *passeur*, will know. You understand 'passeur'?"

"Eh, no."

"It is a man who passes people across the frontier. He will take you to Switzerland. It is his profession."

"If I stay on that platform, then how, how to buy my ticket?" De Witt asked.

"Charles will give it to you tomorrow morning. Now I say good-bye."

They shook hands. "Good luck, my friend," the guide said.

As the guide had said, it was a very long ride. Having left at half past six in the morning, they were in Nancy at four in the afternoon, in Belfort at ten that night. Until Nancy, De Witt had been standing in the corridor. There was one toilet in the train and its floor was soon flooded, its bowl stopped up; the train began to stink. It was all worse when they were standing still, endless, unexplained waits in little stations with no one getting on. When he got off at Belfort, he was staggering on his feet. How marvelous it felt to breathe the sharp night air. He wondered about curfew; he was afraid to ask in his bad French. But the little train to Montbéliard, with just one car, was waiting as he had been told.

When they arrived at Montbéliard, it was almost eleven. By the light of the one blue lamp, he saw that the platform was empty. He went outside. A light rain was falling but there was some light in the sky and he could see the square and the two streets down which the few passengers who had been on the train hurried home.

Across the square he saw the outline of a small van, its blue headlights on. A man was standing beside it. He started to walk toward him, rubbing his eyes, and only when he was about six feet away did he see that the man was a policeman and that the van had the word "Police" painted on its side.

64

That same instant De Witt turned away, but another policeman had come up behind him and grabbed him by the arm.

What was he doing there?

"I'm a foreign worker," De Witt told them. Belgian. Looking for a job.

They studied his Huy ID card. "Better show him to the chief," they said and shoved him into the van, prodding him with their carbines.

Once more De Witt was riding in a police wagon, but the day had been so endless, he was so far from anything familiar, that he was more dazed than worried.

The police chief was standing in the hallway of the police station with his coat on. "I'm on my way home," he announced to his men.

They told him something De Witt did not understand.

"Eh bien," he said impatiently, and to De Witt, gesturing with his hand, "Your pants. Drop them."

"What?"

"Down."

De Witt stared at him.

One of the policemen stepped up, opened De Witt's raincoat, undid his belt, and pulled his trousers and underpants down to his shoes.

"Voilà," the chief said. He pointed at De Witt's genitals. "A Jew, a foreign Jew. To Belfort."

These words De Witt understood. "You're crazy," he said. "I'm not." He pulled up his trousers.

The police chief shrugged and walked toward the exit of the

station. "I'm Christian!" De Witt shouted after him. "I am! Lots of people—" He didn't know how to say "circumcized" in French.

The front door fell shut behind the man.

"Cochon—pig!" De Witt shouted after him, as he buckled his belt.

"Pig?" the policeman asked De Witt. "You're going to Belfort, my friend. You can explain yourself to the Germans there." And he kicked him hard in the groin.

De Witt did not fall. He felt tears come to his eyes, more from anger than from pain.

"Pigs, pigs!" he shouted. "And to think, we studied Victor Hugo in school! And Molière! A whole year! Une année complète!"

The policeman stared at him, too surprised to kick him again.

He was sitting on a bench in a little whitewashed room, while at its center table the other policeman was drinking red wine from the bottle. De Witt kept his hand pushed against his belly to lessen the aching. From what he had understood, they were waiting for the cop who had kicked him and who was going to drive him to the German Gestapo in Belfort.

The wine-drinking cop handed De Witt the bottle without saying a word and motioned that he could take a swig.

There's always a twosome, a brute and a nicer one, De Witt thought. One lesser brute. It's the same kind of crummy damn game everywhere.

He felt the phial of sleeping pills in the right-hand pocket of his raincoat. For a second the idea crossed his mind to take one against the pain. No, that was stupid. He undid the cap with one hand, and the pills spilled out into the pocket. He got hold of several, at least five or six, and palmed them. Then, after waiting a moment, he asked in a low, humble voice, "Monsieur? One more?"

The cop held out the bottle to him, which was now only a third full. De Witt got up to take it with the hand holding the pills and let them slide in. One fell on the floor and he stepped on it as he sat down.

He took a sip without opening his mouth, turned the bottle as if to read the label, took another make-believe sip, and handed it back.

Not long after, the policeman offered him the bottle again and he declined with a polite smile. The man finished it then, put it on the table, and fell asleep in his chair, his carbine still dangling from his shoulder.

De Witt slowly stood up. No reaction. He opened the door of the room as softly as he could and walked the long corridor out of the police station into the Monbéliard night. You fuckers, you can't hold me. I'm no amateur.

On the wall of that station a map of the region had been pinned up, but De Witt hadn't had a chance to look at it. All he knew was that Switzerland lay due east and Montbéliard was the last town before the border and the end of the railway line. I just have to make it, he told himself, on foot. Very simply, to save my skin. I'll worry about the rest of it afterward.

The rain came down in stops and starts. An effusion of soft light penetrated the clouds and hovered over the town. He ran in the opposite direction of where he guessed its center must be, keeping as much as he could to a straight line. Nothing stirred, the streets were empty, the windows dark. The end of the world.

Then he could see that the rows of apartment houses had fallen away. Lonely buildings loomed up, and after them only a black flatness of fields. More light spread from the sky here, and he saw he was following a long stone wall with a wood behind it. Where the wall turned, he hid in a cluster of bushes and trees. He would have to wait for the first light to locate a true easterly direction.

"God help me," he whispered. "Let it be ahead." If east were behind him, he'd have to cross the town again.

He sat huddled under a bush whose foliage kept out most of the rain, and slowly let his pain rise to the surface of his awareness. It feels as if my balls are about to come off. He had read once that an attacking wild animal never aims for that spot. If it's true, he thought, it's one more proof that we're more beastly than beasts, that beasts that kill should be called, humane. He imagined himself coming back to this town, Montbéliard, after the war. I mustn't forget the name, I'll find that same police chief, I'll follow him when he goes to his little café after work, he orders his glass of wine. I'll sit down at his table and say calmly, remember me, monsieur—oh screw. I wonder what became of my passeur.

He toyed with the idea of taking one of his pills and going to sleep, but it seemed too risky. Fumbling in his pocket, he managed to get the pills back into the phial while keeping them dry. He found a sausage skin in the pocket, left over from his provisions, that he hadn't wanted to throw on the floor of the train. Not that its floor hadn't been filthy enough. Virtue its own reward. He started to chew on the skin as slowly as he could.

At three in the morning the sky cleared in places and a half-moon appeared for a moment, low behind the wall. East was not quite where he had prayed for it to be, but it was not on the other side of Montbéliard either: His road had taken him to the southeast. He tied his shoes, dried his neck with his handkerchief, and, cutting through a field of stubble at a forty-five-degree angle to the road, resumed his walk.

When Geertje opened her door to the man who had scrutinized her from the street in the last twilight, she was immediately sorry. She had closed her blackout curtain and turned on the little lamp before going to the door, and she could see now that he was a German. He wasn't in uniform but he was wearing the unmistakable German police raincoat, and when he unbuttoned it she saw he was wearing a pistol on a holster attached to his belt. "Don't worry," he said in Dutch but with a strong accent. "It's a private visit."

"Oh, I'm not worried. In my profession, a man is a man."

He smiled, he liked that.

"My prices are—"

"Don't rush me," he interrupted. "I won't haggle. I like to talk a bit first. May I sit down?"

Talk first—God knows what he wants, she thought. Frieda had told her some hair-raising tales. "Have a cup of herb tea," she said. "You're with the police, right?"

"The *Aussenstelle*. We're more like diplomats than policemen."

"Oh."

"I'll show you some photographs. I'm from Bremen. You know, Bre-men? A port, like Amsterdam. A very fine port. What's your name?"

He pulled out a wallet and showed her pictures of a little house on a suburban, treeless street; of his parents, his wife. "We are so busy, I haven't been home in a year," he said. "I miss her very much."

"Well, why did you come here?" Geertje answered, blushed, and smiled. Jesus, don't make them angry.

But he smiled back. "Why, Marlene? You look a bright girl, but you may not understand."

"It's that complicated?"

"No. You're from the north, right?"

She nodded.

"I can always tell. That'a good dolichocephalic skull you've got, girl. We're here because we're the stronger, it's that simple."

"Oh."

"Look around you. Look around you when you go buy your rations on . . . right across from you, how do you say it, the

Newendyk. All those men—I'm not talking of women, mind you—in the middle of this great Germanic war. They're strolling around, buying this or that, looking for a black-market pack of cigarettes. Three centuries of prosperity have done that. We're steel, they're cotton wool."

He lit a cigarette without offering her one.

"Are they all like that?" she finally asked.

"Yes."

"Then how come they keep the police so busy?" She smiled again, to soften the sharpness of her tone.

But that question did not annoy him either. He shrugged. "Degenerate elements, anarchists who want to profit from the blackout and the shortages." He made a gesture with his left hand. "We'll erase them, they won't leave a trace, and you'll thank us for it."

"Thank you."

He didn't want her to undress, he didn't even want her to touch him; he undid his pants and started to masturbate. "This may not seem very manly to you," he announced while he was doing so, "but manliness is not necessarily demonstrated by . . . by coupling." And when she did not answer, he insisted, "Don't you agree?"

"Oh yes, I do."

She meant it, and he smiled again, but at that moment there was a knock on her window and she looked away, just as he was coming. When she turned her eyes back to him, it was all over, and on his face was an expression of cold fury. He moved his hand to his belt and in that instant she thought, he's going to shoot me for this.

The police officer hitched up his pants, dropped a ten-mark note in the chair, and left without another word.

Geertje sat motionless after he had gone. Imagine. I might have been dead now. For looking away.

I hope Jerome succeeds, I hope he screws up their plot, she thought. It was the first time she had thought this, not from some vague tenderness, but in these precise terms. She had looked on De Witt as an odd, almost pathetic creature, not to be taken quite seriously as a man. Now, suddenly, she was bitterly sorry she had not stayed with him.

She turned off her light and opened the window. "Bastards, fuckers!" she screamed, leaning out. "Steel, my ass! We'll get you!"

67

If Jerome de Witt had known how far it was to the Swiss border and if he had had an inkling that his progress, once there, would not be much easier, he'd probably have given up and knocked on the door of a French farm. That, in this early period of the war, March 1941, when so many people believed in a German victory, would most likely have led to the farmer calling the police and thus to his arrest, prison, the Germans, and death.

But he did not know, and did not look beyond taking each step and then one more and then one more. If only I wasn't in such a beat-up state, he thought, I'd do better. No food, no sleep, hurting like the devil. He didn't know either that he was in better shape than he'd been as mayor of Amsteldyk; he had become tougher—not in his aching muscles but in some other way. Jopie would have recognized it.

When dawn came, he saw that the landscape was quite different from what he had constructed out of the shadows and outlines of the night. He had been climbing up a gently sloping, long, stony hillside, and at only some ten feet from him a white, narrow path followed that same direction. The rain had ended. Gusts of wind from the east carried the sound of barking dogs. The path seemed to lead on to a village; the horizon showed trees and farms, far off but unmistakable against the sunrise, and stretching both north and south. He slowly walked on; now that he could see the slope, the going seemed even rougher. Every so often he saw to the left or to the right of the path little shelters built of stones: nothing but

four walls, a door opening, and a roof usually half caved in—
their purpose a mystery to him. He decided to wait for night-
fall in one of these. The first one he investigated had been used
as an outhouse, but the next one with its earthen floor was dry
and stood empty. He curled up against an inner wall, next to
the door opening, and swallowed one of his pills.

It was twilight when he opened his eyes and painfully
scrambled up into the doorway. To his right, the east was dark,
the farms now invisible; to his left, quite far down the valley
he had come from, a burst of separate sunbeams shone low over
the horizon through a gap in the inky black clouds. The land
around him lay as empty as before. His throat was contracted
with thirst.

He peed and saw blood in his urine. There was a tube of
toothpaste in the left raincoat pocket, and he put some on his
teeth with one finger and tried to make spit, but his mouth was
too dry. His shelter had a raised stone threshold and he had to
make a conscious effort to step over it; but once he was back
on the path, walking was not as difficult as he had feared. He
decided to go straight through the village ahead.

Darkness had fallen again when he passed the first farm. A
chorus of dogs now took up his progress, one starting the
moment another fell silent. Once a shadowy child darted across
the road in front of him. The village was but a hamlet; soon
its dogs and houses were behind him. Here the ground sloped
down, as he realized after a few steps. He stood still.

I can't go on without water, he thought, not another night
for sure. I have to risk it. He turned and very slowly walked
back to the wall of the last farm he had passed. Its windows
were shuttered, he could distinguish that. All was silent but
then, as he took a step into a kind of gateway, a wildly barking
dog rushed at him and came to a halt two feet away, yanked
short by a chain. De Witt jumped back and retreated behind the wall. He heard a man cursing and saw the glimmer of a lamp. Then, again, stillness. Okay, he thought.
So much for that. He turned and continued on his way.
It required less effort going downhill, but now there were

boulders strewn everywhere and he stumbled repeatedly.

Let's think of liquids. I will have a large beer, no, no beer, lemonade. A real one, like when I was a child, in summer, when we sat in the grass and squeezed lemons into a pitcher and filled it with cold water from a tap that was kept running a long time. Okay, lemonade. Now something more interesting. Whiskey, large glasses, filled with ice and the soda brimming over. Swimming in a blue lake and just opening your mouth and drinking. Grapes. God, grapes. Was anything more marvelous ever created. A bar, with its long row of bottles. The Gerstekorrel Bar in Amsterdam, a German soldier offering him a cigar—that stopped his images. Back onto this hellish hillside sloping down into . . . into hell, of course. He giggled.

He walked most of that night. Sometimes he sat down on a boulder, but he stayed awake. It seemed to get warmer toward dawn, and presently a foggy, gray light surrounded him. He was passing a potato field and crawled on his hands and knees till he had found several old potatoes, which he peeled, more or less, with his nail scissors. Then he went on, chewing them until he could swallow again. The path came to a pine wood and turned sharply to the right—south, that was. He decided to continue straight through the trees.

When De Witt emerged from the pine wood, he looked down a grassy slope. Sunlight filtered through the clouds. At the bottom of the slope was a gulley beyond which the ground rose again and another wood began. At the edge of that wood was a small farmhouse with a smoking chimney.

There was little wind here and as he held his breath, he thought he could hear a stream gurgle below him. He started to crawl down the slope, but it was too painful; he stood up again and hurried on in a crouch. The gulley held water, a tiny stream. He had to take off his coat to work his way to it, and then he pushed his head among the stones and drank the ice-cold water. Afterward he lay on his back in the grass.

Some twenty feet away from him at the edge of the gulley stood a milestone with a design on it. After staring at it a while, he realized this design was a Greek cross, four thick arms of equal length. It took him still more time before it penetrated his mind what this meant. He got up, jumped across the gulley, and ran toward the house. A woman and a man appeared in the doorway.

"Switzerland?" he asked hoarsely, in German.

They nodded.

Dear God. And he had never even seen a German patrol. The date was March 25, the day of André de Bock's arrival in Zurich.

The couple made him sit down in the kitchen and gave him a bowl of milk and bread and cheese. They spoke German but it was a dialect, hard to grasp, and De Witt reacted to most of their questions with a smile or a nod. The ground was very hilly; through the window he could see it climb steeply beyond the house. He wondered if they had a horse and cart, if they would drive him to the nearest station. He had only Dutch money but he could give them his watch. "Do you have . . ." he began carefully, just as two soldiers entered the kitchen. They were Swiss, uniforms quite different from the German ones, and with the Swiss white-cross-on-red insignia on their shoulderstraps. They carried rifles.

"What have you done." De Witt cried, standing up.

The farmer smiled. "Okay, okay, good. Good people. Border soldiers."

"How did they know to come here!" De Witt cried.

One of the soldiers gestured for him not to shout. "We sent a child," the farmer said. "We have to. Swiss law. They will take you to their post. All will be good."

"Oh," De Witt said, falling back down in his chair.

"Allez," one of the soldiers said.

"Thanks for the food." And De Witt stumbled out the door with his escort.

But all was not good. At the post, a sergeant and then a lieutenant interrogated him. Yes, if he was Dutch he could enter the country, but he had to prove it.

"I have nothing," De Witt said. "I have a Belgian ID card, one the underground gave me. I couldn't carry two different cards, could I?"

"A false card?" the lieutenant asked, clearly taking a dim view of that. "May I see it?"

But De Witt couldn't find it. It had stayed at the police post in Montbéliard.

"I'm sorry," the lieutenant said, "We must escort you back to the border."

"But you can't do that. You're condemning me to death. The Germans—"

"I must, sir. We have our laws, you have yours."

"Well, what do you want me to do then?"

"Try and get some proof of Dutch nationality. You have a consul in Lyons."

"A consul in Lyons? You're crazy. There's a war on, or didn't you know?"

The lieutenant shrugged and beckoned his men with the fingers of one hand.

Twenty minutes later De Witt was back at the gulley, with the two Swiss soldiers waiting to see him climb back up into the pine wood on the French side of the border.

That day carried an experience for De Witt, different from anything he had known. In past months he had been in danger and he had been afraid, but he had always felt that he was sharing those emotions with others, that his enemies were the enemies of those around him, even if those around him didn't see it that way.

In Holland he had felt he was in trouble *by choice*. At almost any time, he had felt he could give up on that somewhat exorbitant mission he had made his.

In the pine wood on the Swiss border it was different. He wasn't on any mission, he never even thought about the murders and the Indies shares and De Bock in Zurich; all that was part of someone else's life. As he climbed back up that hillside under the pine trees, he thought he could see himself, as if he were looking down on earth from a very great height. A miserable little man, crawling back and forth through a hostile landscape, lost in a world in which there was literally no room for him.

The eyes of those two indifferent Swiss soldiers in his back burned him, as the indignant looks of Buurman, the contemptuous look of the Beauftragte, had not.

He had joined the Jews, the Red Scum, the species Buurman had warned him not to go down the drain with.

No point in wishing I were here or there, he muttered to himself. There isn't any here or there. No point in making Max Geelkerken blush. No point in interrupting Geertje earning her five guilders under a passer-by—his thoughts were whirling so, he lost track of them. He stumbled on for a long time and then, without making any conscious decision, started to cut back down the hillside again, cutting a very wide arc that would lead him far from those soldiers and the farmer with his complacent smile.

"I hate you," he said aloud. I hate the lot of them, Swiss, French, American, German, Dutch, sitting behind the same fucking desk, saying the same fucking things.

He heard the familiar ticking in the trees, and the drops started to hit him. It was raining once more, and hard.

He came to another edge of the wood. A curtain of rain swept toward him across a vast expanse of farmland. In the distance a row of hills filled the horizon and the clouds were so low that they obscured the hilltops.

I'll go look for some potatoes there or turnips, or something. But then he saw a white line cutting through the fields not very far from where he stood; it was a road. On it approached a

German patrol with dogs; he could hear their voices and the barking. He turned and ran. He waited for shouts; he could almost hear the "halt!" already. He waited for the sound of rifle shots. Nothing happened. He tripped over roots, ran on, then fell as his foot went down a hole. He lay still with his face pressed into the wet moss and all he heard were the raindrops hitting his back.

70

The offices of the Amsterdam stock exchange had closed, William Scheltema put some papers in a kid attaché case, picked up his overnight bag, and went out without even locking his desk. It was a day like any other; he could still change his mind.

"Not a single taxi, Mr. Scheltema," the doorman told him.

"That's all right. I'll walk."

Unexpectedly, it had turned into a mild spring afternoon. Better than the wet snow of the morning; not that it made Amsterdam look any better, he thought. The low sun only showed the city's gray shabbiness more cruelly. I wonder how they'll ever get through another war winter. He was struck by the discovery that he had thought "they" and not "we."

He went north on Beurs Street. It wasn't more than five minutes to Central Station, and the night train to Zurich did not leave until six. But the police control often took a very long while and, anyway, it was nice to take your time. When he came to the station square, he saw that most of the telephone booths were unoccupied. How perverse, when you need one, there are lines a mile long. Should I phone Emily? Tell her what? Your husband is off to Java? But am I? Let it be. I'll wire her from Zurich. She won't worry. Urgent trip, great rush, back soon. Leave it open, don't stir up anything.

At the Dutch control in the station he had only to show his ticket; but then they made him enter the German control office, where they wanted to see his passport, exit visa, Swiss entry visa, return ticket, and permit to change money. "You may change up to seventy-five guilders a day into Swiss francs," an official told him. "That should be sufficient for your needs."

"Yes, absolutely." In his inside pocket he carried a sealed letter of credit issued by the German Reich Bank for five million Swiss francs. *I may be selling myself, but not cheaply.*

The train had already been formed and just as he stepped out onto the platform the lights in the cars went on. A porter led him to his compartment in the sleeper. It wasn't the kind of train he used to go look at as a child, dreaming of far journeys; sometimes on a rainy Sunday with nothing to do, his mother had taken him to the station and they watched the international trains leave, cars in beautiful wood with gold lettering, *Compagnie Internationale des Wagons-Lits*—he felt a moment of sentimental tenderness for himself as a child. This train was nice enough, though, blue and white; signs with black letters in German reading "Amsterdam-Köln-Mannheim-Basel-Zürich." A waiter came when he pressed the button in his compartment, and took his order for tea. The platform remained empty for a long time, then a single passenger, an old lady in furs, followed by two porters with luggage, went by. The waiter reappeared with the tea and a plate of cookies wrapped in tissue paper. It was half past five on the station clock, and Scheltema felt that the disheveled city already lay a million miles behind him. *De Bock's second-in-command. His successor, presently. A man creates his own circumstances, his own destiny. Amsterdam was outside history. He had made the right decision.*

71

At eight o'clock in the morning—his watch was still running —De Witt 'marched' into the Swiss village of Bure. He knew its name because here there was a road sign. "Marched," because he was whistling a song and keeping in cadence.

He was carrying a thick tree branch as a cane (or weapon) and had sharpened its end with his scissors. He thought he'd use it on anyone now who might try to question or stop him. No one did. He passed two peasant women who glanced at him over their shoulders and then continued their conversation. Maybe my luck has turned again, he told himself. Maybe they can see I'm better left alone.

A farm cart came up behind him, and he held up his hand for a lift. The farmer slowed down but, after a look at De Witt, speeded up his horse and continued on his way. De Witt tried to think of a French or German curse to shout after him but then decided it was funny that his appearance was too unappetizing even for a ride on a manure cart.

After this encounter, the road remained empty. He crossed a stream on a little wooden bridge and while on it, felt a tremor in its planks. He jumped down the bank and hid in the bushes along the water. A minute later a Swiss army patrol came by, marched heavily across the bridge, and vanished in the direction of the border. The incident did not impress him. Suddenly he was taking it for granted that he would cope with whatever they had in store for him. He accepted the idea that he was hunted; and it was no longer something fearful but a defiance.

It was past noon when he came to a small town. It looked closed up; the people were presumably eating their midday meals behind tightly shut doors and windows. Good. At the first square, a fountain played and he took a long time drinking and washing his face and neck and head, brushing his teeth, cleaning and wiping his raincoat and shoes with tufts of wet grass. He started fumbling for his toilet things to shave, but it seemed too much of an effort. He left his stick carefully pointing upright against the fountain, and continued down the narrowing street leading away from the square. A window displayed overcoats, violins, watches: a pawnshop. Its door was locked but there was a light on in the depths of the store and he knocked. A man came forward, shaking his head and holding up two fingers. De Witt took off his watch and showed it; the door was opened a crack and a hand came out to take it. "Ten francs," the man said.

Ten minutes later De Witt was sitting in the train station with a third-class ticket to Zurich. The town, he had learned, was called Porrentruy, its distance to Zurich some one hundred sixty kilometers. The next train was due at one o'clock. The ticket had cost five francs sixty.

He was perplexed at the luxury, the prewar-ness, of this small railroad station: chocolate bars, pastries, bread rolls on display; a newsstand with several English and American magazines, cigarettes. Things were new and shiny, even the money. For one franc twenty he bought a hard sausage, and for fifty centimes half a load of bread, but as he sat with them in the third-class waiting room he could not eat. He was so weary, he could only stay upright by grabbing hold of his nail scissors in his coat pocket and digging their point into his side.

He had two francs seventy left and some three hundred Dutch guilders. It was Wednesday, March 26, the last full day of André de Bock's stay in Zurich.

72

De Witt fell asleep the instant his train started to move, which was a good thing, for whatever else he might have said or done would have aroused the suspicion of his fellow passengers. In Basel someone shook him; everybody had to change trains there. At a quarter to four in the afternoon they entered Zurich Main Station.

Many people were milling around in the large hall, men who looked like farmers or workmen out of a job, and he felt he was no longer dangerously conspicuous. He went into the toilets, put on the clean underpants he still had in his pocket, and shaved his face and then his head, which had already begun to look bristly. The attendant, whom he gave half a franc, brushed his jacket and trousers for a long time. De Witt tucked his grimy shirt collar in and decided that without his raincoat he did not look disreputable.

He came out onto the station square. A low, lead-colored sky vaulted the town where he had never been. Streetcars were making their turns in the traffic circle and beyond them shone lighted shop windows. A terrifying dizziness seized him; he did not know where he was and felt an urge to kneel on the pavement. The human condition. Aloneness, loneliness—think of Lydia, of Geertje, anyone, a woman's body—the blond girl in the red dress in the Amsteldyk hotel dining room —It passed. He started walking, turning to the right off the square to where the streets looked poorer than those ahead of him. In that first block from the station several shops carried signs, "Checks Cashed," "Money Changed." How dangerous would that be? Would they ask for identification? He turned, entered the most dingy-looking one, and called out loud in German, "Good afternoon!"

A big woman in a black dress appeared. Foreign money? *Dutch* money? She hadn't seen that in a long time, didn't know if she wanted it, there was no rate to look up. She stared at him while talking and he felt prickly heat on his neck; he took a step back, for he thought he must still be smelly. "I've had it for a long time," he muttered. "Souvenir from a trip. But I need cash now."

"I'd rather not, sir."

"Just give me fifty francs."

"Forty."

Obviously he should have asked for much more.

She opened a drawer full of money and took out two twenty-franc notes. He hastened out of the shop without another word, quite certain that she would report this to the police the moment the door closed behind him. He turned a series of corners and then, while walking, transferred most of his possessions from his raincoat to the pockets of his jacket. Forty francs. Only today counts, anyway. He took off his raincoat, rolled it into a ball, and dropped it into a municipal trash basket. One more marker in my now international trail of raincoats.

He walked toward a street where he saw more pedestrians, and a streetcar passing through. He stopped in a café and drank three cups of coffee. He had been worrying about calling the Dutch consulate; they might report an illegal entry to the police. He decided to risk it. It took him a long time to find the number. He let it ring twenty times, but there was no answer. Then he looked up the address of the Hotel Baur au Lac in the telephone directory. It was now twenty past five.

73

He was going down busy streets, the sidewalks were crowded with people who had come out of work and were doing their shopping. For someone from occupied Europe these window displays would be amazing, even more so of course than the little stands in the Porrentruy railroad station, but De Witt was no longer paying attention to his surroundings. He was making a great effort of will to forget all that and to forget, too, his protesting body.

His one preoccupation now should be Jonkheer André de Bock, about to spend his last night in the Hotel Baur au Lac. I did not expect to have so little time. I can't screw up now, though. Let's concentrate on each step in turn.

He looked down at his feet moving across the blue flagstone sidewalk and saw that his shoes, which he had cleaned so carefully at the fountain in Porrentruy, seemed about to fall apart. Clothes first, he thought, I can't enter any hotel like this, let alone the Baur au Lac. He knew the name; it was one of the poshest hotels in Europe. Thirty-eight francs was all he had. Surely it won't buy a wardrobe, not even in a secondhand shop. Or, if it does, it won't look much better than what I've got on. Worse. Jopie spent a lot of money on this and the suit isn't even torn, just dirty, and smelly maybe.

Twilight was falling and everywhere lights were springing up, advertisements first, then the street lamps. Lucky bastards, he thought. They don't know how lucky. He looked up along the houses to the sky, which now appeared black, and saw a

226

flickering neon sign, "Abendkl——mieten." Half the letters were missing. He was below the window of a shop on a second floor, behind whose glass stood a tailor's dummy dressed in a tuxedo. Saved.

He climbed the stairs to the shop and told an old man who was sitting at a table using a foot-pedal sewing machine that he wanted to rent a tuxedo, evening shirt, black tie, shoes. "For one night."

"You go to party?" the old man asked suspiciously. His German was heavily accented.

"No, no." De Witt smiled indulgently. "I got a one-night job as a waiter. At a . . . at a yearly doctors' convention dinner."

"Oh, ach so. Very good." Now the man jumped up, grabbed a tape to measure De Witt's shoulders and legs, and started hunting behind various curtains. "We will fix you up fine."

He came back with his arms full of clothes, put them on the counter, and said, once more looking doubtful, "There is a twenty-franc deposit needed." It seemed he expected that De Witt would now bolt.

"That's okay. I'll leave my suit here too, please."

"Fine then. I have suspenders. I have everything. You don't wear a coat?"

"I'm never cold."

But he was shivering with cold as he came back out and started toward De Bock's hotel. Just nerves, he told himself. A few minutes later he saw the Baur au Lac entrance. It disconcerted him. He had not known it was so close; he needed time to think.

A doorman touched his cap, a page turned the door for him, and he entered the lobby. Quiet. Velvet and brocade. Self-assured wealth. Isn't it strange, he thought, before the war we used to think of Switzerland as a place with stony fields and poor peasants, while we were the fat cats.

He went to the reception desk and asked if Mr. de Bock from Holland was in. "Baron Bock?" Yes, but he had given orders not to be disturbed. What was his room number? They never gave those out.

"I'll leave a note then."

"Very good, sir."

He was handed some hotel stationery and, sitting at one of the little round tables, he put a blank sheet in an envelope and wrote on it, "Jonkeer André de Bock, personal." Back to the reception desk, but the clerk who took the letter had his back to him when the put it away, and De Witt could not see the room number.

He went into the brasserie across the street, took a table by the window, and ordered choucroute garnie, which was only three francs fifty. There he was, in the wall mirror, a drawn but clean face, pale, a shaved head, a badly fitting tuxedo with bulging pockets, the elbows and sleeve ends shiny. I hadn't noticed that in the shop. No wonder they wouldn't give me a baron's room number.

He doesn't look like a waiter, the man in the mirror. Not like a man about town either, however. "He," what do I mean, he. That's me, Jerome. God knows why.

Someone stood beside him and he looked up, expecting to see the waiter with his food. The man standing there, with a friendly, amused smile on his face, was William Scheltema.

74

"May I sit down?" Scheltema asked.

De Witt stared at him in bewilderment. Scheltema, in another three-piece suit, mouse-gray this one, the vest with little white buttons, looked as neat and calm as if they were meeting in his office. He seemed surprised at De Witt's apparel, though.

"Why are you dressed like that, Jerome, and what on earth has happened to your hair? You do look peaked."

"I've been sick." De Witt took a deep breath and shook Scheltema's hand. "William Scheltema. I am very glad to see you. All is forgiven, you are the answer to a working man's prayers. I was at a dead end here. Don't tell me you are not here for the same reason as I am. I always hoped I'd convince you. Imagine your walking in here."

Scheltema bent over to him. "Yes, Jerome, we seem to be comrades-in-arms at last. You don't mind if I call you Jerome? But are you sure you're all right?"

The waiter appeared and put De Witt's choucroute in front of him. "I'll have a beer," Scheltema said. "A light one. You too, Jerome?"

"How did you get here?"

"Well, I'm the Secretary of the Amsterdam Stock Exchange. I've had to make official trips to Switzerland before this. The Germans don't interfere; they give me my exit visa without questions. It's a good train."

"And they trust you to come back?"

"Obviously. What would I do, what would I live on if I stayed here? Leave my job, my wife, everything? But what about you?"

"Oh, you see, General Buurman was a friend of my father's. I said to him, 'General, I'll clear out and you won't have to bother with me ever again.' "

"You don't say."

"You don't believe me, do you, William. Well, you're right not to. I got here illegally. On the sly." De Witt expected further questions, but Scheltema seemed to take the answer in his stride.

"Did you achieve anything so far?" he asked. "How did you know De Bock is sitting across the street?" and he pointed to the Baur au Lac.

"How did you know?"

"It's no secret. The De Bocks always stay there. Where else, they'd say. I took a room in the place myself, and I was going in there just now when I saw you at this window."

"Well, what do you know."

They looked at each other in silence. "I have to digest this," De Witt said. "First of all, why did you change your mind? Why are you on my side now?"

"I never was on any side before, Jerome. I simply believed you had gone off the deep end. But I was wrong and you were right. Right, up to a point. We don't think this business goes to the highest level. We're satisfied there's a conspiracy and with André de Bock as its kingpin, we think it's some kind of SS intrigue. That's what gives us a lever, you see, on De Bock."

"Who are 'we' and 'us'?"

"The inner circle of the board. Working members like me, all of us sensible fellows, no millionaires, just people with horse sense. You won't like this, Jerome, but that's why I'm here, negotiating with André de Bock."

"Negotiating? With that man?"

"We have no choice. I can't have him arrested, can I? He's broken no Swiss law. Besides, you know what they say about the president of Switzerland." And when De Witt didn't answer, he continued, "The German ambassador in Bern—he's the president of Switzerland now. About De Bock, he'd be off tomorrow to Batavia. You want me to knock him down? I do not think the fate of a colonial empire is settled with fisticuffs or pistols. I had one meeting with him and he seemed to hesitate. I've had to tread very carefully and it's all been very hush-hush. To the man in the street the German occupation looks like a solid machine, but the reality is that it's torn by all kinds of internecine strife."

De Witt took a bite of his sauerkraut and tried to swallow. His happiness and relief at seeing Scheltema had gone. Even the deep determination that had filled him, that last night of wandering in the woods of the border, seemed to have been snuffed out. He knew again how tired he was. Nothing had changed, it had all been pointless; he might still be sitting with Scheltema in that café on Damrak arguing. There were no black and white in Scheltema's world, only shades of compromise. The dead would remain dead and, whether in Baarn or in Batavia, De Bock would be driving his Bugatti.

"Poor De Witt, you are all in, aren't you? We owe you a great deal, you know. If you hadn't kept at me, we might not have pursued it, I might not be here. I would have contacted you before leaving, but you were lying low of course and I had no idea where to look for you. I even called that man Smit, your former clerk, but he acted as if he'd never heard of you. We have to tread carefully, as I said, but I'm certain we can get your name cleared."

De Witt smiled sourly and shook his head.

Scheltema put his hand on De Witt's arm. "You must have had a hard time getting here. I think you can still help me."

"You said you can't have him arrested. But why didn't you go to the Dutch consul? There's a consul here, I tried to telephone him."

"You think I don't know that? And what do you think he'd do? War or no war, do you think governments interfere with legal transfers of ownership?"

"People's sense of ownership," De Witt muttered. "Schutte used that expression."

"But it's right they don't interfere. Otherwise where would they be with their propaganda about fighting for justice and democracy? Jerome, you—Do you know the RAF never bombs certain Ruhr factories owned jointly by the British and the Germans?"

"I don't believe it."

A silence.

"You said I could still help," De Witt said.

"De Bock and I have a meeting tonight at nine. He's threatening to leave tomorrow with the certificates and the bearer bonds, you see. I don't think he will, it's a hand he's playing. Don't shake your head. Our negotiations are formal, impersonal. After all, De Bock is the last of a very fine Dutch family. He may respond to an appeal to that, *or* to a financial compromise."

"And I—?"

"Of course, he knows you. I can't introduce you as someone you're not. But we can make that work to our advantage. You were with Buurman once. The Germans wanted your arrest, and now here you are with me. It'll help make him realize he holds only one German card and that there are others in the game. If he leaves, it has to be by Lufthansa, it's the only way out of Europe, Zurich-Stuttgart-Lisbon. 'Maybe I shouldn't show up in Stuttgart with my loot,' he'll say to himself."

De Witt looked thoughtfully at Scheltema, and then started to eat his food with more pleasure.

"Tell me, De Witt, if I hadn't been here already, what would you have done? To stop him, I mean?"

"I didn't know yet."

Scheltema began to laugh, shaking his head. "You're a funny fellow, De Witt. The last romantic. A billion guilders in shares, and he doesn't know yet." It took Scheltema a while to control himself, as he wiped his eyes with his handkerchief. "Sorry. I'm not laughing at you, but you are funny. All right then. You come to the meeting. At nine tonight. To be perfectly frank, I'm not that much at ease. It will be good to have you there, and you deserve it. All right then?"

"Since I'm here, in this far city."

"You won't be sorry. Promise me you'll come."

"I promise."

75

When De Witt knocked on the door of the De Bock suite, it was Scheltema who called, "Come in."

A double door, a foyer, a sitting room very elegantly furnished. Heavy gold-colored curtains had been drawn shut. A fire was burning in a marble-framed fireplace and numerous floor lamps spread a warm light. Scheltema was sitting at a table covered with documents, a brandy snifter in his hand. A chair stood at his right side; across from him another chair had been pushed back and an empty glass stood on the table in front of it.

"De Witt. Good. You came." And, in an undertone, "I've explained your role in this as my helper. Take your cues from me."

"Where's De Bock?"

"He's taking a phone call in his bedroom, 'a private call,' he said. What are all those papers?"

De Witt was carrying various newspapers and notepads. "I figured they'd give me a bit of a . . . well, you know."

"Right. We're drinking a 1908 brandy, specialty of this hotel. Help yourself, it's on the sidetable. And then sit here next to me. But lock the door, will you? Close both doors. This is very sensitive. But don't be nervous. De Bock seems relaxed tonight."

De Witt went over to the marble-topped sidetable, which stood under a gilded mirror. Here's to me, the toilet-escape sleeping-pill artist. He put some of his papers down awkwardly, poured brandy in a glass and, before putting the stopper back, emptied all of his remaining sleeping pills into the carafe.

That was what he had come up with, the only angle he had been able to think of during the long hours of waiting in the brasserie, staring at his stale beer. It was not much of a trump card.

He gave the carafe a shake as he carried it to the table, putting his notepad and glass down next to Scheltema, and then refilling both other glasses.

"Cheers," he said. "Tell me which role I'm supposed to play."

"Cheers. Now then—have you told me everything you know?"

"De Bock received his brother's shares. And all the others, right?"

"And do you know where they are?" Scheltema asked very softly.

"Don't you?"

"No. It would strengthen my hand if we knew. But it's not crucial."

"In a bank here, obviously. But there seem to be about a thousand of them in this city."

"It's not crucial," Scheltema repeated. He paused, drank

some brandy, and hesitated. Then he called, "André!"

Instantly, André de Bock came in from the other room. He was wearing a dark-red smoking jacket and looked at De Witt, and from De Witt to Scheltema. "Good evening," he said.

"Good evening, André," De Witt answered, getting out of his chair. He refilled Scheltema's glass. "Here's to our meeting again." He waited until André picked up his glass and drank.

They both now looked at him with curious half smiles.

Time. Time is what I need. "André," he said, "I've made some truly remarkable mistakes in the past. I owe you an apology for them. Yesterday, when I spoke to the British military attaché in Geneva—"

"What are you talking about?" André de Bock asked.

"Don't worry, gentlemen. Nothing unpleasant. We'll all be friends yet. Comrades-in-arms, as William calls it. Here's to friendship, and here's to the Dutch merchant, in the year 1941 as in the year 1605. Yes, the attaché. He is a man of the old school. Colonel . . . now what the hell is his name. I'm bad at names, it's on the tip of my tongue. O'Hara? O'Connell? O-something. Anyway, he said—"

"William?" De Bock interrupted sharply.

"It's all right, sir. He's just playing around. I've finished with him. He doesn't know anything critical."

"You forget George Canty, the American consul," De Witt cried.

"I talked to him on the phone last week," Scheltema said with a little smile that looked apologetic.

De Bock drained his glass and stepped over to a walnut cabinet. He opened it and turned on a radio. "Der Kleine Kobolt," an announcer's voice said when the sound came on, and music filled the room. De Witt stared at him as De Bock produced a small pistol from the pocket of his dark-red jacket.

"No," De Witt said involuntarily, holding out his hands toward De Bock.

De Bock carefully pointed the pistol in his direction, bringing it down a quarter circle to eye level, like a man at a shooting range. He fired it.

76

When De Witt came to, his first awareness was of the radio playing a German waltz.

He was slouched in his chair. Looking down at himself, he saw a hole in the left of his tuxedo jacket, much like a cigarette burn, and as he looked what seemed a surge of blood spread out from it. Damn, he thought. The tragedy of timing. If they had talked three more minutes. Here I've been shot but I don't seem particularly surprised by it, I seem to be quite chipper. Don't these things hurt more?

He tried to sit upright and felt an excruciating pain in his left hand. He focused on it. It's like a raw chicken leg. Jesus. I must have tried to catch that bullet in mid-air. Well, you cannot do that; it's in my body. Not in my heart, obviously. Who'd have guessed colonial billionaires carry pistols around to shoot people. Or perhaps that is precisely what you should guess.

Only now did he concentrate on his surroundings. André de Bock sat across from him, apparently fast asleep, leaning back in his chair, snoring with open mouth, some spit dribbling from his lower lip. The little pistol was lying in front of him on the table. Beside him, Scheltema, his eyes on De Witt, and retching into a large yellow silk handkerchief. "You poisoned us," Scheltema gasped.

De Witt shook his head, which made him so dizzy that for a moment he feared he'd pass out again. "Just pills," he muttered.

Scheltema leaned over and pulled the pistol toward himself. "What? What did you do?"

De Witt cleared his throat. "I said, 'just pills.' Di-methyl atavine. Strong stuff, I'm a very bad insomniac. You were supposed to be out cold, not to get sick. It works almost immediately."

Scheltema appeared to get a hold on himself now. "Why
. . . ?" he began. He did not finish his question, shrugged, and
said, "The luck of idiots. I'm allergic to certain organic acids.
Before the war. . . . But never mind that." He wiped his mouth,
screwed his handkerchief into a ball, and dropped it on the
floor. He was about to pour himself some brandy, then smiled
at De Witt and put the carafe down. "Now that would have
been a mistake, wouldn't it, Jerome?" He looked at De Bock.
"André always drinks too much brandy anyway."

"You're buddies?"

"Buddies?" Scheltema repeated the word with distaste. He
picked up the pistol, holding it sideways, and studying it with
something like wonder. "V. Bernardelli, Gardone V.T. Made
in Italy," he read out aloud. "Trust André to . . . " He put the
pistol in his pocket. "This isn't my way of doing things,
Jerome. You should know that by now. In fact, I stopped him
from 'making sure of you' as he put it, just before—"

"Just before he conked out."

"Quite so."

"I don't know why you think I've such luck," De Witt
mumbled. He felt nauseous. " 'The luck of idiots.' You should
have conked out too."

Scheltema got up and poured two glasses of water. He put
one in front of De Witt and sat down with the other. "Well,
I didn't. I'm not in the habit of gulping down my liquor. You
are lucky to be alive. You may be bleeding to death, however."

"Why, if you don't approve, do you work for this man?"

"I work with him. Presently I may be working alone. André
de Bock is more interested in, in other things. I need him;
unfortunately, the happenstance of a man's name, a man's
family, still weigh heavier in the scales this world holds up than
the greatest competence or intelligence."

De Witt blinked to clear his vision. The water helped; under
the table he poured some of it over his left hand. It hurt badly
but that helped too. Still confusedly, he thought he saw a path
to follow. I'm not defeated. I'm not.

"Intelligence," he repeated. "I thought you were very

sloppy, in that restaurant. 'No idea where to find me.' I had told you myself I lived on Zeedyk and it registered with you, for you sent the police after me."

Scheltema looked at him and did not answer.

"Do you realize what put me back on my feet?" De Witt continued. "When you said, 'Of course De Bock knows you.' How could *you* have known that, William, unless you two were buddies?"

"All right, Jerome. Clever. My mistake. But you're not on your feet, are you? You are bleeding to death. And I'm very tired."

I'm not, De Witt thought. I feel pretty good now. I'm tougher than I thought. He leaned his head on his right hand, and said hoarsely, "It's not even stuff like that, slips of the tongue, cleverness. I'm sure it never is. It's instinct. I just had to listen to you for a while, you could have talked about anything at all. You see, I've been hunted. Believe it or not, but it's not a bad thing to happen to you. It makes you aware of . . . nuances."

"Hunted. Nuances." Scheltema retched again, turning his head sideways. "Excuse me," he muttered. "Let's come to an agreement, Jerome. If I had had my way, André and I would simply have called the police. You're here illegally, you would have been interned. Maybe even handed over to the German border patrols. I don't know what the Swiss policy of the moment is, it changes all the time. But André has an aversion to 'loose ends' as he calls them." He paused and drank some water. "I have no wish to see you dead. I enjoyed our discussions."

"Me too. I was looking forward to reading that monograph. On the year 1605."

Scheltema even smiled. "Now I can't let you go and I can't have you arrested, because you have a bullet wound in your chest. Your hand—The Zurich police notice such things, and André and I have to leave tomorrow."

"Okay, William. Kill me and hide the body in a trunk."

An audible sigh from Scheltema. "I will help you to my

room, which is on this floor, and put you in my bed. I'll see if I can do something about the bleeding. In exchange, I need your word of honor that you'll not make a move until after eleven tomorrow morning. At eleven you can call for a doctor."

"You'd trust me?"

Scheltema shrugged and patted the pocket with the pistol. "I will insist you drink a glass of this chemical punch you made us. You won't get a better offer, Jerome. I told you, I do not believe the fate of a colonial empire is settled with De Bock-style rough stuff. This is not your business, you should have stayed in Amsteldyk in the first place. But if I have to, I'll shoot you without giving it a second thought."

"Okay, William. You win."

"Your word of honor?" Scheltema asked.

Honor, once more. "Yes."

"Let's go." Scheltema took the pistol in his right hand, the carafe of brandy in his left. "Can you make it?"

"I'll try."

De Witt hoisted himself up and went around the table, leaning on the table top with his right hand. He realized now he was in worse shape than he had thought, but for Scheltema's benefit he even exaggerated the pain and the effort. Three agonizing steps across the open floor brought him to the sidetable under the gilded mirror. "We'll pause here for refreshments," Scheltema announced, and poured a glass of the brandy. He held it out to De Witt.

De Witt looked at his reflection. I look greenish. Can I drink that stuff and then throw it up when I'm alone? He caught Scheltema's eyes in the mirror.

"Here you go," Scheltema said, in a quite friendly voice.

At the edge of his field of vision, De Witt saw a bright glimmer. A golden statue, a naked woman with a quiver of arrows on her back and two hounds at her feet. Diana, the maiden huntress. He stumbled as he turned toward Scheltema, his right hand closed around it and he hit him on the head with it, with all that remained of his strength.

Scheltema fell to the floor; De Witt's knees buckled under him and he fell down beside him.

After a while De Witt opened his eyes. Scheltema's feet, motionless in cordovan oxfords, were only a few inches away. Between them lay one of the gold hounds which had broken off. The huntress had landed on her side, and De Witt stared at her beautiful breasts in the mathematically perfect shapes of parabolae.

The telephone in the room started ringing.

77

Later, De Witt was very grateful for that phone, for it made him get to his feet again without "listening for pain," as he phrased it to himself. He picked up the receiver and a voice said in German, "Herr Baron Bock, would you please turn your radio down. Guests are complaining."

"Of course. I'm sorry."

He was standing up without holding on to anything. He shuffled to the radio cabinet and as he couldn't bend down to the knob, yanked out the cord. Leaning on the thing to rest, he glanced at Scheltema. Scheltema was lying on his back. His face was totally without color but no trace of blood was visible. Could he be dead, could that be all it takes to kill someone? Honor, word of honor. They don't even know, they don't even understand.

He pressed his left arm against his side by holding the wrist with his right hand, and made for the door De Bock had come out of. Blessedly, it was open a crack, and so was the door to the bathroom leading off it. At the foot of the bed stood a wooden valet on rollers. This is a very fine hotel, he said to himself. He hung on to the valet, pushing it along, and made for the bathroom. It's like when I learned to skate. Now just concentrate on other things but hurting. Scheltema is worse off. Prove you're no amateur.

He got out of his jacket; the worst part was when the sleeve slid over his left hand. He opened his shirt. It did not look as alarming as he had expected: a very small hole, much dried blood, more blood still seeping out. One inch over and it would have passed by me. There were mirrors all around him in the bathroom and he saw that the shirt looked burned in the back, too. I hope that means the bullet came out again, he thought, but he couldn't see anything or localize any pain from there. He took a bath towel and bound it around his chest, then focused on his left hand. It was an awful mess. Maybe my hand saved my body. He opened the cold tap and held the hand under it, but the pain was far too much to keep it there, and while he was trying this the towel fell off. Damnation. He peed. No blood there; one hole plugged.

He wheeled himself back to the bedroom with the wooden valet, and to De Bock's dresser. Piles of shirts, underwear, handkerchiefs, clean, soft, silken. He wound a silk handkerchief around his left hand, then another one over that, and tied it in a fashion with his teeth. He succeeded in wrapping a silk shirt around his chest and used the sleeves to bind it tight. Then he sat down on the bed and blacked out again.

That spell did not last long, it seemed to him. He opened his eyes and stared at the ceiling for a while, realizing that lights from outside played over it. No blackout. Switzerland. He sat on the side of the bed. A silver pot stood on De Bock's night table. Cold coffee. He drank from the pot and poured the last in the hollow of his hand and rubbed his face with it, which felt marvelous.

Keep going, he told himself. I need a sling for that left arm, though. Another shirt. Then, with his right arm draped over the valet, he went back into the sitting room and lowered himself into the chair behind a desk standing in the corner, half facing the room. Oh damn, I forgot something. Up again, and to the front door where a "Do Not Disturb" sign was hanging on the inside. Unlock the door, hang it on the outside, now why didn't they think of that. Lock the door, back to the desk. Thank God. Sit. Let's survey the scene.

De Bock had not stirred, his snoring was irregular and sounded awful. There's a medical term for that, I don't remember which. Scheltema had not moved either, but De Witt thought he could see him breathe: the buttons of his vest seemed to move, just very slightly.

The time was a quarter to eleven, on a beautiful antique clock over the fireplace.

78

He opened all the desk drawers and put everything on top. A zippered briefcase contained a thin Hermes portable typewriter. A fat briefcase contained stock certificates such as De Bock had shown him at his house, but each one for ten shares only, in that same Batavian Petroleum Company. De Bock's wallet was there too, his passport, his keys. That was a relief; he had been worrying about having to bend over and search the man's pockets. De Bock had made himself comfortable in his smoking jacket for the reception and death of Jerome de Witt.

A Lufthansa plane ticket Zurich-Stuttgart-Lisbon, for March 27. That day was just about to begin. No mail, no indication what he would do—what he would have done—in Lisbon.

About a hundred Swiss francs. A hundred-dollar bill. A small, leather pocket diary. No addresses. A few scribbled entries, hard to decipher.

Let's look at the keys. A car key—which car? The Bugatti in Baarn? Or could you still rent cars in Switzerland? No matter. One, yes, definitely, one safe-deposit-box key. He'd had one just like it, if smaller, after he was married, when he had had personal papers he felt should be put in safekeeping for the future, children. . . . This key had SBG stamped on it, nothing else. He brought up the telephone directory, which he had left in its drawer, and looked under "banks." SBG could

241

stand only for Schweizerische Bank Gesellschaft. No help, that. He could hardly show up there and try to look like De Bock. Still. . . .

Then he found a folder with hotel stationery. Here was something he could do. Reifeneisen. Two letters. First he put a sheet in the little typewriter, but it was too awkward with the sling. Write them by hand, sign illegibly, as De Bock's secretary.

To Finanzkommissar Fischbein, The Netherlands Bank, Rokin, Amsterdam. Herr André de Bock, who considers the future of Europe of an importance surpassing all considerations of family and persons, as his actions have demonstrated, was gravely perturbed to learn of a German police officer who has enriched himself while in the process of executing certain unavoidable policies. It had been reported to him that a certain Heinz Oberwalt, of the German criminal police in Amsterdam, has been offering stock certificates for sale, certificates that could only be in his possession through theft from the late brother of Herr André de Bock.

We are asking the Finanzkommissar to take the severest measures, and will not hesitate to take the matter to the Reichskommissar himself if need be. Yours truly, for Herr André de Bock, signed illegibly.

Scharfuehrer Heinz Oberwalt
Kriminalpolizei
RAI Building
Ferdinand Bol Street
Amsterdam.
Dear Scharfuehrer,
We are not unaware of an unfortunate attitude of the SD toward your services, leading to a lack of official appreciation of the same. Allow us to send you, as an unofficial token of appreciation of those services for the future of Europe, ten shares in the Batavian Petroleum Company, to use for your comfort and that of your men. To avoid recriminations between two branches of the police, you are ordered to destroy

this letter. The certificate is to bearer and may be freely cashed. Heil Hitler. For Baron Bock, signed illegibly.

There were dozens of stamps. Let's put two francs on each, it couldn't cost more.

He was so pleased with what he had done that he got up without wincing and went to drink several glasses of water. He had been parched with thirst but afraid to move again.

He brought a pillow back from the bedroom and installed himself as painlessly as possible in his chair. He leaned his head back, closed his eyes, but then he felt himself slipping away into something between sleep and a fainting spell. He shook himself. Come on, get with it, he muttered.

It was half past one in the morning.

79

De Witt sat at his desk, half leaning over it, for a very long time.

He was wide awake now and not even particularly aware of his body's miseries. What odd creatures human beings are, he thought, so weak and so tough.

He was studying those two men. Could he try to tie them up, with his one hand? With electrical cord maybe? Should he kill them? The pistol was in Scheltema's jacket.

He had won. Well, he had won so far, inexplicably perhaps, and unfairly, too. Scheltema, just like the general once, had trusted his "word of honor." But no honor was involved, not even the honor between thieves; that "honor" was a little word for a kind of buddy-buddy accomodation, respected only as long as convenient, outside the world of terror and death, a world where twelve hostages were shot to death by German peasants in uniform. And just for the hell of it. It could as easily have been ten hostages. Or a hundred. In a year it would presumably be a hundred, or a thousand, or a whole people.

There was definitely no need to worry about a word of honor to Scheltema. Still, it remained puzzling: It could so easily have happened that De Bock would have killed him, De Witt, that he would no longer exist. Such a fate wasn't really avoided by tricks. Could Scheltema possibly, somehow, not have wanted to win? And if no table had been free at the window of that restaurant, Scheltema wouldn't have seen him. No, that was different again. He, De Witt, would have gotten into De Bock's suite somehow and in better shape than he was in now.

But what do I mean with "winning"? These men are at my mercy now but I don't want them, I want the bonds that make a man own the East Indies, and I can't get those. I'm in no state to walk from this hotel to the next corner and whatever I do or don't do, I'll be in a Swiss jail before long and probably in a German jail not long after. A German grave. And indeed, you must admit, it cannot be that the ex-mayor of an idiotic little town would alter the destiny of a billion guilders (a *billion?*), that in this shiny tuxedo now minus jacket I would have frustrated a colonial enterprise of *Grossdeutschland*.

It's a big enterprise. They wouldn't have bothered with it if it weren't. For the want of any one barrel of oil, one batch of rubber, one more shell or torpedo fired by the German army, the war was lost. Could be lost.

Killing André de Bock and William Scheltema will at least delay the enterprise, that is certain. In the light of eternity there's no justification for killing them, but right now we're not bathing in the light of eternity. I'm in a Swiss hotel room and I'm very close to falling on my face. You'd have to move a long way out into eternity, beyond Venus or Mars, to get to a point where you'd see, it makes no difference if Hitler wins or loses his war.

How much does Scheltema's life weigh, in balance, against the deaths of children? Who are these men? They're living in obliviousness of everything except their own emotions and pleasures, they're as selfish as amoebae, they haven't progressed beyond the amoeba. They're not their brothers' keepers. There's nothing sacred about their bodies.

Sending out bullets to tear through flesh, sending them out

from your own pitiable vulnerability. Just look at this hand of mine. What a pitiable mess the human race is. Let me get up one more time. Let me give William another chance.

De Witt shuffled over to the telephone. It took a long time for the hotel operator to answer. "The British embassy, in Bern," he asked in German. Twenty rings. A voice, in English: "Night duty officer."

I must sit down. He dragged the phone over. "This is important, are you listening?"

"But certainly," the man answered. "Who is calling?"

"My name is De Witt. That's W-i-t-t. I need help, to stop a theft, an act of plunder. I'm from Holland. This is a big German undertaking, a very sensitive, secret, plan."

Silence.

"Are you there?" De Witt asked.

"Yes, indeed. You said it is very sensitive?"

"Yes. Yes. This is serious, it's not a joke."

"I wasn't suggesting that, sir," the man said. "But in that case you'd do better to come here. Our calls are all monitored, you see. By an outside source."

"Come where? To Bern? I can't. I'm—I'm not well."

"I see."

No you don't. I'm not handling this right. De Witt felt giddy. He took a deep breath and slowly looked around the room. All that leather and velvet and gold. It is too warm in here. The fire had died down but the fireplace still held glowing embers, and when he tilted his head he could see their reflection moving in the glass of a portrait facing him, a man in black, with a black hat, who was staring inimically at the world. "Time is short," De Witt said into the phone. A feeling of irreality had crept over him. "There are papers here in Zurich, documents, that represent control over the oil production of the Dutch East Indies. Oil. Rubber. War materials." He said all this very fast. "This call is monitored by an outside source?" he then asked.

"Indeed. By the German embassy, to be undiplomatic but precise." The man chuckled, or made a sound of the kind.

All those folks are too damn genteel, De Witt thought.

"Stolen papers," he said angrily. "Can you people help me do something about it, or not?"

"Are you the owner or one of the owners, sir?"

"No. But I represent them, so to speak. I can't explain on the phone, not if, as you say—"

"Yes, quite. But it is the middle of the night. Have you talked to your own legation, have you filed any kind of court action with the Swiss authorities?"

"No."

"May I ask why not?" The man still sounded polite, but icily so.

"Because they were not literally stolen, that's why not. The owners sold out, but under duress. They—"

"In that case—"

"If I called you," De Witt interrupted loudly, "and not the Dutch, it's because I know what they would say, that war or no war they will not question the property, I mean the propriety, of ownership, and all sorts of crap like that—please don't tell me that in the middle of this great war you're going to sell me the same line." To his disgust he saw that his hand holding the phone was shaking.

"We're quite aware of the fact that we're in the middle of a war, sir, and yes, as you put it, I'm going to sell you exactly that line. I don't think our embassy's brief here in Switzerland is to intervene in ownership disputes, or maybe burglarize people's safes, if that's what you had in mind when you asked for our help. You must excuse me, I must free this line now."

De Witt remained silent.

"However, if you want to take this up with our commercial attaché, the embassy is open to visitors from eleven to one only, five days a week." With that, the night duty officer hung up.

"Were you disconnected, sir?" The hotel operator.

"No, it's all right."

To hell with all of them. All of them. Propriety, that was a good word to use. Still, I sure screwed up that call.

In spite of that, he felt pleased with himself. He was glad he had not argued more.

I'll help myself, and not for them either. Purely for myself.

I will stop this German enterprise if it kills me, and then I'll go happily or unhappily to any Swiss, German, or other jail; I'm simply not going to think that far.

He felt very nauseous now. He made it back to the little desk, though, without accident.

It was four in the morning.

80

At a quarter past five in the morning, on March 27, 1941, as a grayish dawn light began to appear around the edges of the Baur au Lac gold draperies, Jerome de Witt came upon his moment of greatness. Or that is what he called it later—to himself only, though.

For an hour his thoughts had been going around and around. Killing two men would achieve a postponement of the German enterprise, but presumably not even a very long one. Not killing them would achieve that De Bock missed one plane and took the next one. The bonds were in a secret safe at this SBG bank and if De Bock didn't pick them up, they'd sent someone else to claim them and carry them to Java.

De Witt's moment of greatness was, precisely, when he suddenly saw what it said on the page in De Bock's pocket diary, headed Thursday March 27. A pencil scribble that had looked like no language, no words:

tigalimalimasatudelapanampattiga

Which split up as: tiga lima lima satu delapan ampat tiga. Which translated from the Malayan as: three five five one eight four three.

The fate of a colonial empire.

After that, De Witt just sat still, afraid to move, afraid to fall asleep.

At eight in the morning he got to his feet, a sensation as if he were crawling through broken glass. He went to the bedroom in his wooden-valet shuffle. On the way he stood still, slightly swaying, and studied De Bock and Scheltema.

De Bock had slipped to the floor. His mouth was closed now, and the snoring had stopped; he seemed in a very deep sleep. Scheltema was not quite motionless; he had a twitch on his face that came and went. A streak of dried blood showed on his forehead. His face was still chalk white. Was it possible to be unconscious for so long, or could he even be in a coma?

De Witt pushed the wooden valet over to where Scheltema was and lowered himself to his knees. He picked up Diana, the golden huntress, now accompanied by only one hound; he was going to hit Scheltema over the head one more time, and De Bock too. Then he didn't. He kissed the goddess on one of her breasts and put her back on her feet, on the floor.

In the bedroom he looked at himself in the mirror of the wardrobe. His face, still green but respectable: he had shaved late in the afternoon of the previous day. Think of it, that was only yesterday. He meant to tie a clean silk shirt around his chest but the old one stuck and he had to let it stay where it was. His hand he did not dare touch; just looking at it made it hurt even more. A separate heavy pulse seemed to be beating in it.

He picked a lightweight camel coat from the large De Bock collection and got it over his shoulder with his right arm through the sleeve; he kept his left arm in the sling under it. All this was a lengthy endeavor. He wrapped a foulard around his neck and put on a soft hat, which fitted rather well.

Back to the other room. The two letters to Amsterdam, the keys, the Swiss money, all in the coat pocket, plus a little authorization he had written for himself over De Bock's signature copied from his passport. Just in case. Matches. The diary. He'd carry the stock certificates in the briefcase they were in, and which he had put on top of the wooden valet.

Onward, De Witt. Marching as to war. A bad moment at the hall door when he had to let go of the wooden valet. Diana-Artemis, protect me.

He closed the door of the suite behind him, straightened the "Do Not Disturb" sign, and, wearing a frozen smile, marched to the elevator. Pain is a subjective emotion only. A bellboy in the lobby accepted his two letters for mailing. The doorman helped him into a taxi. When he sat down, he realized he had not seen the lobby or the bellboy; he had just walked toward the glare of daylight, holding out his letters. He must have been pretty conspicuous. Never mind. Nothing will go wrong now, it wouldn't make sense if it did.

"To the Schweizerische Bank Gesellschaft. But please stop at a good tobacco shop first." He knew what he was going to do.

When the taxi was in motion, he became very dizzy. He felt he had to throw up; with a tortuous effort he wound down the window on his side. Air. A blue sky. The dizziness passed.

At the tobacco shop, he asked the cab driver to do his errand for him. "I've had an accident," he explained. "I don't move easily. I'm going to the country, and I'd like at least six cans of lighter fluid. I can never get the stuff in the village. And please get me some Monte Cristos if they have them. Get yourself some too. Here's a fifty." In memory of Cremer, for good luck. To lie down in a quiet Swiss jail cell and smoke a Monte Cristo. I'm sure they'll let me.

The driver came back with the cigars and four half-liter cans of lighter fluid. "Only four, sir, they're in short supply. They asked, were you running your car on them. Expensive stuff, six francs a can."

"Thank you. Four will do." He put them in the briefcase.

It was five minutes to nine when they pulled up in front of the bank. "Let me sit here until they open," De Witt said.

They were long minutes.

At nine, the driver helped him out of the cab; De Witt had the fare and tip ready. Then he added another five francs and asked the man to help him inside. He remembered that safe deposit departments are ususally down a staircase, below ground.

The cabbie took his arm and led him down the stairs to the private safes, where a receptionist asked De Witt's name. If either of those two has come out of it, De Witt thought, if De

Bock has phoned here, now I'll know. Guards will appear and quietly ask me to step into some little room. But they didn't, De Bock hadn't.

"Shall I wait, sir?" the cabbie asked.

De Witt gave him a bright smile. "No. Thanks. I'll be picked up."

The bank officer in charge of the department came out. "The safe for Baron Bock," De Witt told the officer. "I'm his private secretary, and I have come to add these shares and to take inventory. Here is the key to our safe, and his authorization."

"Do you have the number, sir? We give access by number only."

"The number is 3551-843."

And so it was.

They conducted him down a long, empty corridor and left him alone in a stately room after putting a number of very large metal boxes on its table. "We've also prepared a wooden case for shipping," they told him, "as the Herr Baron had instructed."

"We won't need that today," De Witt said.

"Very well. Ring the bell when you're finished, sir."

Then De Witt had to sit a while to catch his breath, cope with the pain, hoist up the sling for his left arm, and re-tie the shirt under his coat. But he was all right. It seemed funny to him: from the outside he looked more or less a Swiss gentleman, but underneath the camel coat he was a very odd mess.

It had been a long way from Amsteldyk to the Schweizerische Bank Gesellschaft basement. He took all the shares and certificates out of the boxes, in bundles three or four inches thick, and on the floor he built a tower with them, with openings in between, just as he had done once as a child in Houten with the bricks a mason had left hehind after a job on the house. He couldn't bend over, so he had to drop the foundation of his building into place. Although the thing tottered when it was completed, it did not fall over.

Now he meticulously poured the lighter fluid from the four cans over his tower and set fire to it all around. Soon it burned from bottom to top, from Batavian Petroleum to Banka Tin and Zinc, and the smoke became so thick, he could hardly see his hand in front of his eyes. That was not the reason, or not the only one, for the tears running down his face.

He rang the bell and shuffled to the door, and between his racking coughs he cried, "Finished!"

ABOUT THE AUTHOR

Hans Koning was born Hans Koningsberger in Amsterdam, Holland. He left his country as a student to serve in the British army during World War II, and in 1951 arrived in the United States by way of Indonesia. His first novel, *The Affair,* published in 1958, established him as an American writer, and he has since published eight other novels and half a dozen travel and other nonfiction books. Two of the novels, *A Walk with Love and Death* and *The Revolutionary,* were made into films. He has been a reporter for the *New Yorker* and contributed to the *New York Times,* the *Atlantic Monthly,* the *Nation,* and the *Paris Review.* He makes his home in New York City and in London.